# MASHIAKH,

## RETURN of the WATCHERS

PATRICK ALLAN WHITE

ISBN: 0-692-34006-8
ISBN I3: 978-0-692-34006-6
Library of Congress Control Number: 2011910471
Ariel Lightworker Publications
Bradenton, Florida

# Contents

I will ascend to heaven; I will raise my throne above the stars; I will sit on the mount of assembly on the heights of Zaphon; I will ascend to the tops of the clouds, I will make myself like the Most High.

*—Isaiah 14:12*

# Prologue

In the past, they had been great lords over heaven. There were nine in number, each possessing powers with no limitations. All bowed down in awe of their majesty, and in their majesty they were humble. Except one. A great prince—the chief of those guarding the Tree of Life that stood in the Eternal Sea—whose Light was far brighter than the rest. They called him the son of the dawn, Daystar. The signet of perfection, full of wisdom and perfect in beauty, he built a palace sitting atop the highest peak of the holy mountains among the stones of fire.

Realizing that he was far better than the others, the prince came to desire that all should obey him and him alone, and his heart became filled with pride. He used the power imbedded in the Tree of Life to create an infernal tree, planting in its center unlimited darkness. Absorbing this new source of conscious living-energy into himself, he became supreme lord of the shadows. His name became Samael, in honor of the secret poison he had created allowing him to change good into evil.

He gathered around himself a loyal band of Angelic lords who were attracted by his new dark power. They acknowledged him as the one and only ruler of all things created and uncreated. Two million of the Angelic host flocked to his banner. When he sensed the moment was right, through the force of his will, the mighty prince waged war against the very light he had sworn to protect.

The First War of the Angels had begun. Through his rebellion, Samael caused the uncreated to stir and by doing so brought forth space and time.

Michaela, the leader of the Hosts of Light, raised her sword and cried out to the prince, "I now name you Samael the Black, for you have sinned. I will cast you as a profane thing from the holy mountains and the stones of fire. Your heart is proud because of your beauty, and you have corrupted your wisdom for the sake of splendor."

The war continued, waging back and forth, with no side gaining the advantage over the other. Finally, there was a decisive battle on the plains of Hades. Michaela had driven Samael and his army out of the Northern Mountains where stood the Tree of Life and into the barren foothills that surrounded them. Michaela's name was the war cry of the Angels of Light in the battle. Already, thousands of Angels from both sides had been defeated and thrown into the outer dimensions of creation. Seeing the enemy's exhaustion, Michaela raised her sword high into the air and cried out, "For the Light." She charged directly into Samael's forces without heed for her own safety. The rest of the Angelic host, watching with amazement the bravery of their leader, followed her into the ranks of their dark foes.

The outnumbered legions of Samael, with their backs against the steep walls of the mountain, put up a fierce resistance, but the onslaught proved too much. Sensing the end was near, Samael, along with his lords and chief lieutenant Beelzebub, fled the scene of the battle. He used what was left of his great power to send them all into different dimensions to wait until the time was right for them to return and defeat the Light.

# SCROLL 1

*94-91 BCE*

א

# THE LITTLE FLOWER

"Hannah, Hannah! Where is that girl?"

Hannah came home just as her Aunt Emorun was setting the table for the evening meal. Her aunt looked up as she was putting the bread on the table. "Always sneaking off to pray, and sitting there for hours on end with your eyes closed. If your uncle discovers you doing that again, well, he's already warned you."

Hannah tugged at her aunt's worn-looking apron. "I've wanted to tell you something for the longest time, but haven't been able to find the right moment. It's something important, and concerns the reason I've been gone so much these days."

"What? Don't tell me! You've fallen in love and want to get married! What wonderful news. Who is he? A nice boy from a good family, I hope." Her aunt clasped her hands in front of her and smiled.

"Well yes, in a way. I've found a new friend. But, it's an Angel. At least, that's what I think it is."

"An Angel? Your new friend is an Angel? Have you seen this Angel?"

"Recently, whenever I'm deep in prayer, I hear a voice. It's similar to a human voice, but sweeter and more beautiful. Once or twice I imagined I could even see what she looks like."

Hannah's aunt shook her head. "You'd better be more careful Hannah. It's not normal for people to be hearing, let alone see, Angels. We'd better not mention this to anyone, in particular, to your uncle."

The aunt wiped her hands clean. There was a worried expression on her face. "Now, help me set the table. Your Uncle Stollanus will be coming in any minute. Remember, not a word of this to him. He's not been in a good mood these past weeks since business got bad again. When will these ceaseless wars end?"

Hannah's uncle arrived and they all sat down at the table. After saying some prayers, he looked up at her. "Where have you been all afternoon? Don't you know that your aunt's hands ache with joint pain? She shouldn't be making meals without some help."

"Yes, I know, but I've some good news to share. Today I learned that Aunt Emorun's hand will get well if we can find some Foxglove root and make a salve out of it. We just need to rub it on the hand, and wrap a bandage over it every day for a week. After that, the pain will be gone forever. Isn't that wonderful? I know the pain has been terrible."

The look on her uncle's face changed. "Who did you hear this from? I hope not from that sorcerer who lives on the other side of the lake."

Hannah's aunt passed him some more bread. "I wish you wouldn't call her that. I hear she's a very nice person."

Stollanus gave his wife a stern look. "Who told you that? Don't tell me, I can guess."

Aunt Emorun stared deeply into her husband's eyes while raising her hand. "Don't say a word more about it. She can't be here to defend herself."

He didn't want to argue, so Stollanus stuffed a piece of soft goat cheese into his mouth. "What I hear is, that she'd just as soon cast a spell as look at you, and all for a coin or two."

Hannah appeared embarrassed as she glanced over to her aunt. "No, it wasn't her. I just heard it, that's all."

Aunt Emorun changed the subject. "Stollanus, finish up the bread. I was able to find some raisins at a good price to put in." Then, she looked over at Hannah. "Did you wash your hands?"

Hannah held up her hands. "Yes, I did. It is so written in the laws of our people." Her face took on a serious expression. "We should adhere carefully to the laws, as Aravat, our lord creator, gave them to us. There are many teachers these days who do not observe what they preach. Our high priests are not legitimate and our kings do not belong to David's line."

Aunt Emorun glanced over at her niece with a shocked look on her face. Even Hannah felt a little surprised. What did she know about these matters? She was just a simple uneducated girl from a small rural village.

Stollanus put down his plate with a thud. "Hannah, when will you learn?" her uncle scolded. "You shouldn't talk about such things." He got up to see if anyone was listening through the open window and lowered his voice. "It's dangerous. These days, such talk can get you killed."

"Now be a smart girl," Stollanus continued, "and spend more time learning how to cook and trying to look pretty in order to find a husband. That's real women's work, looking nice and having babies. Just look at yourself. Your hair is uncombed, your clothes a mess, and you can hardly even boil water. You have no interest in boys, and all you want to do is pray. Heaven help us!"

Hannah hung her head. "Yes Uncle Stollanus, I know. You've often told me so."

Uncle Stollanus reached for his goblet and poured more wine into it. "We're a poor family. I must work hard with my hands for our food and keep. Why, some families even consider Hannah the village idiot. It doesn't help me find work. Hannah's at the prime age to find a marriage partner, but it will take a miracle to secure someone suitable. I may need to go to a neighboring village, where they haven't heard about her strange ways to find one."

After a few seconds passed, he reached over and touched Hannah's hand. "In spite of this, child, your uncle loves you very much. Although there are many things odd about you, you're an honest and upright girl. I dare anyone to say otherwise." With that, he hugged her.

"It must be the wine," Hannah said with a grin. The three of them laughed.

Hannah's Aunt Emorun was her deceased mother's younger sister. She married the Hellenized Jew Stollanus while living in Damascus, many years before. Born in Syria and a miller by trade, Stollanus moved his family to northern Galilee to prevent the Seleucid government from drafting him into its army. Their current house sat on the outskirts of town next to a small but fast running stream that provided the water necessary for the struggling milling trade. The stream's fresh, clear water came pouring out of a large wooded area, situated on a sloping hill, not far behind their meager home. The stream grew larger as it meandered through the village of Thella, until finding its home in the shallow waters of Lake Hulata.

When Hannah finished her chores, she often slipped into these woods to pray. These opportunities did not come however, as often as she would have liked. The only child of her aunt and uncle was already married and lived in a different town. Being still at home, Hannah spent much time assisting with the milling work, especially as her uncle's back was getting worse with age.

It wasn't the most suitable time to be searching for spiritual gifts, as war was never far away. The armed conflicts between the supporters of the Sadducees and the Pharisees that served as a proxy war between the Judean Maccabee and Syrian Seleucid kings, continued unabated. Not only had the fighting taken many of the able-bodied men, but it also reduced the number of caravans that passed by on the road connecting Jerusalem to the Syrian hinterland. Both had a disastrous effect on her uncle's business.

* * *

The air was crisp on that early autumn day and the sun was about to set. Hannah sat deep in prayer next to her favorite tree, oblivious to the surroundings. Not even the birds dared disturb her. A soft wind began to blow, stirring up dust from a nearby pile of fallen leaves, causing Hannah to cough. She opened her eyes and noticed a bright light shining through the branches of the trees. She stayed calm and did not move. To her astonishment, a beautiful woman appeared in front of her. Clothed in splendid garments and wrapped in a glowing rainbow of vivid colors, the woman began talking to Hannah in a slow and melodic voice.

"I have come to warn you that a dark evil is approaching. You must flee. Go and warn your relatives." After saying this, the woman disappeared. At first, Hannah thought she was hallucinating. She had not eaten much for lunch and was a little hungry. Perhaps that was the cause. After giving it some thought however, she felt it best to go tell her aunt and uncle about it. Hannah ran as fast as her legs could carry her down the hill and out of the woods into the yard behind her house.

Her uncle was cleaning up after a hard day's work. Hannah could see her aunt inside preparing for the evening meal.

Hannah stopped in front of her uncle. "Finally came back to the land of the living?" he asked with a gentle pat on her shoulder.

Hannah tried to catch her breath. "Uncle Stollanus, I think we should leave this place." She looked around a bit. "Maybe we should hide in the woods!"

"What's this?" he asked. He placed his hands on his hips as he examined his niece from head to toe. "Are you sleepwalking, or has your ceaseless praying caused you to lose your senses? Come now girl, be reasonable and help me move these bags of grain into the barn for the evening. I'm more afraid of the rats than of your silly pranks."

"Uncle Stollanus, please believe me. I think we are in grave danger. We must flee!"

Her aunt came out of the house. "Come on everyone, it's almost time to eat. Finish your work and get cleaned up. You can continue your conversation during dinner."

Hannah ran over and pulled at her skirt. "I had a vision while in prayer. It said we must flee from an approaching danger. Even if Uncle Stollanus won't believe me, I know you will. You know I never tell lies or exaggerate."

A look of concern appeared on her aunt's face. "Are you certain Hannah? Maybe you fell asleep and had a strange dream. These kinds of things do happen, even to prayerful folks like you."

"No, it seemed real." She pulled at their arms, trying to get them to move.

Hannah's uncle appeared agitated. He turned to his wife. "This craziness runs in your family, having conversations with beings from other realms." Stollanus scanned the surrounding. "What happens if someone is looking for her? I never wanted to get involved with your family's situation. They warned me before we wed."

A confused look came across Hannah's face. Who'd be looking for her? She began to panic as a sense of dread began to fill her. "I haven't lost my mind, nor am I hallucinating. You can have me examined by the priests in the temple later if you wish."

"I think we should do as she says," her aunt replied as she looked at Hannah. "If nothing happens, we will at least have had a nice walk. Not a bad idea after all, I say. I could use some good air."

The uncle shot back a look of displeasure. Then, glancing at Hannah while she stood there still pulling at them, he softened up a bit. "All right, but just a short walk. After that, let's eat. I'm as hungry as a wild animal."

The three of them went into the woods. It was a clear day and the dry red leaves that still clung to the tree branches rustled lightly in the wind. Climbing the hill that rose above the clearing where they lived, they were able to see the valley below that stretched to the shore of Lake Hulata.

"You see Hannah, nothing to be scared about," the uncle said after standing there for a few minutes enjoying the beautiful view. "The sun is setting and all is at peace. Do you feel better now? How about returning home and enjoying a nice supper together?"

Hannah's aunt brushed with her fingers the long locks of hair that hung down to Hannah's shoulders. She seemed relieved that it was a false alarm. "There dear, you are young and your mind is still growing. You'll get better at distinguishing between the worlds of the seen and unseen as time goes on. At least you know you can always count on us. Now give your uncle a big hug and thank him for coming here with you."

Hannah turned to her uncle and wrapped her slender arms around his round frame. "I love you so much. I'm very lucky, aren't I?"

Aunt Emorun smiled as she saw a few small tears roll down the cheeks of her burly husband as he basked in the warm embrace. There suddenly came the sound of thundering hooves from strong horses and the shouts of many men. Through the gaps of the few trees, they saw a large troop of mounted soldiers enter their back yard.

"This is the place. Find the girl and the magic stones she carries," their leader shouted out in Latin. His manner was course. "He's promised gold and female slaves for the one who finds them both." They threw lighted torches onto the buildings and grabbed the food that Hannah's aunt had made, gulping it down in a few bites.

One man, heavily armed, wiped his mouth with his dirty sleeve. "There's nobody here. They must have fled."

"Well, keep searching. If we return empty-handed, he won't be happy," the man in charge barked. His large stallion snorted, as if it too was eager to catch their prey. "When you're finished, meet up along the main road. Now, get moving and find them."

Hannah's uncle had learned some Latin while still in Damascus, enough to understand what the soldiers were saying. Looking around in panic, he urged his family to go deeper into the woods. As Hannah was the most familiar with this part of the forest, she led them to a small indention along the side of a large boulder, partially hidden by tall green bushes.

The aunt noticed her husband breathing with difficulty. She slipped her hand into his. "It will be fine," she softly whispered into his ear. "Hannah has special friends."

He looked into his wife's eyes. The very thought of it made him feel even more uneasy. He was just a simple tradesman and wanted no part of it. It was most likely because of her special friends that they were in the present situation.

A few of the mounted soldiers rode into the woods searching for signs of life even though the sun had already set. After some time and not discovering anything, they left to rejoin the main party of soldiers.

The three of them remained hiding. Fearing the soldiers return, they waited some time before going back home. As they walked into the yard, they were horrified to discover that nothing remained but the smoldering ruins of their torched house. Even worse, they had smashed the milling stone into small pieces. Seeing it, Hannah's uncle fell to the ground and wept.

"Now I have no trade, no work to do in this world," he said through his tears. "My father provided the money to buy this from what was left of his meager savings before he died. He wanted me to carry on the family tradition. Now, all is lost. I don't have enough money for a replacement. All is lost." He looked over at his wife's niece. "Is this the repayment I receive from Aravat for agreeing to take the girl in?"

Hannah covered her mouth in shock from his words. She had never heard him say anything like it before.

Hannah's aunt hugged her niece tightly, as if to show how much she cared for her. "Don't speak such nonsense. Hannah's a wonderful girl and you know it." She looked around at the destruction. "All is not lost. We are all still here as a family. Stones can break and be replaced, but not lives, in particular the lives of those we hold most dear."

Stollanus didn't reply.

Hannah's aunt knew it was not safe for Hannah to stay here any longer. Somehow, they had discovered her whereabouts. "Hannah, gather what is left of your belongings," she said in a way that did little to hide her anxiety. "We set out at dawn to consult with someone about your future."

Hannah realized what was happening and felt sad. She walked over to her uncle and touched his shoulder. "Thank you Uncle Stollanus for all that you've done for me. I'm sorry things turned out this way." There were tears running down her young face.

Her uncle didn't look up, but just nodded. Hannah's aunt grabbed her hand and led her away. They would have to find a place to sleep outside. Maybe close to the woods would be best, in case there was further trouble. Fortunately, it was a warm night.

## ב

# ABIDE BY YOUR CALLING

Hannah and Aunt Emorun arrived at the small hut close to noon. The sun was unusually hot. On the way there, they had encountered few people, as most feared to venture to this side of the lake. Tales and legends about Mount Harmon abounded among the common people of northern Galilee. Sitting quietly with her eyes closed underneath the branches of an ancient cedar tree was a lone woman. A dangling mane of silken hair rested loosely on the top of her rounded shoulders. Bushy eyebrows, the same color as her hair and curled at the ends, contrived to give her a mysterious appearance that equaled her reputation. Her spotless white robe had a hood with strange-looking letters sown in gold that bordered its edges. As she stood there gazing at the woman, Hannah felt that she resembled the wandering women healers who occasionally stopped by Thella to sell their herbal salves and charm bracelets.

It seemed to the aunt that the woman was asleep, so she motioned to Hannah not to make too much noise for fear they might wake her.

Suddenly, the woman opened her eyes and greeted them. "Peace be with you," she said in a soft voice. Her face shone as radiant as the midday sun on the brightest of days.

"And with you," the aunt replied with a curtsy. "Are you the one they call Selith?"

The woman smiled. "Yes, I go by that name. The young one who accompanies you is Hannah, is she not?"

Aunt Emorun placed her hand on Hannah's shoulder. "How do you know her? She's not told us that she has come to see you. Although she has many faults, telling falsehoods is not one of them. Or, is it that the rumor of her strangeness has spread even to this deserted place?"

"You are wrong; she is not strange at all. In fact, her body has a wonderful glow about it." The woman kept her gaze fixed on Hannah as she spoke.

"My sister instructed me to bring Hannah here if ever there was danger," she glanced around at the strange surroundings, "although I cannot ponder the reason why." Then Hannah's aunt pulled out a delicately woven blue velvet pouch from inside her robe. "My sister also said that these must stay with Hannah."

A simple bench made from what remained of an old fallen tree was not far away. The woman gestured to it. "Excuse my poor manners. Please both of you have a seat. You must be tired after such a long trip."

A wicker basket sat on top of a transparent green jade stand. "There is some dried fruit and nuts inside." Selith said while pointing to the basket. "I made the wine from grapes that grow wild along the lake. It will refresh both body and spirit without disturbing the head."

Hannah rose to get the basket, but her aunt stopped her. "We didn't come to burden you. This must be what you planned to eat for your midday meal. We can't take it."

Selith insisted, motioning with her hands. "I prepared it when I learned of your coming."

The aunt was beginning to wonder about this woman. "You seem to know everything."

"I also know what happened yesterday." Selith's expression changed. She appeared worried.

Taking the basket, Hannah bowed. "Thank you. I'll say a prayer in thanksgiving for your kindness."

Selith nodded. "Prayers have great power. You should be careful however of what you pray for, you may receive answers you do not expect."

The two eagerly ate. They had only time to drink some thin gruel before departing in the morning. Selith refilled Hannah's cup with some of the wine. "Do you pray often?" she asked.

Putting down the piece of dried fruit she was eating, the aunt answered before Hannah could. "It's all she does. Pray, sit with her eyes closed as you were when we arrived."

Selith appeared pleased.

They finished the food and drink. There was a brief interlude, as if a strange energy moved among them, encouraging them to be at peace. It was very quiet, with only the sound of a few birds singing somewhere off in the distance. The silence ended with Hannah's aunt getting up from her seat. "I have something to ask of you," she said to Selith with a serious expression on her face. "It has bothered me for all these years, but I never had the courage to come find out before. Or perhaps, I didn't want to know the answer. But now I do, because I suspect it may be related to yesterday's events."

Selith waved her hand, displaying various rings on many of the fingers, each inlaid with a small gemstone. "As you wish."

Aunt Emorun sat back down and swallowed hard. "Why did those evil men murder my sister?"

Hannah turned towards the aunt and grabbed her sleeve. "You never told me she was murdered. You said she passed away from the fever."

"Hush now, girl." Aunt Emorun played nervously with the pouch still in her hand. "You are big enough to know that you can't tell children just anything. Let this woman speak. I want to know what happened that day. Was it because of the pouch or because of Hannah?"

Selith gazed into a fine polished ball of clear yellow sapphire that sat on top of her staff. An ancient order of women healers mined this precious gem in the alluvial marble tunnels of the Mogok highlands, long before the Great Flood. "They wanted both," she answered, while still looking into the sapphire.

"It is the curse of my family. My husband often tells me so." Hannah noticed a small line of tears trickle down her aunt's worn face.

Selith stood up. She was very tall, more so than the women of these parts. "It is no curse, but a holy blessing. But with blessings come responsibilities. One cannot just take and not return something for the gift."

Listening to the conversation between her aunt and this woman, Hannah became aware that there was something mysterious about her family and wondered what it all meant.

"She had a friend by the name of Machala that belonged to the same order of Nabiim as your sister and Hannah's father," Selith continued. "On a visit to your sister, the evil ones followed this friend and discovered your sister's whereabouts. After Machala left, they first killed Hannah's father, running a sword through him in front of his wife. It was part of their sinister plan. Your sister, now a widow, their leader made a bargain with her. He would spare the infant Hannah's life if she agreed to marry him and give him the contents of the pouch. She did as he bid, spending the night in his bed. It was a ruse. Before dawn, she silently left their camp, handing Hannah and the pouch over to you before fleeing. The leader sent his men in pursuit. Soon catching up with her, they left her dead. Fearing his anger for finding neither the infant nor the pouch his men told the leader that they had killed Hannah as well as her mother, and that the pouch was lost forever, thrown into the lake before they could get it."

Aunt Emorun shook her head in amazement. "How do you know? Were you there?"

The woman rubbed one of her rings. "It came to me in a dream. Your sister was my student. Because of it, we were connected in a spiritual way."

Hannah's aunt got up and faced Selith. "Why couldn't you save her? On her visits, she often talked about you. She said you were a person of many wonders."

"I was far away and could not make it in time, things happened too fast. And even if I could, I do have the power to deal with so many armed men." Selith bowed her head. "I am so sorry. It was difficult for me too."

Selith pointed to the pouch still in Aunt Emorun's hands. "I have done my best since then to keep their eyes focused elsewhere, until at least Hannah was older. However, it seems that they have grown more powerful, hence the visit yesterday."

"What's in the pouch?" Hannah was beginning to become frightened. "Why not just throw it away and be done with it?"

Selith's smiled at Hannah's innocence. "Yes, that does sound like the best solution. Unfortunately, it is not that simple. The contents of the pouch are very valuable. One cannot discard them just like any common goods. No, that would not do at all. We will have to think of another way."

Pondering it, Aunt Emorun grabbed Hannah by the arm. "Hannah is right. We no longer want the pouch." She threw it on to the ground. "We'll end the family's curse once and for all. It's cost the lives of three generations of my family." She stroked Hannah's hair. "And almost took another."

Selith was at first shocked, but it soon gave way to anger. "You are one of his descendants too. How dare you treat his inheritance in this manner!" She pounded her staff on to the ground with a hard thud. "What were your sister's final words to you?"

Aunt Emorun wrung her hands for a moment before answering. "She said the contents of the pouch were sacred objects and to never let anyone near them, or to tell anyone about them, even if it meant my life." Hannah's aunt then thought about her sister, who had given her life for whatever was inside the pouch. She bent down and slowly picked it off the ground.

A sad look came across Selith's face as she realized how much Hannah resembled her mother. After giving things some thought, Selith walked over to a tree that stood nearby. "Hannah, bring the pouch here." There was some hesitation. Hannah was reluctant to handle it. It seemed all too dangerous. "Hannah, come now, and bring it here." Selith's tone was commanding.

Aunt Emorun urged her to take it. Hannah touched the pouch, half expecting it to strike her dead. Finding it no different however, from a common pouch similar to the ones she often saw at the market in Thella, Hannah took it over to Selith. She secretly was glad, hoping that her family would be finally relieved of guarding it. Selith touched the tree with her staff, and spoke words in a strange language that sounded more like singing than talking. Suddenly, a small hole appeared.

"Place the pouch inside," Selith ordered.

Hannah obeyed. Soon afterwards, the hole disappeared. Hannah rubbed her hand over the bark where the hole had been in amazement.

The sun was getting lower. Aunt Emorun suddenly remembered the events from the previous day. "They say you have the gift of sight," she said to the woman. "What lies ahead for the girl? Is she to die also, just like the others?"

Sensing her doubts, Selith walked over to Aunt Emorun, staff in hand. "Hannah must stay here. It is too dangerous otherwise. The wicked cannot enter this place unbidden," she looked up towards Mount Harmon, "at least, for now."

Calm returned to Aunt Emorun upon hearing Selith's words. Selith looked Hannah's aunt directly in the eyes and spoke in a reassuring manner. "You will have to trust me, and more importantly, have faith in Aravat. Given your linage, that should come easy."

Selith took the aunt by the hand and led her towards the rugged shoreline of Lake Hulata. "You had better get going if you are to catch the ferry," she said. "You must cross the lake by sunset." Hannah followed along.

They soon arrived at a lone pier made from the wood of trees common to this area. Hannah suddenly realized that Aunt Emorun was going to depart without her. "Please don't leave me here." She grabbed at the aunt's arm in desperation. "I want to go home with you?"

"You're all grown up now," the aunt replied, giving her niece one last look. "You should have been married a long time ago with a family of your own. It will be safer here, in this far out-of-the-way place. In any case, I doubt that your uncle would agree to take you back. There just aren't any other good choices, but for you to stay here. You should be grateful that this woman has agreed to take you in." She gave Hannah a warm embrace. "Visit when you can. Our home is close enough."

Selith handed the aunt a small cloth bag. "Inside are some coins. Give it to your husband Take it as payment for her dowry. He can rebuild his mill with it."

The last ferry of the day arrived. As she got onto the flat raft, Hannah's aunt felt a twinge of sadness as the boatman shoved off.

Hannah was about to begin a new life. Standing there on the receding shore was the girl she had raised, nurtured, and loved all these years. Was this really how it was supposed to be? It had all happened so suddenly. Was she right in agreeing to leave Hannah here? She waved one last time. Despite her misgivings, something inside reassured her all would be fine and that it was the right thing to do. It was almost as if somebody was standing next to her on the boat putting her at ease. Perhaps it was one of Hannah's Angel friends. The very thought of it brought a smile to her face.

Hannah shed some tears as she watched the boat fade into the rays of the setting sun. Her youth was ending with the close of the day. Selith slipped her hand into Hannah's in a sign of friendship. She could sense Hanna's sadness and apprehension.

"Today, you begin the first steps of a new life," Selith said, "and have much to learn before you can comprehend fully the inner mysteries of the sacred arts."

Hearing about these sacred arts, something inside of Hannah changed. She suddenly felt a strong desire to learn more about them, enough to calm her anxieties. Selith wasn't surprised. It ran in the family.

"The Light is but one," Selith said as they returned to her hut, "and leads us out of darkness. It is in every person of every religion and every race. It is only through obedience to this Light that one can become its true child. If you dwell in the Light, you will feel the power of it within yourself. But to do so, you must first learn how to be still, how to wait, and to walk in the Light."

Selith would now be Hannah's guide and teacher, just as she had been for her mother. Selith knew however, that the path ahead would as difficult. The evil on the outside would be searching for Hannah and the contents of the pouch. There was however, no other way. Hannah would have to gradually advance up the steep mountain of this new life, one step at a time.

ג

# THERE IS YOUR TEACHER,
# THE LIGHT. OBEY IT

The ebb and tide of the seasons flowed into the river of years. Warm weather had returned to the Golan plateau, and the hills and woods were alive with nature as it rose from winter's slumber. Selith and Hannah sat in a large expanse of clover. Birds sang cheerfully as the bees were busy collecting nectar from the freshly budding flowers. A gentle breeze blew the fragrance of the plants round their heads, intoxicating them with its heavenly scent.

Hannah's life was undergoing a profound transformation. Her personality was changing and her countenance radiated an inner beauty. Few things saddened her for she was happy in her new life. Selith taught Hannah the secrets of the precious stones, along with the healing power of the trees, herbs, and the flowers. She also revealed to Hannah the motion of the sun, moon, and stars as well as the mysteries of the square and circle, of forms, numbers, and signs.

They were resting together after immersing the herbs into a small clay vat filled with olive oil and honey. "It is important to pray," Selith said as she stirred the pot, "for the humble plants that have given their lives to make the salve. The prayers call forth the life force residing inside them. All life on earth depends on the rays of the sun for existence. However, since creatures receive only limited nourishment directly from sunshine, the plants digests it for us, transforming the sun's hidden power into life when humans consume them. Energizing the sun's life force in our food is the real reason behind praying in thanksgiving before meals."

Selith handed Hannah a brightly embroidered flask that contained a special elixir made of Elelisphagon, Ligustikon, and Thymon. "The best way to tame a wild horse, Hannah, is to give it plenty of space to run."

Hannah was surprised at the sudden change of topics. "How'd we get from plants and sunshine to horses?" she asked jokingly.

"We are not talking about animals Hannah but about meditation." Selith had a serious look on her face. "Do not try to force things. Simply lift up your heart during meditation with a gentle love. Desire the Light for its own sake and not for any results. If you insist on having pre-determined goals for your meditation, you will encounter difficulties. Instead, just center all your attention on the Light and let it be the sole concern of your mind."

It amazed Hannah. It was almost as if Selith could read her innermost thoughts. It was true. She was spending more time in mediation and frequently encountered difficulties. It did not bother her though. A new joy was rising from her inner depths, springing suddenly like a spark of fire. Hannah felt that some power was guiding her, almost taking possession of her in such a way that it dominated her every action.

"I find this easier said than done," Hannah answered while sipping some of the elixir.

"Humans are never alone," Selith said as she poured more into Hannah's cup. "They have friends. When you fix your gaze on the Light, and forget everything else, the Angels rejoice and assist you."

Hannah looked over at Selith with excitement. "There are truly such creatures as Angels? Have you ever met any?"

"We can talk about Angels another time. Your lesson for now is to learn to be at home in the emptiness," she said instead. "And return to it as often as you can. If you hope to discover the Light in this lifetime, it must be in that state."

"Yes, I do try to feel only emptiness, but it is hard to stay this way for very long. My mind always wants to wander." Hannah did not want to dwell too much on it. She was content just to love that which was impossible to grasp by knowledge. She only wanted to love the Light, so that by belonging to it she could share somehow in the fellowship of the great prophets of her people.

They got up to go. Selith always made certain they were home before evening. They waded through the shallow marshes close to the shore of Lake Hulata. This was the fastest way back.

Their feet sunk deep into the rich mud. All nature prepared for the end of the day as things became still. Selith continued to instruct Hannah as they went. "Enlightenment is an individual process. The bar is set at different heights for different people. There can be no one standard set by others that all must obtain."

"Will I ever obtain this enlightenment?" Hannah asked as she struggled to keep her clothes dry.

Selith used her hand to pull Hannah out of some mud that reached up to her knees. "The unique spiritual journey that each of us makes to reach this fullness of our own Light, enlightenment, never ends, not even with bodily death, but continues into the joy of eternity."

Selith suddenly raised her hands motioning for them stop. "Get down and do not talk," she whispered. There were only a few reeds nearby but Hannah did her best to hide. Coming close was a group of men chasing a deer through the marsh. The creature was unable to outrun the men because of the water and was still some way from the safety of the forest that bordered the shore. One of the men used his bow to let go an arrow. Selith raised her arm and as she did, the arrow went wide of its mark. Hannah could hear the sound of more arrows whistle through the air causing many birds to scatter in fright. Selith kept her arm extended. Not one arrow hit the deer, allowing it to make it to the trees. With that, the men let out a curse and went away.

"Romans," Selith said after they were gone. "These days there are more and more of them coming to Mount Harmon. The Maccabees and Seleucids are too busy fighting each other to pay any attention. They are up to no good that is for certain." Hannah watched the men as they retreated and heard their voices. It was then she realized that the armed men who came to their house in Thella those many years ago must have been Romans too.

Selith led Hannah to the nearby Jordan River. She said a few words in a language that Hannah couldn't understand. "That should keep them from crossing over into our part of the woods."

Selith urged them on at a faster pace since darkness was now upon them. "Now where did I leave off? Oh, yes, now I remember. Every human is born with a certain measure of Light," Selith said with a look back towards the river, "although at times it does not seem so obvious. It is just that we are all at different stages of the spiritual journey at different times of our lives." Selith saw by the look on her face that Hannah was perplexed. "Do not be overly concerned," Selith quickly added. "No matter what stage we are at on that journey, we have just the right amount of Light needed. When it is time to move on, we receive more Light and proceed to the next level."

Suddenly, a distinct pounding noise came from the direction of Mount Hermon's towering snow-covered peaks. Selith put a hand on Hannah's shoulder "Maybe it is best if you did not go alone in that direction anymore. I wonder if it has anything to do with those Romans." Selith felt uneasy about it all. Things were happening too fast.

# ז

# YOU ARE NEVER ALONE

The day was clear and the sun was about to pass its mid-day point in the sky. Hannah was picking wild berries in a field that lay next to the large forest that separated their huts from the river. With her hands busy plucking the plump ripe fruit off the branches; she was trying to imitate the gay chirping of the birds that were busy watching her from a distance.

"Good day to you young miss," a voice said suddenly from behind her. "Maybe you should share some of your harvest with those birds over there. After all, they were planning on eating it for their lunch."

Hannah was so startled that she dropped the berries on to the ground. She had not heard anyone approaching. She looked down at the berries, now ruined after landing with a splash onto a large rock. "Look at what I've done. Now neither I nor the birds will have anything to eat."

"Do not fret; it will make a fine meal for the little insects. It is important to develop a deep desire to do good not just for humans, but also for all created life."

Hannah looked up to see a woman dressed in a beautiful robe that sparkled in the bright sunlight. With long hair that reached below her waste and barefoot, Hannah thought she looked familiar but was certain they had never met. Hannah seemed embarrassed by her clumsiness and it showed on her face. "Excuse me, are you from around here?" she asked, flustered somewhat.

"Well, not exactly, although I have been spending lots of time recently in these parts," the woman said as she glanced around at the surrounding countryside.

Hannah's curiosity was not yet satisfied. "Do you always walk so quietly? I normally can hear someone coming from quite some distance."

"Yes, I usually do walk quietly," the woman answered with slight nod of the head, "that is if I am walking at all."

Hannah's eyes grew wide on hearing her reply. Realizing she had gotten berry stains on her clothes, Hannah tried wiping it off on to some grass. "Maybe I should go wash."

"That will be fine, let us go." Without saying anything else, the woman walked in the direction of the river.

"How do you know the way?" Hannah queried the stranger while tugging at her arm.

"I always let the Light be my guide."

"What do you know about the Light?"

"I know all that Selith has taught you and even more," the woman replied with another nod as she turned to Hannah.

"You know my teacher? She never mentioned anyone like you before."

Hannah was out of breath. Not watching where she was going, she tripped over a tree root, falling face down on to the ground. Hannah raised her head. "I guess I should let the Light be my guide too. Maybe it will serve me better than my eyes."

They soon reached the river. Hannah waded into its shallow waters to wash while the woman rinsed the stains off her arm. "It is important to embrace sister simplicity, for the more material possessions that bind you to this life, the harder it is to ascend into the Light." The stranger said this as she gazed with fondness at the natural beauty that surrounded the river.

"This woman talks just like Selith," Hannah thought to herself. "I wonder if they're related."

Drying in the warm afternoon sun, the woman asked, "What do you know about the Light?"

"My teacher says it's the very fabric of the Universe, the Ultimate Cosmic Force," Hannah said as she sat on a rock and dangled her feet in the water. "It's limitless, omnipresent and omnipotent."

"Your teacher must be very wise. Did your teacher also mention about it being the repository of infinite wisdom, infinite knowledge, infinite sound, and infinite light?"

"Yes she did, but to be truthful," Hannah said as she bowed her head in embarrassment, "I'm not sure I really understand what it all means. She says it is the ultimate cause of everything. Everything, including every word and every form, begins in the Light, thrives in the Light, and ends in the Light. She once told me that for as long as things receive nourishment from the Light, they can survive. No sooner than the nourishment is withdrawn, there is death." A frown came over her face. "It sounds so complicated. Perhaps I'm a little slow."

"Do not try too hard," the stranger said, as she placed her arm on Hannah's shoulder. "It is something you need to feel and not understand. How can anyone understand that which is beyond understanding."

Hannah looked up with a confused look on her face.

"Take me to see this teacher of yours," the woman said as she took Hannah by the hand. "I am certain she will clear things up for you."

The two of them walked on a path that led through numerous groves of cedar trees, the smell of which filled the air with a delightful fragrance. This was Hannah's favorite part of the forest that separated Lake Hulata from the foothills of Mount Hermon east of the river.

They arrived in the small clearing where their isolated huts sat nestled next to a low field of clover. Hannah received no reply after calling out for Selith. "That's strange, this time of day she is always sitting over there under her favorite tree meditating."

The woman found an old log to sit on. "Did your teacher mention that everything, including letters, words and sentences, are nothing but the Light in essence, all bristling with cosmic power?"

Hannah was not paying any attention. She was too busy searching for her teacher, worried that something might have happened to her.

"And that when you say a prayer, it releases a very strong power that can attract an Angel to you. The reason for this is that in the Light there is no difference between Name and Form. When you say a prayer to an Angel, it reaches the Angel no sooner than the words leave your lips. If you continuously pray to an Angel, often saying its name, you can attract the attention of that Angel and it may even appear right before your eyes."

Hannah stood there exasperated. "Where can she be? This is the first time since I came here years ago that she has left without telling me beforehand. I wonder if it has anything to do with the Romans. They keep coming up to the banks of the river, but none have crossed so far."

As she turned back around towards her new acquaintance, Hannah jumped back several paces in surprise. There was Selith, now sitting on the log instead of the stranger.

Hannah gave Selith a warm hug. "You've returned! I was so worried."

"Did you see that strange woman sitting here?" Hannah asked while looking around. "She claims to know you. It seems today that everyone is coming and going as if they were Angels, including you!" Hannah scratched her head in bewilderment.

"Do you believe in Angels?" Selith asked with a smile on her face.

Hannah sat next to her teacher, still in a good mood after seeing her again. "I suppose I do, I mean, I want to. I think Angels sometimes whisper things in my ears during prayer. In any case, I always do as you instructed and pray to them as often as I can. I haven't noticed any effect though."

"Now you will!" With that, a bright light appeared forcing Hannah to cover her eyes and fall to her knees in fear. "I'm sorry teacher, you must be angry about something. I didn't drop the berries on purpose. I promise I'll do better from now on. You must be patient."

The light subsided. Standing there once more was the stranger. "Rise, Hannah. If you learn nothing else, it must be that your senses constantly lie to you while you walk this earth."

Hannah rubbed her eyes in disbelief. Perhaps she was hallucinating from the frequent fasting. Getting back on her feet, she reached over to touch the stranger to make certain she was not seeing things. "I didn't until now realize the full extent of your powers, teacher."

"It is no magic, Hannah. I am an Angel. We have the ability to change our appearances at will."

"An Angel, a real Angel?" Hannah's hands covered her mouth in astonishment. "I never met a real Angel before, at least not in the flesh. Why didn't you tell me before?"

Selith reverted to her original form. "If I had told you and your aunt that I was Angel, would you be here now? I doubt it. I had to wait until you progressed in your training. One must be careful when dealing with humans. They have serious limitations including an overdependence on their bodily senses. If I went around proclaiming just to anyone that I was Angel, they would consider me insane or possessed by demons. It is impossible for humans to accept the unseen world of the spirit as reality, even though many profess that they do."

Hannah's hands were still shaking. She didn't know what to think about it.

Selith sensed it. "Much that is now hidden will be revealed when you can stand to see more Light. I just hope we have that much time," the Angel said, while looking in the direction of Mount Hermon. "The hour is late and sinister clouds have begun to form."

Seeing that Hannah was still having difficulty in making the transition, Selith reached over and touched her student's head. "Would you feel better to forget that I am an Angel?"

Hannah closed her eyes. After a few minutes, her face became calm again. "No. I trust that you chose this time to reveal your true self for a reason, even if I'm unclear what that reason is. I accept your decision. Now that I know you are Angel, I just hope that I meet your expectations as a student."

Selith nodded in approval. "You just did."

A bright fire blazed out of the peak of Mount Hermon. It made Selith feel uneasy. Selith pointed to the places where they often meditated together. "There is something I need to tell you."

Hannah and Selith sat down together. The Angel gently touched Hannah's hand.

"Have you ever heard of a prophet by the name of Enoch?"

Hannah gave it some thought. She couldn't recall ever hearing anyone mention his name, but that didn't come as a surprise. She was a girl, so she never received any instructions at the temple, and her uncle discouraged Aunt Emorun from discussing religious matters with Hannah.

"Do not use your outer thought processes, but your inner vision. Does the name conjure up any feelings?" Selith kept her gaze fixed on Hannah, as if sending her grace.

"It doesn't seem to be familiar to me."

"When you think of his name, what is the first image that comes to your mind?"

Hannah centered down and emptied her mind of any thoughts. "Relax, relax," the Angel said softly.

"I see stars," Hannah replied, "lots of stars. The entire sky is filled with white bright stars."

"Good. Now listen to what I am about to say with the mind's eye." Selith moved her hand to Hannah's forehead, at the place of her spiritual eye.

"Long ago, in an earlier age, the Angel Ariel took Enoch beyond the Great Eye of Orion to become a Star Walker. There, she showed him all the workings of heaven and earth, the seas, and all the elements. She also revealed to him the secrets of the sun, and the laws of the moon, the twelve constellations of the stars and their passages, the seasons, years, days, and hours. At the end, Ariel gave Enoch objects on which the data were inscribed, instructing him to study them carefully as they contained sound keys that could unlock the Light symbols. Encoded into the very basic fabric of the universe at the time of its creation, these keys were the way the Light communicated with its creation."

"Can you see it all clearly," Selith asked. Hannah nodded her head, yes.

"Fine, then let us continue." There was not a sound in the entire forest. It was as if all of creation had stopped to listen to Selith's tale. "After his return to earth Enoch wrote down all that he had learned. He in turn, gave it to his son Methuselah. To preserve the knowledge given to Enoch, Lamech, the son of Methuselah and the father of Noah, built a temple at Moriah, on top of a mammoth sized Generating Crystal called the Foundation Stone. Utilizing the principles of Sacred Geometry, he constructed inside the temple, nine vaults, each one beneath the other. In the deepest vault, he placed a Record Keeper Crystal that contained everything Enoch leaned when he walked the sky, including the sound keys that held the secrets of the universe. Next to it, he placed a Teacher Crystal upon a white cubical altar. In the form and arrangements of these vaults, he utilized the nine spheres of the ancient mysteries and the nine sacred strata of the earth."

Hannah was starting to understand. "Are these crystals the contents of the pouch that Aunt Emorun gave you?" she asked with her eyes still closed.

"Yes, they are." Selith pressed a little harder on Hannah's spiritual eyes, pouring into it some of her own life force. The Angel wanted Hannah to internalize everything into her own consciousness, as if she had experienced all the things in the tale herself. "Lamech only told the secret of the vault to his son Noah," Selith continued, "who sealed the entrance to save it from the destruction of the flood's waters. After the Great Flood, Noah's descendants passed this knowledge on to the Jebusite seer-priests who became the guardians of the Foundation Stone and the vaults. Ages passed, and with the arrival of David in Jerusalem, the leader of the Jebusites acknowledged him as the crystals new master, after having a vision that reveled David's divine mission. As a pledge of the crystals safekeeping, King David gave in marriage the eldest son of his most senior Levite priest to the daughter of the Jebusite high priest. On top of the Foundation Stone, David built a new temple, eventually anointing as his high priest and its guardian, the eldest son of this union, who took the name of Zadok."

"Hence, it came to pass, that the secret location and formula for using the crystals were handed down over the generations, from eldest son to eldest son within the senior linage of Zadok. To ensure that men as before the flood did not abuse the power embedded in the crystals, the Sons of Zadoks kept secret the formula for their use."

Hannah was very still, her breath even and quiet. Yet, her mind was able to soar high up to the heavens. This ability came though her years of study with Selith, sitting with her under this very tree, absorbing the Angel's life force as she did.

Selith continued. "Time went on. Eventually, the Maccabees usurped the office of high priest from the Zadoks, and the throne from the descendants of David, wishing to unite them under one person, to restore the glory of Israel. Jonathan Maccabee desired the crystals, after a traitor within the Zadoks informed him about them. He wished to use them to defeat his archenemy, the Hellenizing Syrian Seleucids. Learning of it, the last legitimate high priest from the senior line of Zadok removed the crystals from their hiding place and fled into the desert to prevent their misuse. Jonathan pursued him. Before his eventual capture and cruel execution, this last of the Zadok high priests, gave the crystals to his eldest son. This son, your great-grandfather, had no male heirs, passing them on to his only daughter upon his death. As you already know, your grandmother bore two daughters. Your own mother married the

Initiate Phanuel, a member of the Tribe of Asher, belonging to the order her grandfather founded. These were your parents Hannah. Your Aunt Emorun married the miller Stollanus and gave birth to your cousin Sobe."

Hearing this, Hannah's eyes opened. "Why did you wait until now to tell me the tale of the crystals?"

"The evil ones can read a human's mind just as easy as an Angel can. I feared drawing them to you before you were ready."

Hannah gave the situation some thought. "If it is the Maccabees who are so eager for the crystals, what role are the Romans playing?"

"It is not just mortals, there are also fallen Angels who desire the crystals."

Hannah looked over at Selith in surprise. "There are such things as bad Angels?"

"They are called Watchers and their powers are great, perhaps even greater than mine."

"Are they looking for me too?" Hannah shuddered at the thought of it.

"They wish to give the secrets of the crystals to the kings of men, as they once did before the Great Flood. This time however, the damage will be far greater, as humans are more capable than in ages past in their ability to destroy. The Watchers are not united though in their quest. Some Watchers still believe the Maccabees should get the crystals first. Their dynasty is weak and their country surrounded by strong neighbors who look greedily upon their lands. The Maccabees still dream of restoring their people to their former glory and spreading the belief in the one Aravat to all corners of the world. These Watchers believe the Maccabees will strike a bargain in return for the power the crystals would give them. Others though among the Watchers, have no faith in this house. They prefer to give the knowledge contained in the crystals to the Romans, who will use it to build a new world order based on power and money under the tutelage of the Watchers. As down payment, the Romans are providing human females to the Watchers."

Hannah suddenly felt cold. The sun had set and there was a strong breeze blowing in from Mount Harmon. "What will they do with these women? Make them slaves?"

"Worse, they seek to breed them. They will create a new race of Nephilim, who they will raise in Rome to become its rulers. The world is about to enter a new dark age."

Selith stood up and looked toward the now darkened woods that surrounded their little camp. "You must never let them get the crystals. It would be better to die first."

"Why don't you take them?" Hannah rose to be next to the Angel. "You stand a much better chance than me in protecting them?"

"They are not for Angels. You will understand more as time goes on. For now, you will just have to trust me."

Reaching into her robe, Selith pulled out a silver necklace. Engraved on either side were strange markings Hannah did not recognize.

"It is Angelic Script, the eye writings," Selith said as she held it up for Hannah to see. "I am sorry I did not have the time to teach it to you. In times of danger, when all other sources of the Light seem distant, this necklace will offer great protection from the darkness to whoever wears it."

Selith hung the necklace around Hannah's neck.

Selith also gave Hannah some brightly colored gemstones of various shapes and sizes. "These are for healing. Use them as I have taught you."

Selith had Hannah place them in a pouch made in an earlier age spun from strands of woven Angelica bark. Those under the power of the living darkness were unable to see it.

Hannah protested as she placed the pouch back inside her robe. "If you are unable to, how can I defeat so much evil?"

Selith grasped Hannah's hands. "The blood of the Zadoks runs in your veins." The Angel glanced over at Hannah and then at the darkness that surrounded them. "The time has arrived. There is your teacher, the Light. Obey it."

A sudden loud crash came from the direction of the woods. "The Romans are arriving!" Selith said as she pulled Hannah aside. "The Watchers have provided them with a spell to overcome the prayers I used to protect us these last years. They will be here soon." The Angel grabbed Hannah's hand. "Quick now, into the woods we go."

ה

# GOING AFTER STRANGE FLESH

Selith scanned their surroundings. "The Romans are crossing the river now. We cannot escape south because of the lake. The only way is to cross over Mount Hermon and flee into Syria. The Romans dare not so openly violate Seleucid territory, at least not yet. We will make for the Pass of the Oath. It is what they least expect."

Hannah was hesitant to leave. She enjoyed her life here with Selith so much. "Why can't they just leave us in peace? We have nothing to do with them."

"The dark ones will never let you live in peace. They hate peace."

Selith led the way. "Come now, make haste!"

Hannah started to follow Selith. She suddenly halted. "The crystals, we forgot them."

"It is best to leave them here. We do not know what dangers lurk in the shadows."

Hannah followed Selith into the forest. It was very dark. Hannah soon found herself tripping over the hidden things that covered its floor.

"Use your spiritual eyes," Selith said while pulling her up. "You will fall less often."

Far off into the distance, Hannah heard shrill screams, similar to the screech birds of prey make as they dive for the kill. "What's that?" Hannah asked as she looked nervously about.

Selith did not answer. She just motioned them onward. "We must go faster."

They ran without interruption throughout the night. Only once did Selith permit Hannah to stop to drink from a nearby stream. As dawn broke upon the new day, they could see the snowy summit of Mount Hermon looming high on the misty horizon. The sight of it brought back memories to Hannah of the village elders telling stories to the young children of giants and other foul creatures that lived under the shadows of its slopes.

Selith held up her hand as they came to a stop. "From here, the going will be more dangerous," she said with a look of worry on her face. "We will no longer enjoy any cover from our friends the trees. Nergal, the Eye of Beelzebub, is ever watching the mountain for his lord."

They slowly moved toward the steep ledges of Mount Hermon. They followed long-forgotten paths made during the days of the Amorites. Dark clouds of eerie looking smoke hugged the sides of the mountain.

Selith looked uneasy. "We are near the Pass of the Oath," she said with a frown. "It still has the feel of the foul deeds that took place not far from here."

Hannah gazed out into the vast wasteland with a sense of dread. Selith decided it was best not to push Hannah too far. She was after all, a human with a mortal body tied to the natural laws of this realm.

Hannah was young however. After eating a few pieces of dried fruit and seeds from Selith's pouch, they continued on their way. There was no sight of the Romans, so they slowed their pace a bit. Although noted for their hardiness, the Romans were still no match for the Angel's eyes when traveling through such a thick forest.

Selith suddenly pulled back a few paces. "Look," she said, pointing to the ground. "These are footprints of giant Nephilim. Long has it been since I last saw such a creature from the dark." She placed her hands up to her eyes and scanned the sky as if looking for something. "Now I know who made those horrible screeches last night. Wherever there are Nephilim, their foul brothers the Emin are certain not to be far away. They are all descendants of the Watchers."

Hannah opened her mouth wide in surprise. "Giants! Then the old wives tales were true about this place! I'm scared. I don't want to be eaten by such evil things."

Selith looked Hannah over from head to toe. "If we run into any giants, they will not be interested in eating a scrawny thing like you. They will have other things on their minds, and that fate will be more terrible."

The heavy mist parted. As it did, a stone stairway chiseled out of the rugged side of the mountain suddenly appeared in front of them, leading straight upward towards the peak. Selith put her hand on Hannah's shoulder. . "No human female has ever ascended the Stairs of Semyaza of her own free will," she said. "Not even the Ishim dare come near this place."

In spite of this, Selith urged them on. They began to climb the stairs. As they did, Hannah noticed there wasn't a trace of any living thing, other than themselves, on the barren slopes of Mount Harmon. The higher they went, the colder it became. The foreboding darkness returned. It was thicker than before and clung erringly to their bodies. Hannah imagined she could see black hands made of shadowy smoke grabbing for her, as if trying to pull her off the mountain.

They reached a small ledge that appeared worn by the winds of time. Surrounding it, were numerous beds of loose pebbles, making it impossible to step away without sliding off the mountain. Hannah prepared to continue her ascent, when down the side of the mountain came flying towards them a flock of giant raven-like creatures.

Selith dropped to her knees. "Emin, Terrors!" she cried out.

The Emin sent out a horrible screech as they swooped low. "Hannah, quick, cover your ears, they are getting closer. Do not look into their eyes, whatever happens. Your eyes are the portals of your life force and they can steal yours if you do."

Hannah clung to a large boulder and buried her head deep into her arms to avoid looking at them. She was so scared her teeth chattered.

Several times, they swooped low, attempting to grab hold of Hannah and each time, they failed as Selith swung at them with her staff.

"Is this all you can offer, foul offspring of the dark ones?" Selith called out to them, no longer afraid as she stood up. Just then however, a band of armed Romans arrived near to the ledge. Their leader, a fierce looking man, drew his sword. "We've got them lads," he said in Latin. "It's been a long day and they made us work for our prize. Let's have a little fun before we kill them. But first, get the stones."

Selith raised her staff. "You are wasting your time. We do not have the crystals."

"She lies," barked their leader. "Kasdaya said they're inside the pretty one's robe. We can see for ourselves after we relieve her of the task of wearing it." The Roman laughed as he patted his rounded belly.

Selith was distracted with the Romans. Noticing it, an Em swooped down and grabbed hold of Hannah. "Help," she called out to Selith, "I can't get loose of its hold."

It began flying away with her. The Romans were angry. Their prey was escaping. "Hey there, she's ours," their leader shouted out to the Em. "We're the ones who get the stones and not you." They used their crossbows to let go a volley of arrows, but the Em was now out of range.

Hannah closed her eyes. She was afraid of heights. It wasn't long before the Em set her down inside a large cave. To her surprise, it flew away. The cave had a horrible smell to it. Lots of makeshift beds and blankets lay strewn about in a disorderly fashion. "Who'd sleep here?" Hannah asked herself.

"It's not used for sleeping, my pretty one." The voice was gruff and came from somewhere deep inside the cave. It was too dark for Hannah to see. "We use it for breeding." Course laughter followed.

Out of the darkness stepped a vile looking armed warrior. Covering his black armor was a thick layer of rough leather. He came close to Hannah and inspected her closely. "My, oh my, just look at this, what a beauty," he said in a menacing voice. As he spoke, he revealed a mouth full of rotting yellow teeth. "I'd really like to take the time to breed you too, but I've more important things to do first."

The dark Angel held out his hand. "Now give me the stones. If you do, I'll spare your life. I could even entertain the thought of us giving birth to a son. He would be the kings of kings, with the stones in his possession. Be a good girl and hand them over." He put a curved dagger next to her throat. "Otherwise, you are going to be a piece of stinking dead flesh." He was about to slit Hannah's throat when someone hit his arm with a staff. It was Selith.

"No you don't, Kasdaya," Selith said in a way that revealed her inner strength. "Get out of here before I turn you into dust."

The warrior laughed. "You couldn't even prevent a mosquito from biting, let alone stop a lord of the Watchers. Out of my way, or I will send you into the outer realms for good."

Selith hit Kasdaya again with her staff, knocking him against the wall of the cave. He shook his head, and then took out a big black sword. "Say goodbye to your teacher, sweet Hannah. I've had enough of her foolishness."

Kasdaya struck, but to no avail. Selith blocked the blow with her staff. "For the Light," Selith cried out as she hit Kasdaya's sword. The force from it was so strong that Kasdaya lost his balance and fell.

While still on the ground, Kasdaya looked up at Selith. There was a sinister smile on his face. "You're no match for me, light slut. Your power is waning with the fading sun and you know it. Get out of my way, or better yet, join with us. If you do, you can stay around for the next couple of millenniums on earth, enjoying the fun. You can't have this one, but there's more where she came from. You'll look better as a man."

"Run Hannah!" Selith shouted. "I will keep him busy for a while."

Hannah didn't budge. She refused to leave her teacher like this. Selith gave her a hard stare. "Do not be such a foolish human. Go! I command it!"

Kasdaya quickly got back on to his feet. "Run to where?" Kasdaya danced about the rocks. "She's mine," he shouted in glee, "the stones are mine, everything's mine. What a party I'll have tonight."

The Romans suddenly appeared at the entrance of the cave. They immediately noticed Hannah. "You're trying to cheat us," their leader said to Kasdaya. "We chased her all the way to your doorstep, and then you pluck her right from our midst. We're going to hold you to the bargain. You can have the girl, but we want the stones."

Kasdaya seemed agitated. "I give the orders around here. You'll get what I give you and no more."

The Romans drew their swords. They were ready to fight over the spoils. "We'll play fools to nobody."

Kasdaya growled. He wanted both the stones and the girl.

The Romans moved inside the cave to confront Kasdaya. Hannah noticed they weren't paying any attention to her, so she began to make her way ever so slowly back to the entrance of the cave. Once outside again, she immediately took off in the direction of the stone steps that ended at the summit, running as fast she could. She didn't look back, but began climbing back down, using her hands to keep from sliding. She didn't get very far before she caught sight of an Em sitting on a large boulder not far away with its eyes closed.

"Thank goodness, it's asleep," Hannah thought to herself, as she edged by as quietly as possible. Hannah was almost on the other side of him when her foot slid on some loose pebbles, causing her to land on the steps with a hard thud. She paused for a bit, daring not to even breathe out of fear of arousing the creature. Hannah let out a sigh of relief when she saw that he was still sleeping. As she prepared to resume her descent however, the Em opened one of its eyes and looked at Hannah. She curtsied. "I'm sorry to have disturbed you. I was just going for short walk." Hannah tried to smile. The Em let out a large screech, and used its great black wings to fly in Hannah's direction. Hannah raced on her backside down the winding stone stairs, but the Em was soon over her. Using his gigantic claws, he picked her up and began to fly.

Out of the corner of her eye, she now saw Selith on a ledge. Close behind in pursuit, were both the Romans and Kasdaya. Selith took her staff and threw it straight at the Em, hitting the creature in the head. Hannah shook her head in bewilderment as she realized that without the staff, her teacher would be defenseless against her opponents.

The wounded Em began to fly in a disorganized manner, wavering back and forth, at times, almost hitting the side of the mountain. Ever so slowly, the creature floated towards the foot of the mountain before finally letting go of Hannah not far from the ground. Shortly after, the Em collapsed in a heap near to where the stone stairs began. A thick cloud of grey putrid-smelling smoke surrounded the Em's body. When the smoke finally cleared, all that remained was a pile of burnt ashes.

Hannah went over to examine the remains of the Em. A small breeze scattered the ashes around her feet, making them feel as cold as ice. Hannah shivered. She looked up at the stone stairs chiseled onto the side of the mountain. She wanted desperately to help her teacher, so she placed her foot onto its first step. The second going would be more difficult that then the first, since she now knew where the stairs led.

Hannah got only a few steps up, when she heard shouts coming from the forest. She quickly turned around and saw a large group of armed Romans running towards her. An arrow whizzed past her head. Hannah realized there was no way to outrun them up the stairs. They would kill her before she got very far. Her best chance was to try to lose them in the woods.

She jumped down to the base of the stairs, and made a mad dash to the forest. At its edge, she paused to see where the sun was, but found it nearly impossible. Although well past dawn, it lay hidden somewhere behind the wall of smoky haze that still clung to the earth. Hannah resumed her run until she reached a newly made clearing. What was left of the mighty trees that once guarded the entrance to the mountain in the days of the Amorites was now nothing other than a few bare stumps. The Romans were using the timber to build ever-increasing settlements below the mountain, out of sight of both the Syrian Seleucids and the Judean Maccabees.

Catching her breath for a few short moments, an intense remorse penetrated into the deepest recesses of Hannah's spirit as she pondered the fate of her teacher. Hannah used her sleeve to wipe the tears as she thought of Selith, fighting to the last to save her. What became of Angels after they died, she wondered.

Her teacher was now gone and she was alone. Where was this new teacher, the Light, she was supposed to follow? Where could she find it? Hannah deeply longed for the peace that permeated all life, even if only for a few brief minutes. Instead, though, she only heard what seemed like Selith's voice, urging her on.

ו

# CROSSING THE RUBICON

Hannah kept running throughout the day and into the night. Only after a long while did she realize she had not slept or eaten for days. She wanted to rest, but fear drove her onward.

It was nearing dawn once more. Hannah turned a sharp bend in the path and tripped over a tree stump, landing in a big pile of leaves. She rested there for a second as she caught her breath. The leaves' pleasant odor reminded her of the wonderful years spent among nature in prayer and meditation while studying with Selith. Tired and struggling to stay awake, Hannah was about to doze off when she felt something hard poking up into her. Reaching inside the leaves, she found to her delight a couple of big red apples.

"These must have been buried by some squirrels for a rainy day," she thought aloud. "I hope you don't mind, but I'm famished." She ate them all. The apples gave her a renewed feeling of energy, enough for the remaining journey.

Hannah arrived back at their camp just as the sun was rising. Remembering Selith's instructions, she went directly over to the tree situated in the center of their small compound. She recited the prayers exactly as Selith instructed. A hole suddenly appeared on the side that received the most sunlight during the day. Hannah reached in and retrieved the pouch that contained the two quartz crystals.

Curious, Hannah reached into the pouch and pulled out the crystals. She peered through their transparent surfaces into the heart of the gemstones. "Yes, there're certainly beautiful, but I don't see what's so special about them." She began rolling them around on the palm of her hand. As she did however, they began to glow and making sounds, unlike any that Hannah had ever heard before. Her eyes froze, as strange images began appearing on their surfaces. She turned away. Not wishing to look at them any longer out of fear, Hannah slowly put the two crystals inside the special pouch Selith had given her.

Hannah kept hoping that Selith would suddenly show up, but she never did. She tidied up their huts one last time and swept the numerous sanctuaries built for the little creatures that lived nearby. They had built these out of stone, to protect them against the weather. In the middle of their small camp stood a long uncut marble table they used for special ceremonies, such as welcoming the yearly solstices. Hannah wiped it clean and placed her hands on it in prayer. She was thankful for the time she had with Selith. Glancing around one last time, Hannah wondered if she would ever return. She made a farewell offering and gathered up her few belongings. Hannah finally departed, feeling apprehensive about the road ahead.

Hannah decided to go back to her former home in Thella, not knowing where else to go. She was not an adventurer by nature, not having travelled outside of northern Galilee. From the trading caravans in Thella, she had heard that to the south in Judea many people didn't even speak Aramaic, preferring Greek or Hebrew instead. Although both her aunt and uncle could speak Greek from their days living in Syria, they never used it at home while Hannah was growing up. Her Uncle Stollanus being a Hellenized Jew and moving to a small town didn't want to stick out, especially being so dependent on his neighbors for the success of his milling business.

The sun had begun its rise over the Hulata Valley. It would take the good part of a day to reach Thella, going at a fast pace. Hannah walked north along the east bank of the wide creek that would eventually become the Jordan River, until reaching a place where the young wild stream was shallow enough to cross. Reaching the other side, Hannah veered due south, walking along the picturesque eastern base of the Upper Galilean Naftali Mountains. She loved this part of Galilee, as nature was still plentiful and human settlements few. Familiar sights and smells of these hills brought back pleasant memories of her youth. It ended all too soon as she arrived at the path that led westward down into the Thella Valley. Hannah picked up her pace, so she could arrive before the sun set.

Entering the outskirts of Thella, Hannah saw one of the men of the village walking towards her. He appeared taken aback, as if not expecting to see her. He tried to avoid eye contact.

"Greetings Hannah!" he said with his head lowered. "Still living with that witch on the other side of the lake? What a pity you never found a husband, someone who could have protected your poor aunt and uncle. Yes, so sad things turned out the way they did." Saying this, he quickly slipped into the small building that served as the village slaughterhouse. A foul odor came out of the door as he went in.

Surprised by his words, Hannah turned back to look at him. She saw him peeking out of the door at her. Hannah knew this man. His name was Daresiel, and had a reputation for being a petty crook, the kind willing to do anything for a coin or two.

Once, he cheated her Uncle Stollanus by selling him some stolen tools, although her uncle didn't know they were someone else's at the time. The rightful owner eventually discovered their location and demanded their return. Her uncle gave them back with due apologies, then insisted on getting his money back from Daresiel. However, the swindler claimed he had been the one cheated and refused. Her uncle didn't want to involve the district Seleucid officials, because of the uncertainty of the outcome in dealing with the foreigners' law. It was just as likely they would accuse him of stealing the tools, and threaten him with jail or something worse, if he didn't pay them a bribe. As a result, her uncle took the financial loss himself.

Hannah didn't reply to Daresiel, but continued on to her old home. After a short while, she approached the simple structure her uncle had re-built on the burnt ruins of their old house with the money Selith had provided. Arriving, she immediately felt something was amiss. A small group of men stood close to the front door. As Hannah came near, they suddenly turned to face her. Seeing Hannah, a few even became angry. "You're too late," a man with a fine robe said. Hannah had never seen anyone as finely dressed before. "You're a disgrace to your family. If I had my way, I'd have you publically flogged for your neglect of them. It's totally against the commandments." The other men nodded in agreement.

Hannah wanted to get past the man, but he prevented it. "How are you going to pay for the burials? The one held yesterday," he paused to look into the house, "and the other to be held soon enough."

Hannah opened her mouth wide in shock. "What has happened? Who has died?"

"You mean you don't know?" The man seemed surprised. "We just assumed you knew and that's why you're returning."

Hannah pushed the man aside and went inside the house. It was a mess. Hannah saw her uncle lying on his bed. She ran over and dropped on her knees next to him. "Uncle Stollanus, Uncle Stollanus," Hannah shook him as she called out his name, "Where's Aunt Emorun?"

He didn't reply. He wasn't conscious.

The other men left. Hannah fetched some water, wiping her uncle's forehead. At a loss what to do, out of habit, she prayed. Then, she suddenly remembered something. Hannah removed her pouch and took out some of the healing gems Selith gave her. Over the years while her student, Selith had taught her many of their usages. She picked out a blue gemstone with little gold spots speckled about its smooth surface. "Azurite, the Stone of Heaven," Hannah said as she held it up. Selith had told her it was a sapphire much favored in Egypt by the ancient healers in the time before the Great Flood.

Hannah placed it in her uncle's hand, and folded it over his heart. She prayed again and waited. After a short period, he regained consciousness. When he opened his eyes and saw Hannah, he became frightened. "You've returned." Her uncle attempted to push her away, but was too weak. "Get out of here."

Hannah was perplexed. "Uncle Stollanus, where's Aunt Emorun?"

Stollanus turned his head away. There were tears rolling down his face. "What a mistake it was, marrying into your aunt's family," he mumbled. "I should have listened to my father. He said it would only bring me trouble and it did." His voice was so frail, that Hannah was having a hard time understanding him.

Hannah gently patted her uncle's arm. "Uncle Stollanus, please tell me, what happened?"

Stollanus remained silent for a while. Finally, he reluctantly turned to face Hannah. "They came looking for a pouch, they said, thinking that your aunt had it. We told them she didn't but they didn't believe us. After they ransacked the house," her uncle waited for a bit before continuing, "they bound me. I was forced to watch as they did mean things to your aunt, thinking I would tell them where they were." He cried some more. "I'm sorry Hannah, but I couldn't take it any longer. Her pitiful screams tore my heart in two. I broke down. I would have said anything to get them to stop. I told them perhaps you had it. I told them too, where you lived. It was just a few days ago." Stollanus started to breathe heavily. "It's the fault of that old swindler Daresiel. He's in their service."

Now Hannah understood why the Romans attacked their camp when they did. Hannah was trying to sort it all out when she noticed his tunic had bloodstains on it. She lifted it up. The wound was still oozing blood. Stollanus turned his head away again and closed his eyes. "Before they left, they killed your aunt and left me for dead."

Hannah tried to use the Azurite stone to stop the bleeding, but it did little to help. Her uncle had already lost too much blood. She stood up. "I'm going for a physician."

Stollanus feebly waved his hand. "It's no use, they're all afraid to come. Since the attack, they think our house is cursed."

Her uncle suddenly sat up.

"What's the matter Uncle Stollanus?" Hannah quickly asked.

"Hannah, save me." He grabbed her arm in panic. "I don't want to die. Spare me this agony."

Hannah put her soft hand on his perspiring forehead and prayed. While she did, she used her other hand to gently stroke the necklace that Selith gave her, now hanging around her neck. Suddenly a bright light appeared. Out of it walked a woman, dressed in a splendid white robe, with golden trim sewn around its edges. "Peace be with you!" she said. "I am Azraela." The tone was sweet and reassuring.

Hannah looked at the necklace with a new reverence.

The Angel gazed down at Hannah's uncle. "Is it because of this mortal?"

"Can you save him?"

The Angel shook her head no. "It would be wrong to interfere with the natural laws of your earth. Do not be sad. He is going to a better place. He just does not know it yet."

At once, the smell of fragrant roses filled the air.

"Stollanus, gaze upon me," Azraela said as she held out her hand. "I have come to take you home, into the everlasting Light."

Her uncle saw the Angel and smiled. "Where are we going?" There was no longer any hint of panic in his voice.

"We are going to a place where sits a splendorous tree in the vast sea of eternity. I promise, you will be happy for ever and ever." Stollanus grasped Azraela's hand. There was a flash of light and the Angel vanished. After she was gone, Hannah saw her uncle lying on the bed, with arms folded over his chest and a smile on his face. There was no breath. He had passed on.

Hannah went over to the table and rested for a spell. She regretted not asking the Angel for some advice. She thought about touching her necklace to summon another one, but decided not to abuse the privilege. They could always take it back, she mused. Better to save it for real emergencies.

Hannah noticed an old loaf of bread still on the table. She saw that it had walnuts in it. "How strange," she thought to herself. "Uncle Stollanus hates walnut bread. In the past, she only made it for me, and on special occasions. Perhaps Aunt Emorun had foreknowledge of what was about to take place and meant it as a message of some sort for me. She too was after all, a descendant of the Great Teacher. She may have inherited some of his special powers."

Hannah didn't give it more consideration, as she needed time to prepare for her uncle's burial. Less than a day was all she had. Hannah tidied the house up a bit and went out. Her uncle was correct. The villagers were afraid to talk to her. The Romans had roughed up some of the men and taken a few of the young women as hostages, saying they would kill them if they informed the Seleucid government about their coming. Hannah feared for the worse, as most likely, the Romans sold them to the Watchers for breeding. So Hannah went directly to the religious authorities. There, she discovered that the men she had run into at her home were from the temple. The one with the fine robe was an exiled Sadducee from Jerusalem. He eyed her with suspicion and inquired into her family background. They were reluctant to come without first getting their money, thinking Hannah might leave town without paying, once things were finished, since she no longer lived there. She paid them right there, to ease their concerns, from the few coins she still had.

Returning home, Hannah stood looking around, taking stock of the situation. Grief began to creep into her mind. Both her aunt and uncle were now dead and perhaps Selith too, if Angels did indeed die. She was beginning to dislike the crystals, so many had died because of them. Maybe her aunt was correct. They were more a curse than a blessing.

There was a knock on the door. Assuming it was neighbors wishing to express their condolences, Hannah quickly opened it only to see it was Daresiel.

He rubbed his bony hands together and craned his skinny neck to get a look at inside the house. "Sorry to hear about your aunt and uncle. Too bad they lived such hard lives, and for what? In the end, those who should have helped them in their old age ran off to spend a life of leisure in the woods. Are you going to invite an old friend of the family in? Or are you going to let me stand at the door like some stranger."

Remembering what her uncle had told her about Daresiel's role in the attack, Hannah did not trust him. "I appreciate your calling on me," she said while gently closing the door, "but I'm feeling rather out of sorts. My aunt and uncle's passing has been a great strain. Please come back some other time."

Just as the door was about to shut, Daresiel put out his foot preventing it. "Well, well. A little uppity are we now. You're pretty, that's for sure. I hear say the Romans living up around the mountain are paying a dear price for young maidens." Daresiel looked her up and down. "Better yet, we can marry. Then, you can share those pleasures with me instead. You've no man to protect you, and I've no wife. You don't have any dowry to speak of, but I'm willing to take a little shame in exchange for a beauty. What do you say? Are you going to let me in or not?"

Angry, Hannah slammed the door against his foot, forcing him to remove it. Instead of leaving though, he used his body to ram the door, forcing it back open and breaking its hinges in the process. Strutting in while pushing the broken door aside, he began ogling Hannah's body in a way that made her feel uncomfortable.

"Now that we're alone and there's nobody to protect you, can't you not see how vulnerable you are? Why, if you can't protect yourself against me, how will you be able to do so from them? Let's join forces. It's been ages and I'm more than ready!"

Hannah ran behind the kitchen table to get away from him. "Get out of here, right now!"

Mad with lust, Daresiel followed her. He grabbed her arm and threw her onto the bed. Not wasting time, he jumped on top of Hannah and tore at her robe.

Hannah pushed him away and rolled off the bed. She grabbed a broom and began to beat him. Daresiel pulled out a knife. "You think you're so smart, don't you. Well, let's get to the point. I want those magic stones." Daresiel let out a laugh. "Yes, I know all about them. I overheard the Romans discussing the situation. They didn't think I understood their mutt of a language. Now, hand them over like a good girl and I'll spare your life. Still better, marry me and we can run off together until I can figure out how to use them. Just think about it Hannah. The poor, despised, Daresiel, would one day be sitting on a throne, and you'd be my queen, just like in the tales of old."

Hannah was desperate to figure out what to do. Just then, the Sadducee exile from Jerusalem came to the door. He saw Hannah with the broom still in her hand. "Young woman, your neighbors say that you're an orphan without any family. Maybe I can better your situation." The Sadducee walked into the house. He caught sight of Daresiel with the knife in his hand. "What's going on here?"

Hannah ran over to the Sadducee. "Please help me. This mean man is trying to force me into marrying him."

"Is he now?" The Sadducee put his overweight body in front of Hannah, as if to protect her. "Now be reasonable and put the knife away." He looked Daresiel straight in the eyes.

"Mind your own business," Daresiel sneered. "You only want her for yourself. You're on good terms with those Romans and would do anything to take revenge on the Maccabees who sent you to this miserable outpost. How much do you think you can get for her?"

"Nonsense," the Sadducee replied. His fat cheeks wobbled as he spoke. "My intentions are honorable. She's a pretty one without any family. A match with me would be a step up."

Daresiel came closer to the Sadducee. "Out of my way, fat priest, I can kill two just as easily as one." Daresiel was a butcher by trade.

The Sadducee took hold of a stool and threw it at Daresiel. Daresiel ducked and lunged at the priest. They both fell to the ground and began fighting. Hannah took advantage of the turmoil to flee. As she ran towards the center of the small village, it seemed to Hannah that her foes were everywhere.

ז

# WILD BEASTS,
# GENTLE SHEPHERDS

Situated along one of the minor caravan routes between Judea and Damascus, Thella was a place where traders often met up. With the civil war between the Pharisees and Sadducees winding down, and commerce slowly returning to normal, the small village's business activity took place at the marketplace every day except Sabbath. Trade caravans often preferred to use less traveled routes, like the one that ran through Thella, to avoid the more heavily patrolled thoroughfares along the coast of the Great Sea. Well known among all traders in the region was the reputation soldiers had for reducing their life's savings to an empty bag or wagon. Worse still were the hated tax collectors, who would not only confiscate their goods, but also might sell them or their family into slavery over trumped-up unpaid tax charges.

Hannah went directly to the village square. She quickly joined up with a small group of merchants going to Jerusalem on business who agreed to hire her as caretaker for the animals. Being from Thella, the traders had heard about Hannah's reputation as a hermit and at first hesitated to take her on. In the end, however, they gave into Hannah's persistence. Although unmarried, attractive, and appearing to be in a desperate situation, Hannah felt protected by this very same reputation. Nobody would dare harm her out of fear she would cast a spell on them.

The small caravan had been on the road south for a day when it stopped to water the animals along the northern shore of the Sea of Galilee. Hannah had unloaded the heavy bags off the sore backs of the pack animals when she noticed some foreign looking men going from caravan to caravan, as if searching for someone. Hannah wasn't certain, but they seemed to be Romans. So far, she hadn't seen anybody else that looked like these men on the journey. Hannah spotted the Sadducee from Thella among them. He appeared to be leading the small group in their search.

As they neared her caravan, Hannah grabbed one of the mules and took it to the shoreline. She began washing it in the cool waters of the shallow sea, using it as a shield to hide behind.

The strangers began asking questions of the men who were traveling with her. The caravan leader pointed over to the pack animals that were lazily nibbling on the few scrappy-looking bushes that lined the rocky banks of the sea. Knee deep in water, Hannah could see the men go over and search among the animals. She knew it would just be a matter of time before they caught sight of her. Hannah wondered where she might flee. She was not a good swimmer, so there was no hope in using the sea as an escape route.

Hannah looked at her necklace and wondered if she should use it. She closed her eyes to pray about it for just a second, for she reckoned that was all the time she had. Suddenly the mule she was hiding behind began to move without any prompting. Hannah thought it ever so strange. This mule was the most stubborn of the bunch, always needing cajoling to get it to do anything. And now, it was acting more like a docile lamb, walking ever so slowly along the bank of the sea towards a clump of small bushes. Hannah walked in synchronization with the legs of the animal, making it nearly impossible for those on the banks to notice her. Once arriving at the bushes, Hannah laid belly down in the water, hiding behind them.

Hannah stayed this way for some while. Thinking enough time had passed; she got up and looked around. They were gone. Getting back on shore, Hannah noticed that deep dark brown mud stained the front of her robe. She looked a mess. The people in the other camps mocked her as she walked by. Most already had a poor opinion of people from Galilee, considering them for the most part poor and uneducated. Her appearance only solidified their impression. Arriving back at her own camp however, Hannah was surprised to discover that the robe had turned a clean bright white, as if newly bought.

In a good mood, Hannah petted one of the other pack mules. It was happy for the attention. She then glanced down once more at the necklace. "But I didn't touch it," Hannah said to the mules, as she got ready to sleep. "How can it be?" Giving it no more thought, she dozed off into a deep slumber.

* * *

The small group arrived outside Jerusalem towards midnight of the third day, making it too late to pass through the closed gates of the city. Needing to wait until morning, they made camp near a place with water for the animals. As they had been riding hard for most of the day under the scorching sun, everyone felt tired, including Hannah. Spreading out their blankets on the hard ground, under a sky now covered with clouds, the men went to sleep as soon as their heads hit the bits of straw that served as their pillows. Hannah wanted to do the same, but instead took care to make sure the animals were bedded down. By the time she went to sleep, it was nearly dawn.

Hannah was rudely awakened by a kick to her side. She got up to find that the troupe had left without her. A big man was standing there with his hands on his hips, staring down at her. "What happened?" he asked in a mocking tone. "The men all left. I hope they paid before their departure."

At first, she did not understand the meaning of his words, but then it struck her. He assumed she was a woman of the night and had found some customers among the traders.

"No, sir, I'm not that kind of person," she said while rubbing the sleep from her eyes, "but a woman of Aravat."

"That's right and I'm Moses," he replied with a grin. "You're a young pretty thing, so you'd better get moving along before the guards see you here. They might force you to give them something for free."

As soon as he left, she looked around for the bag with her belongings, only to discover that the traders had stolen it. What was she to do? She knew not a single person in this large, strange city, and now had no money, nor even one small piece of fruit to eat. After giving it some thought, Hannah decided to go to the temple area and try to secure assistance there.

Approaching the main gate into the city, a burly guard with a short black beard told her stop. He held up his large hands. "What's your business here? I can tell by your clothes you are from Galilee. Where are the rest of your fellow travelers?"

Hannah was respectful to the guard. "I wish to go to the temple. Can you be so kind as to tell me the way?"

"To the temple," he shot back. "And what business do you have at the temple? It is no high holy day. Is there someone you wish to visit?"

"No sir, I just want to see it. And perhaps seek gainful employment."

At this, the guard bristled. "Now I see your meaning. You've come to either beg, steal, or to sell something else. Although, I don't think you will get much at the start for that something else, looking the way you do in those dirty clothes."

Hannah fell to one of her knees. "Dear sir," she pleaded, "if you're a man of Aravat, you can feel in your heart that I' m not any of the things you mentioned. I am seeking answers that only Aravat can provide, if he is merciful. Please, let me in."

The guard scrutinized her closely. "All right, you may enter," he finally said with a tone of resignation. "The temple is near the center of the city. Keep walking down this road until you see a large grey building. That's the merchant's pavilion. Turn to the left and not too far from there, you'll see it. You can't miss it. I wish you success in your search. However, be warned. It's not safe for young unaccompanied women, in particular those from the wild areas of the north, to be wandering about the city unless they are up to no good. Find your answer as quickly as possible, and after that go home where it's safe."

Hannah looked more closely at the grungy guard and felt he was nearer to the spirit than he was willing to admit himself. She gave him a curtsy. "Thank you for your kindness, sir. Your children, and your children's children, will rise up and call you blessed." With that, she ran past the guard and into the holy city of Jerusalem.

It was going to be a hot day. By mid-morning, the sun was already sending down blistering rays of eye piercing light, forcing Hannah to walk in places that provided shade. Her stomach was complaining from its emptiness, and her lips cracking from thirst. Hannah asked an old woman she met along the way, who had a kind face, where she could find a well to get some water. Laughing at her naïve question, the woman informed her there were no such wells inside the city, unlike in the countryside.

Feeling extremely tired, Hannah decided to sit and rest for a while before proceeding to the temple. Thus far, she had encoun- tered nothing but difficulties since her separation from Selith.

Hannah was beginning to lose confidence. Then she remembered the necklace. Hannah hesitated. Was she wrong to use it now? She couldn't make up her mind. As she sat there, confused, two young women came walking up to her.

"Peace be with you!" they said in perfect Aramaic. "We see that you are a stranger to these parts. May we be of any assistance?"

Surprised, Hannah wasn't sure how to reply. "Yes, you are right," she finally said after regaining her composure. "Do I really look that different from everyone else here?" As she said it, Hannah stood up and looked at herself. "Maybe I wasn't smart in coming here. But I seemed to be led by an inner guide."

One of the women let out a joyous laugh. "It is always wise to follow a leading, that is, if you know what one is. As for looking different, do not worry. How is it possible to be a prophet while looking the same as everyone else? The problem with following the herd is stepping in all the droppings!"

The young women giggled in unison. Hannah surveyed them more closely. Taller than most women of Palestine, they wore spotless white robes and each carried a cloth satchel. They pulled some fresh fruit and honey from the bags. "Here, take some," they said in joyful tones as they handed them to Hannah. "Eat and be refreshed."

Hannah readily accepted their offerings, eating everything quickly. "Famished, it seems!" said the fatter of the two. "Here, wash it down with this. It was made by our friends, the bees."

Hannah drank some. It was delicious. She knew by its taste that it was mead. It made her feel refreshed without causing her head to be either cloudy or sleepy.

Hannah began feeling like her usual self. "Where do you live?" She was curious and wanted to find out more about these interesting women. "What form of work do you do here? I'm looking for a position myself. Maybe you can refer me to some kind persons that would be willing to take me on as a servant. I'm a very hard worker, and honest too."

They both bowed. "We live neither here nor there," the taller of the two answered. "And our work, we are simple herders. As to finding suitable employment, well, that is a path that only you can take."

Although their answers were confusing, their cheerful dispositions made Hannah glad at heart. They moved closer to Hannah's ear. "You must be careful," one of them said. "Do not judge scrolls by their sheaths," said the other. "Those who appear good on the outside are often friends of the dark ones, and those who appear rough may well be tender inside."

With that, they started to go. Before getting too far, one of them suddenly turned back around. "Oh my, I almost forgot. We ran into a group of men, traders by the looks of it, from the same place as you. They were early this morning just inside the city gate and were involved in some dealings of business with smuggled goods. Their hearts were simple, but had taken shadowed roads recently, perhaps too hungry for quick, if ill-gotten, gains in their business dealings. With a money-tainted life force surrounding their bodies, he who commands the black hearts noticed them right away. Greed is the bait to entice the unsuspecting into his foul embrace. We wanted to help, but it was not possible to overcome their stronger desire for money. Hence, these traders from the north all went off for some drinking, gambling, and whoring with their new dark friend. That is, all but one." She paused for a moment.

"He was a kind man, and a father of some few daughters. He feared for his spirit and prayed for assistance upon learning the true intentions of his newfound associates. We heard his prayers, as they were full of the spirit of true repentance. When we approached him to inquire about his condition, he said that he did not know in advance that this trading venture would turn to such evil ways, as it was his first foray into business, being but a simple artisan by trade. The harsh conditions of the war between the Sadducees and Pharisees had brought disaster to his family, forcing him into seeking other ways of surviving. He readily admitted that he was not used to dealing with shrewd businessmen."

The taller of the two continued where the other had left off. "From the start, he was suspicious that this business venture might not be to his liking. However, the final realization came today before dawn, when the others cheated the woman who they had hired to care for the pack animals. A kind soul noted for her sanctity he said, they had left without paying her wages and even stole her few belongings. He tearfully spoke about his situation, finally handing us this poor looking bundle. He described what the owner looked like, and asked if we would try to find and return it to her. We promised we would do our best, telling him that he should return to his village and never associate with these bad men again. He agreed and left at once."

She smiled, holding out the bundle. "And, here you are! This is yours, is it not?"

Hannah gladly acknowledged ownership and thanked them for their kindness.

"We can give you some friendly advice if you are willing to accept it," one of them said to Hannah. "Mind the Light as it condemns all its deceivers who have turned from it. You cannot find what you are seeking as long as you rely on only visible things. As temples of the Living Light, the voice of Aravat is already within people's hearts. What need do you have going to the temple that is without and not the one within?"

They waved their hands. "Be of good cheer and go in peace!" they said in unison. There were smiles on their faces as they departed. Hannah shook her head in wonderment. She wondered if they were Angels too. But it seemed odd. Unlike the other Angels she had met so far, these were more human-like. Looking up, Hannah noticed that the sun had passed the halfway point in the sky. Most people in the city were napping, escaping the heat. Hannah thought it would be a good time to go to the temple, since with fewer visitors it would be easier to find a quiet place to pray in what might otherwise be a busy environment.

Hannah felt awkward as she approached the outside of the great temple wall. She had imagined that its splendor and magnificence would awe and inspire her. It was after all, the holiest of holies, and the earthly sign of the special relationship between the people of Israel and Aravat. Instead, all that she saw were the numerous beggars and poor peddlers hawking cheap goods to the visitors. Standing there, she watched as the wealthy and powerful indifferently strode past these impoverished folk in their rich robes without even a glance or acknowledgment of their humanity. She saw some poorly clad peasant woman drop a few coins in their simple clay cups and did the same before going on.

As Hannah walked closer to the main gate that was covered with tall golden vines and grape-clusters, she noticed a large veil embroidered in blue, white, scarlet, and purple, that marked the boundary to the outer temple. Going inside under the scrutiny of stiff standing guards, Hannah climbed a series of large stone steps until she arrived at the interior court. This was the beginning of the sanctuary.

She wanted to touch the breastwork of stone that encircled the area at the level of the steps but was afraid of what the guards might do if she did. Instead, she peered curiously at the inscriptions placed at frequent intervals in Greek and Hebrew. They were warnings for non-Jews not to go any further. The penalty was death.

Hannah covered her head and went into the inner court with its two divisions, one for women, and one for men. She instinctively went into the eastern court reserved for women, as it was the same for any temple of her people. All knew the strict prohibition against women entering the temple proper.

Inside, there stood a few women gathered together in small groups. They seemed to be talking about nothing of any importance. Walking closer, Hannah overheard a haggard-looking middle-aged woman complain about the neighbor's husband and his late night escapades with the young girl who worked at the wine shop. Not interested in hearing more, Hannah located a suitable place to sit far away from the others. She sat on a small hard stool near the minor gate leading into the western courtyard and closed her eyes.

Hannah found it difficult to center down. There was a deep unsettledness blocking access to that silent realm of the spirit. Normally within minutes, she would penetrate the cloud of unknowing. Instead, Hannah felt drowsy and even worse, agitated. Perhaps it was the thought of those poor beggars sitting pitifully outside the gate that bothered her. She had gazed into their sad eyes. Hannah's mind continued to drift. Over-tired by the past day's events, she fell asleep.

When Hannah awoke, it was close to dark. The guards were asking everyone to leave. Hannah picked up her things and went back out into the outer courtyard. There was a buzz of activity as people were going home for their evening meal. Hannah prepared to leave when she noticed a mean-faced guard accompanying a rotund looking Sadducee, dressed in eloquent robes, to the place she was standing. She rubbed her eyes in astonishment. It was none other than the same Sadducee who had pursued her from Thella.

"Is this the woman you were talking about?" the Sadducee asked the guard.

"Yes sir, she's the one."

His voice was stern as he addressed Hannah. "Is this true? In front of everyone, you insulted the holiest of holies by sleeping in the temple. Do you know the penalty for such an act? What manner of person are you? By your clothes, it's easy to see you are a peasant from the north. Don't they teach you basic etiquette in those poor, rural areas?"

Taken by surprise, Hannah didn't know how to reply. "You don't recognize me, sir? I'm the girl from Thella. I must have fallen asleep by accident."

His face now red with anger, he waggled his fingers in her face. "I never met you before in my life. How can you tell lies, in this, the holiest of places?"

"I never tell lies. I came here to pray."

"You were praying? Who instructed an ignorant girl like you how to pray? Why, just listen to that vulgar Galilean Aramaic spewing out of your mouth. Did no one ever teach you to speak proper Hebrew? I'm certain you can't read either. More likely, you were looking for a free place to sleep, or you're hiding from the authorities."

Hannah was confused. Could it be that this really wasn't the same man? Didn't they say in Thella that the victorious Pharisees exiled him from Jerusalem? If it was true, how could he return? Hannah tried to explain her situation. "Oh no sir, I'm not looking for such a place, for I have sufficient funds for a room. And I'm not guilty of any wrongdoing."

"I know this type of woman, sir," the guard said to the priest as he closely scrutinized her. "They come to the temple all the time. Once inside, they either pick your pocket or try to get some unsuspecting man to bed them for a coin or two."

The priest grabbed Hannah by the arm with a firm grip and twisted it until she winced from the pain. "Where's your husband? I wish to speak to him to clear things up."

"I'm unmarried sir."

The expression on the Sadducee's face changed. "What, at this age and already a widow? Where are your other relatives? Surely there must be others that will vouch for your character?"

Hannah replied directly, in a very simple and innocent manner. "I've never been married, and I came by myself. I'm an orphan from Galilee."

With that, the guard smirked. "I told you, she's a tramp and up to no good. I say we teach her a lesson. We must get the word out that we'll not tolerate these types before the High Holy Days. Otherwise, when it gets crowded, we'll have real trouble on our hands."

Hannah struggled to get free of the Sadducee's grip, but instead he pushed her down to the floor. "Take her away. Put her in the temple prison. After spending time in there, she'll know we mean it when we say the likes of her aren't welcome."

Hannah got on her knees and pleaded with them both. "I am not what you think. I'm not guilty of any wrongdoing. I only came to pray."

The Sadducee waved his hand. "Put her in the side cell, next to the back stairs far from the others. There, no one will hear or notice her."

The guard looked at the Sadducee and shot him a knowing grin. "Yes sir. I'll do as you say."

As the guard escorted Hannah away, the Sadducee smiled.

The beggars and peddlers outside the gate shook their heads in amazement as they watched the guard lead Hannah to the temple prison. What possible wrong did the young woman do to deserve such treatment? The common people of the land had no hope against the whims of the powerful.

The cell was damp and dark. It was not large, containing only a single hard cot without bedding. Because there were no windows, there was little light, and no sounds were heard anywhere as it was far removed from the other cells. The guards tied Hannah to the bed. The ropes were such that she couldn't move or use her hands.

The guard lifted her robe. "Nice body and something pretty to look at," the guard said to himself as he walked away. "He said I could have some too, after he's done with her. I hope he keeps his word. I need a change from the old hag I'm married to."

A wave of anxiety surged over Hannah. She tried desperately to touch Selith's necklace, but couldn't with her hands tied. So instead, she closed her eyes in prayer. Hannah was not only afraid of their evil plans, but also that they might discover the crystals while in the act.

It was well past midnight and very dark. Only a small sliver of moonlight shone through a narrow window in an outer chamber. Hannah heard the door to her section open with the squeak of its rusty hinges. There was the sound of a heavy man's footsteps getting close. The steps halted in front of her iron door allowing Hannah to see the shadowy figure of a man in a hooded robe. The man pulled out some keys and unlocked the door. He walked in and stood next to her. It was the Sadducee.

"You thought you were so smart, running away like that, didn't you?" The Sadducee put the torch he was carrying inside a worn base attached to the musty smelling stone wall. "You should have stayed around to see that poor dog Daresiel fall on his knife. It went right through his heart. It was too embarrassing to explain the situation to the authorities, so I had to tell them that you did it and ran away. They're looking for you."

The Sadducee began to massage Hannah's breasts. "The Romans will pay a high price for you, although they won't say why." His voice became excited as he lifted up her robe. "They can wait a few days while I have my fun first. I can try to discover the mystery of your worth afterwards. Maybe others will pay an even higher price."

Hannah closed her eyes as the Sadducee disrobed. Getting on the bed with her, he started to kiss her neck. As he did, the

Sadducee caught sight of the necklace. He stopped to examine it closer. It looked valuable. They only thing stronger than his lust was his love of money. "Where did you steal that?" His eyes grew wide. "It's a sacred object and must be worth a fortune." As he was about to take it from Hannah the cell suddenly filled with a bright white light. So intense it was that Hannah couldn't see anything else. The Sadducee shielded his face. "Who's there? Put out that light. Is this some a trick? Haven't I given enough money for the privacy, or are you trying to force me to pay more?"

The light became even brighter. Through its radiance, Hannah could make out a beautiful woman. She was extremely tall, with hair tied into tight braids that ended on her shoulders. She wore a long, soft, blue robe, and a transparent glow surrounded her body. It grew in strength nearer to the head.

"Too long you have made a mockery of the Light," she said with her hand raised. "See how the girl does not need to shield her eyes? You cannot look at it for it has condemned you. Ask your master to come save you now! I think he dare not, for you are not worth the fight. You already belong to him."

The woman touched the Sadducee with an ancient looking staff that had a carved serpent at its top. He let out a loud and painful scream. The Sadducee writhed in agony on the stone floor. "No, no!" he cried out. "Spare me!"

He went still. Nothing more came from him. His naked body lay motionless on the cold stone floor.

Looking up, Hannah saw the light diminish as the woman put the staff back under her robe. Hannah stared at her with wide-open eyes. "Are you an Angel?"

"Yes. My name is Metatron." The Angel untied Hannah, who immediately pulled her robe down. "Surprised by my visit?" the Angel asked.

Hannah straightened up a bit. "I didn't realize there were so many Angels. It seems there is one on almost every street corner."

"You are closer to the truth than you think." the Angel replied while examining Hannah closer.

Hannah bent over the still body of the Sadducee. "Is he dead?"

"He will recover now that the evil spirit occupying his body has departed. When he awakens, there will be many questions asked. He used the money that the Romans paid him for you to bribe his way back to Jerusalem. Things will not go easy with him. Come now and make haste, we must go. The new day's sun will soon rise."

With that, the Angel took Hannah's hand. Pushing open the door of her cell, they felt the way with their hands along the dark corridor. After climbing some steps they discovered that the way to the outside was unlocked, allowing them to go out into the fresh air. Seeing they were beyond the walls of the temple, Metatron urged Hannah to run as fast as she could. They soon reached the same gate Hannah had entered the city through, less than twenty-four hours before.

The first rays of the sun were beginning to peek through some small white clouds. Arriving, Hannah was happy to find the same guard who had let her in. She greeted him with a smile. "Good morning to you, kind sir."

"And to you!" he replied. Remembering her, his eyes began to shine. "I hope your day in our city was eventful."

"Oh it was eventful enough. I'm taking your advice, though, and leaving. If you will allow me, that is."

He waved her through the gate and raised his hand in farewell. "May your journey be fruitful, wherever it leads."

Hannah thanked him, and without even a glance back to the city, left Jerusalem. "He is a good man," Metatron said as they departed. "Even though his pay is meager, he owns the world."

"I don't think he saw you."

Metatron just nodded her head yes, but gave no further explanation. "I apologize for arriving late, but I was delayed by other matters."

"We were supposed to meet? Who informed you about my coming?" Hannah covered her mouth with her hand. "Oh, I forgot you're an Angel. I guess you know everything. And I thought it had something to so with the necklace." Hannah fingered it. "It seems that I don't even need to touch it. Just wearing it is enough to call them."

Metatron urged Hannah on as they walked. "Maybe you are discovering the connection between prayer and thought. Is there any real difference between the two? Everything is connected. Did not Selith talk to you about this before?"

Hannah tugged excitingly at the Angel's arm. "You know Selith? Is she still alive?"

The Angel sighed. "Things are not going well."

Metatron looked at Hannah's confused expression. "You will understand more as time goes on. For now, it will suffice if you remember her last words. Trust in the Light."

ח

# ONLY ANGELS HAVE WINGS

Leaving Jerusalem behind, they walked at a fast pace, almost running at times. Tired and bewildered, Hannah longed for the peace and serenity of her old life. The sun was high in the sky as they climbed a hill to get a look at the surrounding countryside that spread out below. They were near a wooded area filled with rocks and low-cropped bushes. It did not seem very welcoming.

Hannah shook her head. She was despondent. "Where are we headed? Are you allowed to tell me, or is it a secret?"

The Angel waited for a second or two before answering. "There are no secrets between us. We are heading to the Negev to meet up with some companions."

"The Negev?" Hannah shook her head. "Why do we need to go there? In Galilee, they say most people never return once they enter that foreboding place. I've even heard that horrible creatures dwell there. The last time I went on an adventure with an Angel, the results were not good."

Metatron placed her arm on this frail, poorly clad woman's shoulder. "Allow faith to be your staff."

"Let us start." Metatron looked off into the distance. "We must reach the Springs of Zin before the sun appears on the morrow's cusp."

On reaching the northern edge of the Negev, they turned due east, traveling through its barren gullies and low deserted mountains. Had she not seen it with her own eyes, Hannah would have never imagined a more eerie place. Nevertheless, she forced herself to keep going in spite of her misgivings.

The landscape changed as they arrived at the soft, moon-like Zin Valley. After searching for a while, Metatron found an oasis inside one of the numerous springs in which to rest.

"From this very place the twelve spies were sent by Moses to scout out the Promised Land," Metatron explained as they walked into it. "The force of the Shekhinah is strong here, and will shield us from Nergal, the Eye of Beelzebub."

Hannah nervously looked out into the dark desert night. "This is not the first time an Angel has mentioned this eye."

Before Metatron could answer, Hannah laughed. "I know. There is no time for details. I will understand more as time goes on."

Although Angels did not share with humans a sense of humor, Metatron was nevertheless pleased to know Hannah was feeling more at ease. Metatron led Hannah to a place where she could find refreshment from the healing waters that gushed out of the deep springs.

They sat under the bright, star-lit night for the few hours that remained of the evening. Metatron closed her eyes. Hannah did not know if the Angel was asleep or praying. In any case, she was hungry and decided to go see if any of the trees had fruit to share. Spotting a large Date tree, Hannah shimmied up its narrow trunk, just like the boys in her village used to do to get ripe apples in the fall. After plucking a few, she dropped back on to the ground to view her plunder.

"Thank you sister tree for this treat," Hannah said as she bit into one of the green dates. It did not stay in her mouth for long. "It's so bitter!" she said, spitting it out. Being the first time seeing a fresh date, she did not realize that it was weeks away from fully ripening. In the north, they only ate dried ones provided by the traveling caravans.

Hannah did not know what to do. She was hungry and her stomach would not cease its complaining. Thinking it over, Hannah reached into her robe and pulled out Selith's pouch. She then took out the two crystals. "Maybe your magic powers can help me. If you are able to ripen this fruit, I'll know your true value."

Hannah began rubbing the crystals on to the dates. As she did, the crystals lit up and began to make strange sounds again.

"Hannah, what are you doing with those crystals?" The voice was stern.

Hannah turned to see Metatron, hands on hips and her face red in anger. Hannah lowered her head in shame. "I'm sorry. I was hungry."

"Humans can be such fools at times. It is no wonder they are facing a predicament." The Angel calmed down. "Hannah, you must be more careful. There are many who will do anything to get the crystals, including killing you. Once outside that pouch, their power will draw the Great Eye to them. You must keep them safe at all cost, if you can do nothing else."

Hannah held out the two crystals. "If they possess this kind of power, I think the wrong person is carrying them. They should be under the care of great Angels."

Metatron folded Hannah's hand over the stones. "No Hannah, they are not for Angels. We do not need them. We have powers enough in this dimension. Bad Angels however, desire to place them once more in the hands of men."

Hannah stood there as the sun began making its early-morning march over the horizon. She thought about the dangerous cargo she was carrying, still unable to understand why they would entrust such valuable items to her care, even if she was some great teacher's descendant. Hannah didn't have much to time to ponder it more, as she soon became aware of voices.

"Someone approaches," Hannah said, looking up at the Angel with a surprised expression on her face. "Do we need to hide?"

Metatron appeared undisturbed. "These are some acquaintances of ours. You should go out to greet them. They have traveled far to be here."

Hannah used her hand to shade her eyes from the glaring white desert sand and wondered at the riddle. Who was it they both knew? Perhaps it was Selith. The very thought of it excited her. After a few minutes, Hannah saw walking out of the bright morning sunlight and into the coolness of the oasis two young women, both wearing white robes. They carried cloth satchels in their arms. Hannah instantly recognized them as the same two she had briefly met in Jerusalem.

Striding up to Hannah, they greeted her in perfect unison. Their voices were both joyful and melodious. "Peace be with you, Hannah!" They raised their hands with open palms facing her in greeting. "What gladness it brings our hearts that you escaped the city unscathed. We hope you are enjoying your stay at these wonderful springs. There are no sweeter waters on your earth."

"So you are Angels! I thought so." Hannah moved closer to examine them in amazement.

Metatron greeted them with the same raised hand. "Daylight is upon us, and tomorrow's journey will be long." Metatron motioned for Hannah to stand by her side. "These are Ishim," she told Hannah.

"They are Angels, although they have a body similar to humans." Metatron patted the shorter one on the head. "Her name in your language is Dara, and her sister there is Nissa."

Both bowed. Hannah smiled at them in return. She felt wonderful to be in the company of the Angels. "It is not that wonderful," Dara said while picking up her cloth satchel. "The journey will become more difficult from here on. We are in the dark lord's lands now."

Her words took Hannah by surprise. Talk about some dark lord reminded her of Mount Harmon. Besides, Hannah felt the Angel could read her mind, a trait Selith often displayed.

Metatron took Hannah by the hand. "Be at peace and rest for now."

The Angel's words made Hannah's eyes heavy. A great desire to sleep overcame her. The three Angels led Hannah to a soft bed of grass on to which she immediately laid down on, soon drifting into a deep sleep.

ט

# THERE WERE GIANTS
# ON THE EARTH IN THOSE DAYS

The sun had already set when Hannah awoke. She saw the two Ishim talking in low voices with Metatron towards the edge of the small oasis where they had taken shelter. Hannah noticed how tall and strong Metatron was. With piercing eyes and strong facial features, she never imagined an Angel could look as noble as she did just now. Hannah rose and went to where the others were standing. "I'm now rested, how about you? Or I suppose, Angels never sleep?"

"We have no need to sleep in the manner of the things on this planet," Metatron said as she placed Hannah's hand in hers. "We rest in the arms of the eternal for our source of life through prayer and meditation. When you sleep, it is the same as when we pray. In both states, the Light refreshes the spirit. Perhaps you might like to know that just like Angels humans can also find refreshment using prayer and meditation."

Nissa looked up towards the sky. "Shall we get going? It is a wonderful night for walking underneath the stars. See how clear it is?"

Metatron waved the small group forward. "We must cross the Negev westward tonight in order to reach Mount Karkom before sunrise. We must tread carefully to avoid discovery. Nergal is desperate to learn of our whereabouts."

Dara peered out into the dark night, and then partially closed her eyes, as if trying to feel for something with her mind. "You are right, Metatron. It is getting more dangerous with each day's passing. Yesterday we tracked a band of Anaks as we entered the Negev. They were heading south into the land of the Nabataeans. We dared not keep on their trail for fear of delaying our meeting with you here."

"There are many sinister forces stalking the lands once more." Metatron's face became shadowed with worry while speaking. "Beelzebub is awakening the foul races, long dormant since the Great Flood, to secure his hold on men."

With great speed, they began their race to the west through the cool desert night. The Ishim had put some water from the Zin Valley Springs into a woven cotton flask, lined with strange looking leaves, for Hannah. It was wonderful stuff. With each few sips, Hannah would feel a new burst of energy. She would have never believed that she could run this fast, and for so long without taking a break. The Ishim could run even faster and longer. Hannah discovered they had other skills as well.

Often spotting a fig tree far away into the dark night, they would run ahead in order to pick some ripened fruit to eat and share with Hannah, to avoid stopping. Hannah felt that these two Ishim were the most beautiful things she had ever set her eyes on. Fair, slender, feminine, with soft features and song-like voices, they were so different from the strong and noble Metatron. She wondered how men kept their lustful hands off them.

It was near to daybreak. Metatron raised her hand. "It is as I had feared. We cannot make it in one go. We will have to wait one more day."

She turned to the Ishim. "You two are swift of foot and not easily seen. Go ahead and tell the others we shall arrive soon. They should start making preparations. See to it that Hannah has something to eat and drink. Alas, she may be in great need of it by the time we end this exhausting journey."

Without a word, the two Ishim disappeared into the rays of the early dawn. Hannah watched as they departed. Within a few seconds, they vanished over the horizon as if the desert had swallowed them up.

"Who are we to meet up with next?" Hannah asked. "What are they preparing for?"

Metatron had a grim look on her face as she continued to stare into the desert, as if still following the movements of the Ishim. "There is to be a meeting of the Angelic Council to discuss the present situation."

Close by were some small caves. Metatron found one suitable for Hannah to rest in during the hot daylight hours. Placing Hannah securely inside, she went off to a secluded place to pray.

Many hours passed. The sound of blowing sand roused Hannah from a deep sleep. The rock walls that encased her body seemed to tremble as the wind increased in strength. Through the small opening of the cave, Hannah could hear the sound of howling coming from within the sand storm.

"That's strange, "Hannah said to herself. "Why would wolves be prowling about, in broad daylight, and during a sand storm?"

As she stared into the thick curtain of sand, Hannah saw a large figure making its way towards the cave. Rubbing her eyes, Hannah thought that perhaps the sand was playing tricks on her. The figure was the size of a small tree. It had sharp pointed ears and hair-covered scales encased its entire body. In one hand, there was a black curved sword stained red with blood, while in the other it clutched a partly devoured dead animal.

The creature stopped and sniffed the air. Then it let out a loud screech. The creature suddenly tossed down the half-eaten animal and ran to the where Hannah was lying. Peering into the small cave, he caught sight of Hannah. With its free hand, the creature tried to grab her.

Hannah was able to dodge his grasps by moving from side to side. Frustrated, the creature put his face up the entrance. His rancid breath smelt of rotting flesh. Out of desperation, Hannah reached inside her robe for the pouch. If the magic crystals were to be of any use, now was the time to show their real power. As she placed her hands on them though, she remembered Metatron's warning and hesitated.

The creature did not delay. He grabbed hold of Hannah's feet and pulled. As she came out into the still raging sand storm, the creature tossed Hannah about like a toy doll. For a moment, she laid there, still. They looked at each other. He rubbed his large belly and began to drool, revealing his intentions. She was going to be his next meal. Hannah began rolling around in the sand to avoid his attempts to pin her down, but to no avail. The creature grabbed hold of her hair and pulled hard. Hannah screamed in pain. Just about to begin, the creature caught sight of Selith's necklace. Half covering his eyes, he threw Hannah down with a hard thud in frustration. Although sore from the rough handling, she used this opportunity to run away. He was preparing to give chase when suddenly he stopped and began searching the surrounding hills. Raising his curved sword into the air, the creature let out a loud howl. He had thought Hannah was alone.

There, standing on top of a small rounded hill made of course sand, was Metatron. Not wasting a second the creature charged toward her in a fit of rage. As he swung his sword, Metatron used her staff to block the blow. The sheer strength of the thrust however jarred the staff out of the Angel's hand, allowing the creature to jump at her, hoping to overpower Metatron by the force of his weight. With the creature now on top of her, Metatron grabbed his arm and threw him against a large boulder. Realizing the Angel's strength, the creature decided to flee, but found it impossible as Metatron would not release him from her firm grasp. Panicked, he grabbed her throat, squeezing as hard as possible to weaken her hold. Metatron tried taking hold of her staff that lay only a few paces away, but found it just beyond her reach. Hannah, trying to figure out how she could help Metatron, noticed the Angel's dilemma. She ran over and picked up Metatron's staff.

Realizing that Hannah would soon give it to Metatron, the creature dropped the Angel. Running away, it soon disappeared back into the desert.

"I never imagined such things stalked the earth." Hannah was still shaking.

The sandstorm was quieting down. Metatron gazed off into the desert as she pondered the meaning of the encounter. "He is a Gibbori," the Angel answered, "a giant offspring of the Watchers from a previous age. The Anaks that Nissa and Dara were tracking are also descendants of the Watchers. All are cruel creatures of the dark."

The answer so surprised Hannah that she backed away a few paces. "Are these not the things of legends?"

"They are not legends. The Watchers are fallen Angels who desire to rule the world through men. In a previous age, they bred human females. Their offspring they called the Nephilim. After the Second Angelic War, and the flood that came of it, we banned the Watchers from the earth. They have now returned from exile and are calling back their offspring from the dark places where they have been living in secret all these many years."

"We must make haste." Metatron appeared anxious. "I can feel it. The Light force has shifted. They must have learned we are in the Negev from the Anaks who spotted our tracks. Let us depart at once."

ט

# WHERE PROPHETS
# DARED TO TREAD

As the fading sun retreated, they once more set out. Every now
and then, Metatron would stop to listen, shifting her head
slowly from side to side, appearing to Hannah as if the Angel
had many sets of invisible ears attached to all parts of her head.
Other times, Metatron would just stare into the desert, not moving
her head at all. Afterwards, they often changed course to confuse
unseen foes following somewhere behind. Throughout much of the
night, it was the same, with Metatron never once allowing Hannah
to take a full rest.

With the coming of dawn, Hannah noticed there were more
clouds than the previous day, and they were turning darker. Metatron
urged them on, even though it was now day. The sun began climbing over the horizon revealing that they were standing on a mesa.
One mountain stood higher than the others. Overwhelmed by its
beauty, Hannah halted.

"That is Mount Karkom, the mountain of saffron," Metatron
said while gazing at its barren peak. "It is a sacred space and one of

great power, for it is an earthly vortex of the life force. It was from here that Enoch ascended bodily into the heavenly dimensions, and Moses spoke with Aravat. There are two other vortexes, one on Mount Carmel from which Elijah went bodily into the Light, and on Mount Tabor, which binds the power of the other two together to make a strong life force."

Metatron pointed to the ground. "We have now entered one of the few timeless places on earth. You can see the proof with your own eyes. As you look about, you will notice that the small pebbles underneath your feet have not been disturbed from the effects of time. The surface has remained unchanged since humans first arrived."

Hannah felt overwhelmed by the powerful surge of life force emitting from Mount Karkom. It was so strong that she had an intense desire to sit down and absorb some of it into her own tired body.

"No time for delays," Metatron said, encouraging her to move on. "The enemy knows our plan. We must reach our destination before the sun rises fully in the sky, and we still have some way to travel."

Hannah's body felt as light as a feather as they crossed into the sacred vortex, as if she were walking on air.

"This must be what it feels like to fly," she said to Metatron while bouncing along over the various small rocks and pebbles.

Metatron glanced back over her shoulder to Hannah. "Then unfold your wings of Light to travel faster. They are never far behind. Luckily, they will have difficulty dealing with the vortex. It may prevent them from following us any further."

A few hours passed. Hannah was just beginning to get used to running on air when they reached some large, sandstone, anthropomorphic-shaped boulders standing guard at the foot the mountain. The entire area felt like an ancient sanctuary.

Metatron raised her hand, motioning them to stop. "This marks the path that will take us to the sacred crypt hidden deep inside the mountain. Jedaiah priestesses built this place long ago, under the direction of the Ofanin. On one of the boulders is inscribed the words that will open the crypt when we arrive at its door."

Curious as to what it looked like, Hannah began inspecting the various boulders. After repeated attempts, she was still unable to find it.

Metatron didn't seem surprised. "Reality, at least as humans perceive it, is projected illusion coming through the eye, acting as a lens for time. The Light, as the source of consciousness, uses the eye as a way through which to experience life. So, try using both eyes together, the eye of the senses and the eye of the spirit."

Hannah did as instructed. Walking around the various shaped boulders, she followed her inner guide until she spotted a large pointy rock that did not look particularly different from the rest of the surrounding terrain, or particularly special. Standing in front of it, she gazed at its rough surface for a few moments. "I see it! I see it! It's wonderful! The writing is so beautiful! There are circles, and lines in the form of small flames. It looks similar to the markings on my necklace."

Metatron stood next to Hannah. "It is written in an Angelic language. If you want to read it, now is the time to use your crystals."

Hannah removed the crystals from the pouch. "There are two of them. Which one do I use?"

Metatron touched the double terminated tabular cluster. "This is a Teacher Crystal. It is here to teach. If you peer deep inside, you will discover a multi-dimensional universe."

The Angel pointed to a place between Hannah's eyes. "Put the crystal there and try again to read the script with your mind."

At first, Hannah could still not decipher the markings. Persisting, she decided to try using the same method Selith taught her for seeing the life force surrounding people's bodies.

"I'm beginning to see it more clearly." Somewhat frustrated, Hannah removed the crystal from the place between her eyes. "But I still can't understand their meaning."

Metatron looked back anxiously. "I am sorry but we must keep moving."

Metatron led them onward, trying to explain some of the mystery as they walked. "What you saw was not part of an ordinary alphabet, but a tool allowing humans to connect with the symbolism of the Hebrew alphabet. It blends language tones with symbols, symbols that are encoded messages of Light."

The mountain was beginning to slope steeply, making it difficult for Hannah to walk without occasionally using her hands to grab hold of nearby rocks. It didn't seem to bother her though, as she was intent on listening to Metatron.

"In the beginning of time," Metatron continued, "only Divine Sound existed, and it was one with the Light. Divine languages are contained within the matrix of this Divine Sound, and are what Angels use to put the Light into all creation. It also opens a pathway for Angels to project their image directly into the body, mind, and life force of the human."

Hannah paused her climbing and looked up at Metatron with an expression that revealed she was indeed thinking about what the Angel was saying. "Is it possible for me to discover this special pathway, made for us by the Angels?"

"Humans enter this pathway whenever they join with the sound matrix through prayers, sacred songs, chants, and the like."

Metatron looked up at the mid-morning sky with concern. "We need to walk faster."

As they continued their arduous climb through the rugged mesa terrain, Hannah spotted numerous rock-engravings placed along various stages of their accent.

"Thesy were made by the Ishim at the beginning of the ages as records of the humans' past," Metatron explained. "For those who have eyes to see, they mark the way to our destination."

A few of the markings had almost faded away with the passage of time. When inspected closer however, Hannah was able to make out the figures engraved on them. Some showed hunting scenes of men taking the lives of their innocent animal prey. On others were engraved the Eye of Aravat, and the snake on Aaron's staff. These she recognized from her studies with Selith. The one Hannah liked the best was the outline of a tablet divided into two parts, resembling Moses' tablet of the law. As she rubbed her fingers over the marks, Hannah felt a tingle from the life force embedded within the lines.

They reached an old abandoned well. "This is Beer Karkom." Metatron traced for Hannah some markings on the ground. "This is where the original Tent of the Meeting, the Mishkan, stood."

Hannah stayed close to Metatron out of fear of stepping on something sacred. "If you observe closely," Metatron explained, "you will see that the etchings in the ground are an exact match of the description of the Tabernacle that housed the Ark. The position of every peg is still marked by precisely aligned stones."

"You were right," Hannah said in a tone that revealed her excitement. "This holy ground leaves an undisturbed record of every event that has taken place on its soil." Gladness filled her heart knowing she was standing on the very spot Moses had communicated with Aravat inside the Ark.

As the sun rose higher in the sky, its beams brightened the sides of Mount Karkom. It appeared as a beacon of light, rising above a valley shrouded in an ever-increasing blanket of a thick, foul smelling fog.

After a short walk, they arrived at a large monolithic rock perched on the summit of the mountain, inclined slightly backwards, and surrounded by an artificial wall. Next to the wall was an old altar with a small group of steles. Moving her eyes around the vast complex, Hannah felt the power of the Shekhinah. It was so strong it made her body shake.

"It was named the Altar of the Golden Calf by those who wandered through the desert for forty years with Moses," Metatron said. "King Solomon once prayed here."

Hannah saw a rectangular temple-like structure made up of natural stones and a flat grey slab lying inside it. She recognized the faded engravings etched on to the old stone tablets as Angelic Script. On its upper side, lichens now hid parts of its ancient surface. Without even touching it, the sacred force that had made the markings was still strong enough to knock down a grown adult if they were too close to it.

Metatron took Hannah over to a small group of high boulders that rose out of the flat surface of the summit. "I've grown tired from the long journey, and am unable to see anything else with my spiritual eyes. If there is something of importance, you'll need to point it out." Hannah assumed that Metatron was about to show her some more ancient relics.

Metatron smiled. "There is indeed something important. We have arrived at our destination."

Metatron said something in a language that Hannah could not understand. It was beautiful and sounded closer to singing than talking. A large door appeared out of nowhere. There was a woman standing at its entrance. She was stout and very short, even more so than most of the children in Palestine.

"Peace be with you, Anafiela!" Metatron turned towards Hannah as she continued to speak. "This is Hannah of Galilee. She does not speak our language, at least not yet, hence my use of the common tongue." Metatron extended her right arm, with an open palm facing out.

"And to you Otmon," Anafiela replied, while she did the same so that their two palms could make physical contact. Hannah was now familiar with the way Angels greeted each other.

"Have the others arrived?" Metatron asked. "I am late. It took some time as the place was full of Nephilim."

"They are waiting for you," Anafiela replied. "The two Ishim arrived last night and informed us of your coming." The Angel kept her eyes fixed on Metatron's guest. She was chief warden of the Great Light Seal and the keys to the Tree of Life. She rarely materialized in this dimension and it was her first encounter with a human.

Anafiela took out a set of large keys carved from transparent Emerald and inserted them into a lock that suddenly appeared out of nowhere. With that, the door swung open. Hannah saw that they stood at the entrance to a large cave. This was the first time she had seen such a geological formation, although she had heard tales about them from the traveling merchants in Thella. Hannah was afraid to go in, especially after hearing Metatron say that those horrible descendants of the Watchers lived inside caves.

Metatron stepped in first and waited for Hannah to follow. As she hesitated, Metatron held out her hand. "Do not be afraid, Hannah of Galilee. We are entering a most holy of places. Deep inside the bowels of the Angel of the Earth are buried many of the patriarchs of old. It was to this very spot that our sister Hadraniela guided both Moses and Elijah."

Hearing it, Hannah's fear disappeared. Hannah was amazed at the effect the Angel's words had on her. The two of them traveled down the long corridor into the deeper chambers. Metatron used a crystal that glowed to provide light for Hannah.

"Do not be confused by what others call me, for I have many names. However, you should refer to me as I have instructed. Metatron is my formal name. It is a good lesson in not attaching too much importance to names and forms. They are nothing real in and of themselves. Most of the problems for the human mind stems from attachments to illusionary things that will not survive their deaths."

They traveled on through the deep caverns. There were many chambers; each guarded by beautiful Angels dressed in magnificent robes. Metatron took Hannah to a place that had stone stools and pointed to a polished marble slab. "Have a seat and rest. I need to go and look for the others. Later, I will send someone. Do not move, otherwise you might get lost or even worse, cause trouble by getting in the way. Peace be with you!"

"And with you!" Hannah replied, with a smile.

Metatron disappeared around the corner into a dark corridor leaving Hannah sitting by herself. She felt overwhelmed by the sight of so many holy Angels.

"Maybe this is what heaven is like," Hannah thought to herself.

"Heaven is not at all like this," said a cheerful voice from behind her. Hannah turned around and was surprised to see someone standing there. It was Nissa.

"Peace be with you, Hannah!" The Ishite's voice always had a melodic quality to it. "I hope you are comfortable in your new surroundings."

"Oh, I'm fine enough," Hannah answered. "At least as well I can be, surrounded by so many wonderful Angels." She sensed that the Ishim must be beings of great kindness.

"There are many things about Angels you are about to discover," Nissa said with a slight laugh, "like, there are many types and ranks of Angels."

Nissa pointed to the opening of the chamber that led back out into the main hallway. "We need to be off. There is much to show you, and even more to explain. Allow me escort you to a place where you will be able to rest and have a bite to eat. You have been on quite a journey these last few days. You must be tired."

"I was. Now however, I feel happy and full of energy and not the least bit hungry either. It's a miracle!"

Nissa laughed again. "Life can be full of miracles, that is, if one is willing to open the door to their possibility. Come, let us start out."

The two of them went hand-in-hand down a narrow passageway until they reached a great hall with high walls lined with precious stones of various colors that reflected the light of the torch Nissa carried. Hannah already noticed that none of the other Angels needed light to see by inside the caves. Far off into the distance was a waterfall whose waters fell into a small stream that flowed out of the cavern. Rows of gigantic polished marble pillars lined the sides, leading up to a grand-looking throne that sat at the far end of the hall. Scurrying about were Angels busy arranging high stools into neat lines just in front of the throne.

"This is where the Angelic Council will meet," Nissa said as they walked through the hall.

"What's it all about?" Hannah asked.

Nissa opened her eyes in surprise. "You do not know yet?" Realizing what she had said, Nissa placed her hands over her mouth in embarrassment. "Maybe I spoke too soon. We should wait until the others arrive."

Hannah curiosity was aroused. Metatron had told her so little. "Why can't you tell me now?"

They had left the hall and were walking down a narrow causeway. Scattered about its floor were thousands of small pebble-sized crystals. The intensity of the life force was so strong that it caused the crystals inside Hannah's pouch to vibrate. "Do you know why the Watchers want to mate with human females?" the Ishite asked, as she pulled closer to Hannah.

Hannah noticed Nissa's face became serious. It was a rare sight indeed. "Beelzebub, Samael's chief captain," Nissa said, speaking softly, "seeks to breed a new race of Nephilim to rule men in the approaching age of darkness. To accomplish this, he has allied himself with the Irin, the Watchers. We have heard reports that some of these new Nephilim have already been born on Mount Hermon, and more will be coming from the great deserts in the south if we cannot prevent it. Unlike before, this new breed looks like any ordinary human male. It is treachery from the evil prince Beelzebub."

They moved at a faster pace, deeper into the caverns. Hannah struggled to keep up.

"What is this approaching age of darkness?" Hannah asked between breathes. "Is the sun about to fall out of the sky?"

Nissa was glad that Hannah showed an interest. Oftentimes, spiritually gifted humans had little interest in the affairs of the world, preferring instead to frequent quiet halls to meditate and pray inside.

"How to explain it in such little time." The Ishite furrowed her eyebrows while giving it some thought. "The earth's sun orbits its own mother sun located at the Galactic Center in a twenty-five thousand year cycle. The closer your sun gets to its own, the more spiritually illuminated the minds of humans, and the more power the Daughters of Light have. During the First Age of the current great orbital cycle, when it was very close, the human spirit thrived. Little use did they have for material possessions. The spiritual development of humans of those times was very high. They did not even need to speak to communicate. Instead, they read each other's minds and even predicted future events through their dreams." Nissa's face changed, as if remembering something from long ago.

"You know so much about the stars," Hannah said. She appeared awed by this Angel's great knowledge.

"Unfortunately," Nissa continued, "as the earth's sun moved further away from its own sun, human material culture progressed, but at the expense of the spirit. The age of the Angels began to fade into the age of the prophets, and the strength of the dark forces increased. Human males began to dominate females, and their hunger for the flesh of slain beasts grew unabated. It was during these times that Angels taught their daughters on earth how to use the sound keys as the building block for human language, since the human race could no longer communicate mind to mind. We are now entering the era when the sun will be at its maximum distance from the Galactic Center, and at its full spiritual debilitation. The spiritual Light is dimming and the age of the prophets is ending all over the world. In a few hundred earth years hence, we will reach the summit of darkness as the sun reaches the halfway point in its orbit around the Galactic Center." Nissa looked over at Hannah with eyes that looked both very old and grave.

"Beelzebub has been waiting for this moment. Now that we Angels are losing the source of our power in the Light, he plans to exile us, finish off the remaining prophets, and use the Watcher's new race of Nephilim to give men the tools they need to destroy the world on his master Samael's behalf."

Hannah shook her head in disbelief. "How can this be? What role do I have in all this?"

"Your great ancestor had use of the crystals and knew it also. That is why he was so determined to prevent them from falling into the wrong hands."

Nissa halted in front of a door. "We have arrived. This is where you will stay for the time being. I will bring you something to drink and eat in short order. For now, you should take the time to rest. You have heard much already, and will learn more as time progresses. I will return in a while."

The Ishite disappeared down the hall. Once more alone, Hannah laid down on the soft bed next to the wall. She rubbed the crystals inside her robe and tried to make sense of it all. Her eyes however, would not cooperate and she soon fell fast asleep.

# THE SOUND WILL BECOME FLESH AND ENLIGHTEN THE WORLD

Hannah awoke to find that someone had put a small table next to her bed. It was laden with a wide assortment of fruit, seeds, and nuts, as well as a large clay pot filled with fragrant honey. Hannah was famished and quickly began to eat. Just finishing, Nissa popped in. "It is about time you decided to get out of bed," she said with a warm smile on her face. "We thought maybe you had had enough of all this and passed on to the other life. Come, we need to go now."

Standing slightly behind Nissa Hannah saw two Angels donning full suits of armor made from fine polished white platinum. She marveled at it exquisiteness. "These are Angelic princesses sent to accompany us to the meeting," Nissa said by way of introduction. "Satqiela hails from Second Heaven, and Shatqiela from the Third."

"Nice to meet you," Hannah said as she stood up to greet them.

Satqiela nodded her head in return. "It is rare indeed to see a human attending a gathering of the Angels."

"It is rare because it is forbidden," Shatqiela replied as if unhappy with this breach of the rules. "The last time was when Enoch walked among the stars. Moreover, if you recall, the result was only more work for us. There are reasons for regulations, you know."

"Enough," Nissa said. "We shall all know soon enough why she was summoned. In the meantime, we should treat her with all the respect and courtesy due a friend."

"I, too, am curious as to why I was invited," Hannah replied. "Perhaps you can put in a word to send me back home where I belong."

Nissa scolded the two Angels. "There, you see, you have made Hannah nervous." Turning to Hannah she said, "As for you, you do not have a home at the moment. Do you think you can hide from the dark ones on your own?"

The words of the Ishite reminded Hannah once more about her present circumstances. She thought about the parents she never knew and her aunt and uncle. So many people had died already for the cargo she now carried. Would she be next? Hannah then looked at the two Angel's beautiful clothes and then at her own shabby robe, and felt even worse.

"We need to go," the two Angels said in unison as they motioned for Hannah to follow. Straightening her robe, and putting one last piece of fruit in her pocket, Hannah accompanied Nissa and the two Angels back into the mountain's deepest chambers.

Soon they arrived in the grand hall they had passed through earlier. At the entrance awaited Anafiela. "I bid you an official welcome, Hannah of Galilee."

With that, Anafiela used the same Emerald keys as before to unlock yet another door. Hannah wanted to say something in return, but Nissa took her by the hand and led her inside without giving her the chance.

After finding their seats, Nissa got close to Hannah's ear. "This must be an important meeting of the Angelic Council. Just look, attending are representatives from the seven heavenly dimensions, as well as from the ten ranks of Angelic beings. You have already met two Ishim," Nissa said with a smile, "and also Metatron, who is from the highest order, the Hayot Ha Kodesh, or in the common tongue, the Holy Living Ones."

Many small bells started to ring as an Angel of great splendor entered the hall, escorted by a small group of other noble-looking Angelic beings. Walking behind her was Metatron and another Angel, whose white robe glowed as bright as the midday sun.

"This is her majesty Rikbiela, Princess Regent, the highest of all Angels," Nissa said in a low voice.

The Angel with the glowing white robe strode over to Hannah. "I am Ariel, a member of the Ophanim. I serve as the guardian of the Light and the throne it rests upon."

Hannah stood up and bowed out of respect. Standing next to Ariel, and holding up her hand in greeting, was Princess Regent Rikbiela. "You are most welcome, Hannah of Galilee. I am delighted to meet you."

Mesmerized by the sweet tone of this Angel's melodious voice, Hannah neither moved nor replied. Never in her wildest dreams did she think it possible to hear such an enchanting sound. As she stood there, Hannah could hear heard Rikbiela's voice inside her head. "There is no need to be afraid of us, Hannah," it said. "We will do you no harm."

Rikbiela then turned away and walked to her throne. Nissa tapped Hannah on the shoulder. They needed to sit down. As they did, Hannah noticed Rikbiela eyeing her from the throne chair.

Metatron went over to the princess regent and lowered his head in respect. "Your majesty, I desire your consent to begin the proceedings."

Rikbiela nodded. "You have my permission. But use the common tongue of the humans so that Hannah can understand."

Metatron turned to face the Angelic host. "Sisters, as we know, the human race is facing a crisis. We must act quickly, and decisively, if we are to be of any help. Beelzebub's and his allies are sparing no effort to finish off the last of the prophets and their followers. They are enticing men through promises of power, wealth, lechery, the consumption of flesh, and drunkenness, to swear oaths of loyalty to them. As in the age before the Great Flood, empires led by strong warriors have sprung up, and great armies are on the march. Without the Light to guide them, the human race will be no match for Beelzebub in the age to come."

An Angel rose from her chair. "I say this to you Beelzebub, we fear you not! Even if you align yourself with the Watchers, you are still no match for my Ofanim. We defeated the Watchers once before, and we can do it again. Let us confront these traitors and outcasts while we still have the strength."

Metatron beckoned her to sit back down. "We honor your bravery, good Ofaniela of the Erelim. You have proven your courage often in times past and those who belong to your sacred order will attest to it. Unfortunately, the world we once knew is no more and will not return for thousands of years. Our power is waning. It will not be we, who wage war against the darkness. It will be for the humans to decide their own fate by their own efforts. Our part in this will be small indeed."

Another Angel stood up and looked around in a stern manner. "Neither I, or any of my fellow Seraphim for that matter, have met any human able to fulfill such a task. Why, if even Michaela, the mightiest of Archangels cannot defeat Samael and his legions, how is it possible that a human is capable of doing so?"

Metatron's face became agitated at hearing this grave prognosis. She wanted to say something in return, but Rikbiela raised her miter. "Phanuela, continue, if you have more to say."

Bowing in acknowledgment of Rikbiela words, Metatron sat down. "You are right, Metatron," Phanuela continued. "These are no longer the times of ages past. With the spiritual weakening of the sun, Beelzebub now has the advantage. However, unlike the previous era when humans and Angels forged an alliance to defeat the living darkness, they are now almost blind to the world of the spirit, unable to see the approaching danger."

Rikbiela turned to Metatron. "What are our options?"

"Long have we feared such an ending for the earth," Metatron replied, returning to her feet. Her voice revealed a sense of dread that rose from deep inside her spiritual being. "With the return of the Watchers, our only hope lies in implanting a portion of the Light here. Those few with access to it might have a chance to keep men from destroying earth until the sun regains its strength in the next age cycle."

Phanuela pounded her staff in anger. "What utter foolishness! Your plan is doomed to failure. The rulers of men will crush any followers of the Light in the dark times to come. You place too much confidence in these weak creatures."

"What do you suggest?" Metatron walked closer to Phanuela. "That we leave earth and give Beelzebub his victory?"

"At least it would conserve our resources for another day." Phanuela pulled a red cape around her strong shoulders. "We should choose our battles more carefully. There are other dimensions to care for, no need to waste too much energy on this place. Our problems here all began when we failed to stop the Watchers from mating with the human female. Through this, they planted Samael's darkness inside the basic matrix of their human offspring. I say, let men destroy it and good riddance."

Satqiela and Shatqiela now both stood up. "We will take our myriads of ministering Angels and go with you," Shatqiela said while Satqiela nodded her head in agreement. Most of the other Angels appeared to side with them. Rikbiela looked over in frustration at Metatron. Was this to be the end of earth and the human race?

"No, no! You can't leave the world now." It was a voice different from the Angels. "You cannot! You must not go and leave us to this horrible fate!" Now off her stool, Hannah walked towards Rikbiela.

"Hannah, you must not speak," Nissa said, attempting to silence Hannah by pulling at her arm. "Please sit down. This is a discussion for Angels, and not humans. Come now and be good."

Hannah resisted and now stood in front of Rikbiela. "You can't leave us to our doom at the hands of these dark Angels. You cannot go. You must not go!"

Some Angels gawked at this intruder, while others were clearly unhappy with Hannah's lack of etiquette. A few began to laugh and poke fun at this shabbily dressed human.

Hannah became confused. Perhaps she had made a mistake. She had a sudden urge to run away.

"Be at peace Hannah." Rikbiela spoke in a way that calmed Hannah's anxieties. "We will listen to you, this one time. Angels have pledged to protect the human race."

"I'm sorry. I've behaved badly," Hannah said, wiping a few tears with her sleeve. She looked around at the rest of the Angels. "I can be of no help in this matter. If there is indeed such a human to save the human race, it must be a hero, and not a weak girl."

The other Angels became very quiet. They sat back down in their seats. Even Nissa, who was next to Hannah, was at a loss what to do next.

Metatron turned to Rikbiela. "Perhaps there is a way."

Metatron took Hannah by the hand and walked into the midst of the Angelic host. "Hannah, take out the crystals." Hannah did as instructed.

The Angelic host rose in astonishment. "I did not know they still existed," Phanuela said as she peered closer. "What if they were to fall into the wrong hands? Now I understand why the Watchers are pursing this girl." Phanuela turned to face the princess regent. "I think it unsafe to have such powerful gems in the hands of a frail, uneducated, peasant girl."

Ariel stood up. "You are wrong, Phanuela. Beelzebub would never suspect that we would entrust such powerful crystals to somebody like Hannah. Besides, he assumes we are searching for a champion who will wield the crystals' power to wage war against him and the Watchers."

"Then what is your plan Metatron?" Phanuela asked while looking more closely at Hannah.

Metatron placed her hands on Hannah's head. "Do not be fooled by appearances. Hannah, hold the crystals higher." Hannah did as instructed. A bright white light emitted from their transparent centers. The rays fell on Hannah, surrounding her in a sea of light. The Angels were awed.

"Hannah is a direct descendant of the great Teacher of Righteousness, our old and trusted friend. Only one such as her could hold them, unfazed by their magnificence and power. She will use the secrets of the sound keys embedded in them to unite the three vortexes. With this, the Light Gate will once more open, as it did with the creation of the earth, and through it will come the Light in the body of a human—a Mashiakh. The Mashiakh's life force will be one with the Shekinah, the presence of the Living Consciousness immanent in the cosmos and will be the Light Incarnate. The Mashiakh will teach humans how to transform and reintegrate their own life force consciously, and with full knowledge, into the universal Light. He will show the way to the Light to any willing to receive it. Using this Light as a source of power, perhaps a few lone souls can prevent men from destroying the earth in the darkness to come, the age of men. With the sun fading in spiritual power and with it, our own source of energy in this dimension, this is all we can do. The rest will be up to the human. Their destiny is now in their own hands."

After hearing Metatron's plan, Hannah became very nervous, "Perhaps that holy Angel was correct. I'm nothing but a poor and uneducated girl from Galilee. I can only endanger such a great mission."

Rikbiela got up from her chair. She walked over to a beautifully adorned marble altar. A clear Tourmaline staff rested on its top. Engraved near its crown were angelic holographic symbols representing the Ten Plagues of Egypt, while on its side was an inscription in Hiburu that read, 'To the extent of the Light let these come to pass.' The staff channeled the life force in such a way that it transcended the physical laws of nature, making it capable of performing many miracles.

Rikbiela held out the tourmaline staff to Hannah. "You will not go alone," she said with much solemnity. "Take it. With this staff, Jacob crossed the Jordan, Aaron performed wonders before Pharaoh, and Moses parted the sea. David carried it with him when he slayed the giant Goliath. It is now for you, Hannah to use and later pass on to the Mashiakh as a sign of his authority. It will be a friend when all others have failed."

Metatron looked Hannah in the face. "What say you, Hannah, Zadok's heir? Are you willing?"

Hannah was nervous and hesitated. Something inside though seemed to nudge her to accept. Perhaps it was her glorious ancestors beckoning, although she knew nothing of these Zadoks. Hannah decided to follow her feelings. Looking around at all the Angels,

Hannah bowed her head and crossed her arms in front of her chest. "I will follow the Living Light."

Rikbiela gently touched the top of Hannah's head. "I will bless her with holy oil, so that all, whose spiritual eyes are open, will know she has been anointed for this task."

With the sacred balm in her hand, Rikbiela used her thumb to put some oil on Hannah's forehead.

Finished, Rikbiela said in a clear and loud voice, "Rise, Hannah of Galilee. May the Light be with you!"

Ariel came up. "I wish to be the first to congratulate and bless this woman. It has been many ages, since the time of Enoch, that we have placed so much trust in a human."

Applause rang out from the Angelic host. There was still a chance if the gate, closed since the birth of men, could reopen for a Mashiakh to enter the stream of life on earth. Hannah wished that Selith could have witnessed the glorious Angels of Heaven cheering for her student.

Just as Rikbiela put the staff in Hannah's hand, an Angel came running into the hall. She was out of breath and panted heavily. "Kasdaya has led a band of Watchers here and are besieging the caverns. I fear they are too much for us. Our strength is fast waning with the weakening sun."

A look of urgency came over Metatron's face. "We must get Hannah and the crystals to safety. Clearly, it is they that they seek."

Rikbiela turned to the Angelic host, her face firm with determination. "They will get neither, not as long as I stand."

Ofaniela raised her sword high. "Let us see what mischief we can cause these unwelcome intruders. They will discover that we are not a spent force yet."

Metatron and Nissa led Hannah away. They didn't get far before Dara joined up with them. She had a satchel in her hand. "We still need food and drink."

"Are you going with us too?" Hannah asked.

"Who will make the stubborn mule move the next time you are hiding behind one?" Dara was having a difficult time hiding the smile on her face.

Hannah's mouth opened in astonishment. "It was you who did that trick?"

"They are sometimes referred to as miracles. But we will not mince words over terminology, will we?"

Both Nissa and Dara chuckled. Metatron however, was not amused. "Legions of evil demons are pursing Hannah, and you have time for jokes?"

Dara glanced over at Hannah. "This is the perfect time, in fact."

The small company wound their way through the many caverns inside the mountain until they arrived at a small door. It was barley large enough to let Hannah go through it. Nissa was about to open it, when suddenly Rikbiela and Ariel appeared.

Rikbiela extended her arm, palm facing out, in the manner of Angels. There was a short pause, while the others waited for Hannah's reaction. Hannah hesitated, but then reached out her hand in the same way, until their palms touched. A strong surge of life force shot up Hannah's arm. "May the Light always be with you, Hannah, daughter of Zadok," Rikbiela said to Hannah, mind to mind.

Ariel bowed to Hannah. "And may it be your teacher in all things."

Saying this, the two Angels vanished as quickly as they had appeared.

Metatron turned to Hannah. "I am sorry, but I must join Rikbiela and Ariel. There are too few of us to deal with the Watchers."

Hannah threw her arms around the Angel's waste. "Please do not leave me. First, it was Selith, and now you. How am I to accomplish my task alone?"

Metatron lovingly stroked Hannah's head. "There will be others who will assist you on your journey into the Light. Value their friendship and learn from them."

Nara pulled at Hannah. "Come, there is no time to spare."

Metatron gave Hannah a gentle shove. Hannah began to follow the two Ishim as they left the deep caverns hidden inside Mount Karkom. She turned back to gaze once more upon Metatron, but discovered the Angel was already gone. Wiping a few tears from her face, Hannah and the Ishim walked into the dry desert air. She once more found herself fleeing into a dark starless night from an unseen enemy.

בי

# TWILIGHT OF THE ANGELS

They retraced the steps Hannah and Metatron had taken earlier on their way up to Mount Karkom. Hannah looked up to the sky, then to Nissa.

"The weather seems fouler than yesterday. The stink is worse, and it is darker. How could such a change take place in a single day?"

"It has been longer than a day since you entered Mount Karkom," Nissa replied as she helped Hannah navigate through an area covered with thick brush.

"Did I sleep that long?"

"Mount Karkom is timeless," Dara answered. She was walking behind Hannah for protection. "It is similar to those who pursue a life of meditation and prayer, since they are frequently in a state that insulates their bodies from the ravages of time. They live years beyond the normal lifespan. Time and the living darkness were created together in the same instant. Before that, there was only pure Light. With the birth of duality, came decay and death."

Hannah was not happy to leave the energy vortex. She ever so desired to savor this holy place, feeling its sacredness in her bones.

Hannah relished the thought that, from here, Enoch ascended bodily into the stars, and Moses spoke with the living consciousness. How she longed for some of that special life force to come and comfort her now.

They came to the place where stood the boulders inscribed with Angelic Script. Nissa noticed Hannah looking at them as they passed by.

"There is a connection between Sacred Sounds and Sacred Geometry," the Angel said while rubbing the boulders with her soft hand, "as they both represent the higher template of creation. Sacred Geometry reveals, through forms, our relationship with the Light, and its study unfolds the secrets of the universe. Possessed with the knowledge of the Scared Sounds and Sacred Geometry, the Jedaiah priestesses built these structures inside this energy vortex to serve as a place where humans such as Enoch and Moses could enter the other dimensions to converse with the Angels and the living consciousness. Sacred Geometry provides the door and the Sacred Sounds are the keys that open it."

They were nearing the border of the vortex. Hannah turned to give the holy mountain one last look. She led her heart to a prayerful place and silently put into the Light the desire to return one day to bathe in the flow of the graceful life force that poured forth from here.

There was no time for Hannah however, to relish the moment. After passing through the outer boundary of the vortex, Nissa ordered the group to halt. She looked back towards Mount Karkom. "There is something happening. I can feel it. Great spiritual energies are at war. Will the Light prevail?"

Dara stood still for a moment, sensing for something. "We cannot wait to find out, in case it bodes ill for us. Come now, we should travel southeasterly through the Negev, until we are due south of the Dead Sea. From there, we can go up its western shore until we arrive at Qumran. We have a friend there. I think it is the best route."

Nissa looked up at the sky. "No time to waste. The night will begin to fade in a few hours, and we must be at a safe place by then."

They dashed onto the hot barren sands, now home to many dark creatures. As the sun rose, they scouted for a suitable spot to rest and hide. Dara noticed some large rocks in the distance. "How about over there?"

A couple of old grey boulders stood scattered about, most worn from the many ages of blowing sand grinding against their sides. After they arrived, Dara took a few pieces of dried fruit from her pouch and encouraged Hannah to eat some. Even though she had been running for quite some time, Hannah had little appetite and just wanted to rest.

Nissa climbed a high boulder to keep watch. Dara and Hannah sat down on the hard ground and stared out into the desert wastelands of the Negev. "Perhaps you do not know," Dara said quietly, looking over at Hannah, "but at the beginning of the time cycles in this dimension, we Ishim tended the creatures of the earth."

Nissa called down to Hannah. "You had better be careful. Dara likes nothing more than to tell tales of Angelic lore."

Dara ignored the comment with a smile. "With the close of the Light Gate after the fall of the Watchers, we trained a few human females in the methods for protecting the earth and its creatures. We gave them the title of Jedaiah priestesses and imparted to them a language of Light represented by encoded symbols similar to the Angelic Scripts. The power imbedded in sound, in the form of words, allowed the Jedaiah to use these original Light languages to tune the world as if it were a giant harmonic bell. The ancient angelic form of your language, called Hiburu, was one of these. It was a harmonic language and a true language of the Light."

Nissa was watching Hannah's reaction from where she stood. "Do you wish to hear more?"

Hannah nodded her head, agreeing eagerly.

"Fine," Dara said, looking up at Nissa, "then let us continue. The Watchers though desired to become masters of the earth. They and their foul offspring, the Nephilim, began to thwart the Jedaiah priestesses. The Jedaiah were no match against the brute power and strength of the Watchers and the Nephilim. It was then that the higher orders of Angels intervened, taking Enoch beyond the Great Eye of Orion to become a Star Walker. As you know, Ariel gave Enoch the crystals that you now carry containing the sound keys that can unlock the Light symbols. Encoded into the very basic fabric of the universe at the time of its birth, these keys were the way the Light communicated with its creation."

Hannah pulled at Dara's sleeve. "Please go on, tell me more." Hearing it from her high spot, Nissa turned away to hide a smile. She was glad Hannah was interested.

"Returning to earth, Enoch wrote down everything he had learned. Using Hiburu as its basis, he gave to his people their first language. The language that you use now is not exactly the same as Hiburu. To make it easier to understand by humans, the Jedaiah priestesses re-tuned it to make it vibrate slower. Then Enoch taught the sound keys to his son, Methuselah, who used their secrets to live to be some nine hundred and sixty years of age."

"Why is it that we do not live that long now?" Hannah's wanted to learn more about these things. She felt it might be useful in the work in preparing for the Mashiakh. "What happened to the secrets?"

Dara lowered her voice. "Through a ruse, the Watchers took some of the information from the crystals and passed them on to the kings of men. It was enough to allow the kings of old to build great civilizations. Not satisfied, these kings thirsted for ever more wealth and power, finally waging a terrible war against each other to gain mastery over the world." Dara looked pained as she told this part.

"As the wars spread, so did the destruction. Large swaths of the earth lay in utter waste as men were on the verge of accomplishing Samael's long cherished goal of destroying every living thing on earth. In a desperate act to save creation, the living consciousness imbedded in the Light, that which your people call Aravat, caused the rain to fall for forty days and nights to end the fighting and destroy the world men had built using the keys. In doing so, the last traces of these lost civilizations perished forever, except in tales passed down through the generations. After the Great Deluge, the Angels banished the Watchers and their foul offspring to prevent them from causing trouble again."

Hannah rubbed the pouch hidden beneath her robe. "The secrets of the keys remained however, embedded into the Record Keeper."

Dara frowned. "Yes, and with the sun now spiritually weaker, Samael desires once more for men to destroy the earth. Without the keys though, men must relearn the secrets using the slow and tedious path of time, hence their quest for the crystals. If men ever again regain this knowledge, they will wage war with each other for supremacy, just like before."

"But now," Hannah said, "there will be no Angels to help as in the days of old."

"Even if we could it would matter little," Nissa said as she jumped down into their midst. "In the age to come, humans will deny that Angels ever existed, just as they forgot the gigantic trees that once covered the earth."

Nara got closer to Hannah. "To obtain a long life, as did your prophets in ages past, one must live like the Ishim. Do not consume flesh. Instead, eat directly from the table of the Angels of the Earth without using fire to cook. For fire destroys the life force inside the food. In addition, perform physical and spiritual exercises which renew your life force, and never forget to daily pray and meditate."

Nara gazed upward into the heavens. "In the earlier ages," she said, "we lived among the gigantic trees. Their branches reached far into the clouds. Within the shadows of the tress, all creation lived in harmony with nature. Through the large tracts of forests flowed the Eternal River and in the center of this river stood the Tree of Life. Now, human civilization covers much of the earth and the giant trees are nothing but ash."

The angelic tales made Hannah drowsy. She closed her eyes for what seemed like a few short moments. Opening them again, Hannah was surprised to discover that it was night once more. She noticed the two Ishim gazing up into the heavens. Doing the same, Hannah noticed that it appeared as if the stars were falling from the sky. Long white streaks of light danced across the wide horizon. She had never witnessed anything like it before.

"The Watchers have prevailed, at least for the moment," Dara said with her eyes still fixed on the stars. "The life force of this dimension has spit asunder making it impossible for the upper angelic orders to remain. They will soon starve, being deprived of sufficient Light energy to sustain their high powers." Dara's tone of voice revealed a deep sorrow.

Hannah pointed upward. "There is a fine mist, streaming from end to end through the galaxy. It looks like a river. What does it signify?"

"Touch your necklace. You will be able to see more clearly," Nissa answered.

Hannah placed her hand reverently on the necklace. The mist transformed instantly into a long line of Angelic beings, walking ever so slowly in a single line through the heavens. "Look, there is

Metatron." Hannah waved frantically. "Metatron, do not leave," she cried out. "Please come back."

Nissa touched her shoulder. "She can no longer hear you. Allow her to depart in peace. Their time is over, only to be remembered in tales told to children."

Hannah shook her head. She was unsure what it meant. "Henceforth," Dara said in response to Hannah's thoughts, "only the lower angelic orders, like the Cherubim and Ishim will remain here on your earth. Being closer to humans in form, they can survive with less spiritual energy from the sun."

"Hannah, do you think you can make the remainder of the journey yourself?" Nissa asked, looking in the direction of Mount Karkom. "Dara and I should return to the holy mountain to make certain the bodies of the great prophets are still undisturbed. We may need to remain with them for a while until it is safe again."

"Of course, I can." Hannah tried putting on a brave face.

"Kasdaya and his Nephilim cannot be far behind," Dara added. "It will prove a useful distraction if we are traveling in opposite directions. They will feel our life force more than yours and follow us. This can give you a better chance of escaping his grasp, at least for a time."

Nissa drew a map in the sand. "Follow the sun and go due east. You will make it to the Dead Sea in a few days' time. There you will encounter another Ishite who will assist you. Use your staff if the occasion calls for it, but do not carry it openly. Display it only in times of dire need. It is a staff of great angelic power, and its use will attract the enemy."

Nissa placed her hand on Hannah's shoulders. "Keep your profile low. For now at least, you are once more a simple peasant girl."

Dara handed Hannah a satchel. "Here is what is left of the food and water."

Nissa and Dara extended their arms, palms facing out in the manner of Angels. Hannah was now used to it and did likewise. "You are a daughter of the Light," Nissa said with their hands still touching, "and a true heir of Zadok. It saddens me to leave when your need is the greatest, but there is no other option. We must return to Mount Karkom. Go, Hannah of Galilee, and be at peace, no matter the circumstances that confront you. Remember that the Light is your teacher. Obey it! We will soon enough meet again."

The Angels started out. As they set out towards the west and into the sunset, it seemed to Hannah that the Ishim were transparent, as if fading away.

Hannah was sad that her new friends were gone and realized that she was on her own again. Just days ago, she had been in the company of grand Angels, deliberating on the fate of humankind. Now, she was once more a poor nobody from the north of Galilee. Maybe it was all a dream. How was it possible for a lone girl to open the way for the Mashiakh, in order to save the world from the claws of the demon prince Beelzebub? The other Angels had reason to doubt Metatron's plan. Perhaps she would find that the caves along the Dead Sea were a good place to rest and pray, before setting off on any new adventures. "That", Hannah thought, "would be wonderful."

י

# THE TRUTH
# WILL SET THEM FREE

Hannah slowly made her way to the northwest coast of the Dead Sea, following the route Nissa had instructed. The terrain around the sea was barren with few signs of life, and Hannah was having difficulty adjusting to the smell of the salt water and the aridness of the land. Snakes and desert spiders were everywhere, as were the dreaded red ants. Hannah had heard tales as a child from the trading caravans that often stopped in Thella about the red ants living along the shores of the Dead Sea. Some reported that these were perhaps the most deadly in the world. It was said that if you were unlucky enough to have an encounter with them, they would, without warning, swarm all over the body, biting with great fervor any exposed piece of flesh. She remembered in particular one old traveler who took great joy in scaring the children of her village with stories about the ants devouring an entire person in a single night, while they slept peacefully in their bed. The very thought of it sent shivers down her spine.

For the first three days after Nissa and Dara had departed, Hannah continued to sleep during the day to avoid detection, and to escape the scorching rays of the sun. By now, however, it was the fifth day, and not a drop of water or single piece of dried fruit remained of her meager rations. Exhausted from her wandering, and dizzy from hunger and thirst, Hannah found a solitary tree to sit under on the bank of the sea. She began praying, while fingering the precious stones Selith had given her. As she did, Hannah felt the burden of her task sit heavy on her shoulders. Fatigued from stress and lack of nourishment, she fell fast asleep.

Hannah woke with a shout as a sharp pain shot up her leg. She looked down to see thousands of ants biting her. Grabbing the blanket she was carrying, she tried to wipe them off, but they were too many. For every bunch she got rid of, twice their number had already replaced them.

Fearing that if she delayed much longer there would soon be no leg left Hannah sprang to her feet and jumped into the salty waters of the Dead Sea. As she swam about the warm, green-blue waters, the ants let go of her leg. Hannah watched as they tried unsuccessfully to swim back to shore. Realizing they would all die in a matter of minutes, Hannah grabbed an old rotting log floating close to shore, and put it into the water next to the ants that were desperately attempting to save themselves from drowning. Soon, almost every single red ant was resting on it.

Going over to the log and waving her finger at the ants, Hannah scolded them. "You are a bunch of nasty, mean creatures. I should have allowed you all to drown. However, it is not in my hands to decide the fate of another's life. Now, you can redeem yourselves. As I have saved you, you must in return agree never to bite a creature that does not partake in the eating of flesh! As they do not eat you, you should not eat them either."

She pushed the log onto the shore. Once there, the ants jumped off to the safety of dry land. It did not take long before they had all disappeared back into the sand.

Hannah climbed back on to shore and sat down, inspecting the sand to make certain no more of the annoying ants were around. Turning her attention back to herself, she discovered that her legs had begun to swell and were painful to the touch. Hannah did not fear sickness or death, but was concerned that if something happened she would be unable to accomplish the mission the Angels had entrusted her with.

Limping back to her few belongings, Hannah took out of her pouch a small vile of herbal balm made from the petals of beautiful marigold flowers and the leaves of selfheal. She rubbed it over the numerous ant bites. As she waited for the swelling to subside, she thought back to that day sitting in the sunshine near a field of red clover, when she and Selith had made the salve.

Hannah repeated Selith's teaching aloud with a smile. "Oftentimes, plants work best on the physical plane, for the hurts of the body, while precious stones can be used for the pains of the spirit, as their energies work more on the subtle plane."

Watching the swelling recede on her leg, Hannah could feel her body recovering. She saw a spot that provided more shade and had grass to sit on, so she got up to move. Just as she began walking towards it, she heard someone calling out to her, singing almost.

"Hannah? Hannah? I have been looking all over the place for you. What took you so long to get here?"

Surprised, Hannah looked up to see a young girl herding three small goats. Wearing a dirty woolen tunic with a cloth belt tied around her narrow waist, the girl was not wearing sandals but walking barefoot on the hard stones of the beach. Although her attire was poor, she had a beautiful glow about her body. Her hair was long and flowing, and shone in the glare of the midday sun.

Hannah returned the greeting with equal cheer. "What brings you to these parts, mistress herder? Surely there is nothing here that any goat in its right mind would want to eat."

The herder gracefully bowed and replied with a smile. "There are different kinds of herders, are there not, one for animals and another for people. I have left my flock to go looking for one who is lost. I have found you, and my task is accomplished. Let us rejoice!"

The herder handed Hannah some water from her flask. "Why did you not use your staff to beckon me? It would have made things a lot easier for the both of us."

Hannah seemed surprised by her question. "How would you know about my staff? How do you know my name?"

The herder grinned. "Oh, a little bird, for that matter, told me all about you. That is how I knew where to find you."

"A bird? What kind of bird?"

The herder laughed while she picked up Hannah's things. "You know, those special birds that talk to our inner selves when we allow them too."

Hannah began to suspect something. "What is your name mistress herder?"

"The locals call me Wolf. You can call me the same if you wish."

"But why Wolf? You do not seem all that dangerous to me?"

"It is not because I am dangerous, but because I come and go without anyone noticing. However, I will reveal to you my other name. I am also called Radweriela, the Keeper of the Scrolls."

"The right to guard something as important as scrolls is solely granted by the king, and only in Jerusalem. What scrolls are you keeping watch over?"

"The scrolls that will prove the redactors were liars in league with the dark one," the herder replied. There was a determined look on her face. "Before the scrolls reveal the Truth, the malefics who lust for power and control will don the garb of religion to fool those who have not opened their spiritual eyes. When the time is right however, I will reveal the Truth through the scrolls. It will not be all at once, but bit by bit over the years. They will discover the scrolls in hot sands, in caves, a few through visions and revelation, and some even in the belly of the beast himself. When found out, the evil men who seek to control people's minds for their own dark purposes will groan in agony and gnash their teeth as the veil lifts to expose their real identities. And when this stream of the Truth is rediscovered, it will merge with the many Truths into the eternal ocean of Light to form the One Truth."

Hannah's face lit up. "You must be an Angel!"

The herder bowed her head in acknowledgment. "I am an Ishite. I think you have met some of my order already."

The expression on Hannah's face faced turned from joy to sadness. "Maybe it is not such a good idea for us to be together. Thus far, any Angel that has kept my company has come to a bad end."

Radweriela did not reply but pointed to a rather steep slope on the side of a hill. "That is our destination. Shall we fly or walk?"

Radweriela quickly began scrambling up its side. Hannah realized that her belly was empty and her leg still recovering from the ant bites. It would not be easy to keep up. Nonetheless, picking herself off the ground, she determined to do her best.

It was already dark when they reached a place that seemed like a good spot to rest near the top of the mountain. Radweriela looked at Hannah. "How about this for a home? It certainly has a wonderful view!"

Hannah was perplexed, as they were sitting on a narrow ledge far from the bottom. "Well, if you insist, I guess it will have to do," she replied with a hint of resignation.

Just as Hannah was about to sit down, Radweriela said, "Oh no, we cannot stop here! It would be too easy for evil things to see us. Let us go inside. It is much more comfortable there."

Radweriela turned and disappeared. Hannah twisted her tired body around to see where she was off to, and to her surprise saw that they were directly in front of an entrance to a cleverly hidden cave.

Into the dark cave she went, following close behind Radweriela. The Angel lit two torches that were lying against the wall of the entrance. It was a limestone cave and had a bad smell to it.

"Is this to be my new home? I prefer the sands of the Dead Sea, thank you," Hannah said to the Angel.

Not disturbed in the least by her lack of faith, Radweriela grabbed Hannah's hand and led her further into the cavern. "This way my good lady," she said. "This is just the front room, designed to keep the best hidden from those whose eyes have not been opened."

Hand in hand, they wound themselves through various hidden chambers until they reached a large cavern some distance from the entrance. It was the most spectacular site that Hannah had ever set her eyes on. Glistering stones lined the walls, some common and native to this land, but many were rare precious gems. Placed in even rows were gigantic stalagmites, stretching from front to back so that the entire chamber looked more like the inside of a grand temple rather than a cave. Towards the front was an elevated slab of smooth brown granite, and to its side were twelve stone stools, six on either side.

Hannah turned to the Angel. "It is either feast or famine. The entrance is too dim and dank for anyone to live in, and this is too grand for one person. Is there not something in between?"

"Who said this chamber is for one person?" Radweriela whispered, grasping her hand a little tighter.

"You mean we are going to live here together?" queried Hannah.

The Angel cackled. "Angels are not of this world, so we need nothing to shelter us from the elements. And your home is not to be this place."

"Then, who are *we*?"

"The *we*, dear lady, are neither you nor me, but those who be in need of shelter in the years to come!"

Now Hannah was confused. "I need to sit for a spell. I am very hungry."

"Yes, outside the sun has already set. It is time to rest, and you must be famished. You have not eaten for days."

Radweriela went over to an indentation in the wall near the granite alter and pulled out a large blue bag made from fine linen. She took it over to a long stone bench.

"Come, Hannah, and sup," Radweriela said as she waved a hand over the table to increase the life force. Hannah was amazed. There was a large selection of seeds, nuts, berries, fresh and dried fruits. In addition, there were also stacks of delicious looking honeycombs and several clay vats filled to the brim with bright rich-smelling honey.

Hannah ate until no more could fit into her stomach. To help wash it down, Radweriela gave her a large bowl of refreshing wine made from fruit and honey. When she had finished, Hannah leaned back against the wall of the cavern to take in the beauty of the magnificent hall. She wondered who had made it, and how long had it been here hidden from people's eyes, and who were the writers of the scrolls to be?

"Time to go mistress," Radweriela said, shaking Hannah out of her daydream.

This time Hannah would not obey. "I am too tired to travel any more. I must rest first. Unlike Angels, I need to sleep."

Radweriela stood there giving it some thought. "Yes, I suppose you are right." The Angel proceeded to sit down next to Hannah.

Hannah yawned as she fought off sleep. "How did the Watchers become bad Angels?" she asked.

"I thought you were going to rest?" Radweriela smiled as he said it.

"I will, but first answer my question. Please?"

Radweriela re-filled Hannah's wooden mug with honey wine. "Here, have some more. It will make you feel comfortable." Hannah was thirsty and drank it down in a few gulps. Shortly after, her head felt dizzy. Hannah rubbed her eyes, as it seemed that Radweriela had an exact twin sitting next to her. "It must be the effect from the wine," Hannah thought to herself. She closed her eyes, thinking that in a short while her head would be clear again. When she opened them, Hannah discovered that she was no longer in the cave. Instead, she was inside a dense forest of very large trees. She ran over to touch one. "These are magnificent, just like Dara described," Hannah said as she patted its thick dark brown bark. "I am having a wonderful dream."

There was a tap on Hannah's shoulders. She jumped back in surprise. It was Nissa and Dara. "No fair sneaking up on me!" Hannah said with her hand over her heart. It was beating wildly. "Where did you two come from?"

The two Ishim giggled as they grabbed Hannah's hand. "Follow us," they said in unison, guiding Hannah along a winding green path up to a hill where they could have a better view of the lush forest. It was full of wildlife. Hannah caught sight of a lion sleeping next to a little white lamb beneath a sprawling cypress tree. Not far away were some humans, resting peacefully under the sprawling branches of the gigantic trees. Hannah thought it so interesting that none of the animals of the forest seemed afraid of them as they walked nearby.

"We have traveled back to the first days of the world," Dara said as she pointed to an open valley below. "Look over there, they are our sisters." Hannah saw many beautiful beings, similar to Nissa and Dara, participating in a running game. Radweriela was there among them and waved to Hannah. Their laughter instantly brought joy to Hannah's heart. "While having the life force of

Angels," Nissa said, "the Ishim take physical form in the likeness of the creatures of the earth, to serve as stewards and gentle Shepherds of all created things."

It felt wonderful to Hannah, as peace reigned everywhere. "We lived in these forests," Nissa continued, "eating only from the fruits of the trees, the grasses of the fields, the milk of beasts, and the honey from bees. Because of it, we never experienced disease, or old age."

"We were even strangers to the pangs of birth," Dara added.

It was so nice living here that Hannah soon forgot about all her former troubles.

Hannah soon discovered that the Watchers guarded this dimensions and all creation for the Light. They were so powerful that humans regarded them as gods. One day, observing creation, the Watchers noticed how beautiful the daughters of men were who lived in this wonderful garden. Standing on top of a high mountain, one of them said, "Come, let us choose wives for ourselves from among the human females and beget children." Thinking about the very act, they were unable to resist the lust that took hold of them.

"I fear that you will not consent that this deed should be done, and I alone will become responsible for the great sin," Samyaza, their leader, said in reply, for forbidden it was, for Angels to have this kind of relationship with the creatures of the earth.

"Let us all swear an oath," his followers responded in the heat of the moment. "We will bind ourselves by a curse, not to abandon this suggestion but to do the deed." They were altogether two hundred, and all swore together, and bound one another by the curse. Through it, they fell from grace and into the power of Samael and the living darkness, taking the likeness of human males in order to satisfy their lust.

Having agreed, they swept down on the daughters of men and began to chase them in earnest. One spotted Hannah, and pursued her.

Hannah ran into the woods. "This place seems all too familiar," she said to herself. "I have been here before." Hannah came to a winding stone stairway that led up the side of a mountain. She shook her heads in panic. "Mount Hermon! This is the Stairs of Samyaza."

Glancing behind her, Hannah saw the pursuing Angel not far behind. Not waiting, she quickly ascended the stairs. Unlike before, she was able to climb without difficulty. Hannah soon found herself at the summit, but was unprepared for the sight she beheld. There were scores of young women, some just barely of age, lying there with the Watchers doing cruel things to them. Wails filled the air. Hannah wanted to help, but was unable as the pursuing Angel caught up with her. Grabbing Hannah's arm, he threw her on the ground. Before he could start though, a strong arm pulled him away. "What the hell is going on here?" the startled Watcher said. He was clearly unhappy that somebody was interrupting his fun.

"This one belongs to me," was the reply. Hannah thought she recognized the voice. She looked up. It was Kasdaya. Seeing Hannah lying there helpless, he grinned.

The other Watcher spat on the ground. "She's mine," he growled. "I got her first. Go catch one for yourself."

"I want this one. She's special. Now get going," Kasdaya said in reply, his large rough hand clutching the hilt of his curved sword. It was the same Hannah had seen in the cave on Mount Hermon.

"I say we fight for her," the other replied, pulling a black sword out of its worn leather scabbard with much force. Sparks flew as metal clashed with metal. As the two fought, Nissa and Dara ran over to Hannah out of a nearby patch of trees. "Run Hannah," Dara said as she pulled her up. "Come with us. There is not a moment to lose."

They ran back down the Stairs of Samyaza and into the woods at the base of the mountain. It felt to Hannah that she was now flying, as they soon arrived at the place where Hannah and Selith lived before. Nissa handed her a cup. "Drink this and return to your own time. You have seen enough." Hannah wanted to say something, but Dara put the rim to her lips. Hannah took a few sips and quickly fell asleep again. When she awoke, Radweriela was still sitting there, just as before.

Hannah rubbed her eyes in bewilderment. "Was it all a dream?"

"You can call it that if you wish. What is a dream other than travel into another dimension. Everything is an illusion. You should get used to it."

Hannah still felt uneasy.

"The Watchers made their evil pledge on the summit of Mount Hermon," Radweriela said, "whose name means the mountain of the oath. They took the human females as wives through violence. This great sin caused the Gate of Light that had opened with the creation of the earth to close. Humans and all creation were exiled from the garden."

"And after that?"

"The wives of the Watchers gave birth to the race of Nephilim. They were foul creatures, some you have already encountered. Samyaza named his first son Og."

Hannah felt sad. The garden was such a nice place.

"The world was no longer the same," Radweriela continued. "The fallen Angels taught men how to invoke the power of Samael by eating the flesh of beasts, for those who eat the flesh of slain animals eats the body of death and become death itself. From this time onward, animals began to fear the human. A Watcher named Asa'el, then instructed men in the dark ways of forging swords, knives, shields, and breastplates, and taught them how to organize into groups for fighting battles. Using these sills, men waged war and killed in cold blood. Asa'el then showed men how to adorn their women with bracelets, decorations, and ornaments, and paint their faces, to increase the power of their male lust."

Radweriela stood up. "The sons of men have since that time, waged war against the earthly garden and the Light, exiling themselves from both. In its place, they have built houses of stone and wood, hiding behind great walls, cutting themselves off from the loving arms of nature."

Radweriela picked up a stick that was lying on the cavern floor and began striking at the air is if fighting some unseen enemy.

"Is this not what a male child does by nature, without learning it from any others? Men fill the ranks of armies, jails, and prisons, and fight with each other in sporting contests when there are no real wars. Who is it that competes for wealth, power, and position among themselves with great zeal? They kill animals for sport, beat their family members when in bad temper, relish the sounds of foul words, and force themselves onto women regardless if they are willing or not."

"But this is not always the case," Hannah said, "that men are always evil and women good. Maybe it would be more accurate to say that women are by nature good, but can also turn to the darkness under the right circumstances. And although males are by nature, as you have rightly pointed out, prone to evil ways, they have the ability to work on themselves, and with the aid of grace, turn to the Living Light."

"By saying this, I see that you have realized a great truth," Radweriela said. "However, be warned. Through the influence of the Watchers and their offspring, there is always some measure of the darkness lurking in the male. It is when their violent nature goes unchecked by the Light that they are most dangerous. Samael desires to use the inherent darkness in them to destroy this world. He knows that as men master the secrets of nature, they will possess the ability to destroy all life. There must be some measure of the Light available if this sad fate is to be avoided." Radweriela faced Hannah, her face grave. "Do you have the crystals?"

"They are here," Hannah said while patting the pouch hidden beneath her robe with her hand.

"Good. Take them out. I will show you how to use them."

Hannah took out the two transparent crystals, both fitting in her palm. Radweriela pointed to one. "This is the Record Keeper. Every Record Keeper has a sacred symbol engraved on one of its facets."

Hannah began scrutinizing the crystal to see if she could find it. "They are not easily seen," Radweriela added. "Those whose spiritual eyes are not open will need a bright light in order to see it."

"There are some markings. They look like Angelic Script."

"Yes. It is written in Malach, the language of the Angels," Radweriela confirmed. "Next to it you should see a triangle, as all Record Keepers have a triangle on one of the six facets, forming the termination. The triangle represents trinity, the symbol of divinity in unity. It also represents the proper balance between the emotional, mental, and physical bodies that form the foundation of inner peace for the human. Rub the crystal Hannah. Do you feel the triangle? When Enoch walked the sky, Ariel etched it onto its surface. The triangle is also a symbol of the inner eye. To use it, the triangle must make contact with the place between your eyes that serves as the doorway into the mystical wisdom of the universe."

Now Hannah understood why Metatron had her do this when she first saw the angelic etchings on the rocks on Mount Karkom.

Radweriela's face became more serious. "Remember this Hannah; the staff was given to you to protect the crystals."

Hannah shook her head in agreement and rubbed her hand over the fine etchings on the staff. It was so magnificent. She then turned her attention back to the crystals. "Did Moses use them to communicate with the Living Consciousness, Aravat?"

"Moses used the Ark of the Covenant to communicate with the other dimensions."

Hannah picked up the other crystal. "What about this one? I have some experience using it."

"Yes, I know, I felt it. Teacher Crystals grant access to the vast stores of universal knowledge. Their only mission is to teach and show us the proper way forward."

"Do I use it the same way as the other one?" Hannah asked while putting it close to her spiritual eye.

"There is no single way to use it. It will teach in a manner that best suits the situation, in a way no one can predict. It is better to keep it near your body, in whatever way is comfortable, so that it can communicate clearly when it needs to. If you are in particular need of its wisdom, you can place it on the heavenly eye or in your hand during meditation. You can even put it under your pillow while you sleep."

Hannah returned the crystals to her pouch.

All of the sudden, Radweriela turned to face the entrance into the chamber. "I want you to meet a friend of mine." She spoke into the shadows.

Hannah was surprised. She had not heard or seen anyone arrive. "Are you always this interesting, Mistress Angel?"

Radweriela grinned. "While you may call me interesting, the redactors will not be so kind in their description."

"And what will they say about you?" a voice asked out of nowhere.

"Do not be so rude," Radweriela replied with a laugh. "Show yourself so that my new friend can see you too."

An Angel appeared next to Hannah. She had a beautiful smile and held up her hand in greeting.

"Peace be with you!"

Hannah leaned back against the wall of the cave, trying not to faint. Regaining her composure, she jumped up and gave the Angel a long and warm hug. It was Selith. "You are safe, I was so worried."

Hannah rubbed her eyes and touched the Angel again. "How is it that I can see you? Nissa and Dara said that Angels could no longer materialize."

"The higher order of Angel, the more difficult it is." Selith's face became grave. "At least for those of us who still remain here." The Angel inspected Hannah more closely, trying to see the changes in Hannah's life force since their separation. "As the power of the sun's debilitation increases, all Angelic beings will feel the effect. I am however, a Cherub. At least for now, while not as easy as before, Cherubim can still materialize and be seen by humans. I just need to be selective to conserve my life force."

Radweriela handed Hannah a cloth satchel containing various dried fruits, nuts, and seeds. "You are about to begin the first part of your journey to re-open the gate, long since closed, to allow the Mashiakh to come. You will soon depart the world of Angels, and re-enter that of men. It is a road fraught with dangers lurking behind dark shadows. Along the way, you will make many friends and encounter none-too-few enemies."

The Ishite bowed to Selith. "You are fortunate Hannah of Galilee, for this wise Cherub will be your companion throughout the journey."

Selith rested her hands on Hannah's shoulders. "You have been given three treasures to assist you: the necklace, the staff, and the crystals. Use them carefully. Never before has a single human been entrusted with so much power. You could rule the world if you so desired."

Hannah let out an audible sigh. "I would gladly trade them for a quiet place to spend the rest of my life in prayer and meditation."

Radweriela chuckled. "And that is why you are their bearers." The Ishite pointed to the crystals in Hannah's pouch. "You are to travel to a place near Jerusalem to deliver a message to an order of holy prophets."

"What message?"

Radweriela raised her hand in farewell, in the manner of Angels. "There is your teacher, the Light. Listen to it carefully and you will find the answer to all your questions!"

Selith pointed towards the cave's entrance. "The first rays of the sun are arriving. It is time to depart this place."

As she prepared to leave with Selith, Hannah wondered where the next steps of her journey would lead her.

# י״ד

# WE AWAIT HIS RETURN

The sky had cleared, and the sun was about to rise. The suffering people of Palestine were on the road, walking in a long line. They staggered along slowly—soldiers maimed in battle, the sick, and the innocent female victims of the wars, many with their children, conceived in violence, in tow. All were wandering about with the hope that somebody would take pity on them and perhaps give them a few morsels of bread to survive another day. The cause of this misery was the frequent wars waged by the Maccabee kings to expand their territories.

Among them was a man, barely able to limp along, hanging on to his frail looking wife. As they dragged themselves forward the wife caught sight of two women walking past them at a fast pace. The wife raised her hands. "Please, help us," she called out to them, "for the sake of Aravat. Have mercy on us!"

The two women came to a sudden halt. The wife took her husband and went over to one of them and grabbed hold of her arm. "Daughter of the highest Aravat, my husband is dying from a putrid disease, and his suffering is great. I have served Aravat faithfully my entire life and have asked for his help, but none has come.

I can see that you are blessed with many gifts. Please assist us in our time of dire need."

"Why do you address me as such?" the woman asked in return. "Everyone has a measure of the Light, making us equals in its presence. If I am a daughter of the highest, then you are too, and so is every woman you see here."

The wife of the sick man was unable to reply in any meaningful way. "Help us," she pleaded, "for I have followed all of our traditions as prescribed by the priests in the temples. Surely Aravat can repay me with a miracle, if he so chooses."

"Your meaning is that Aravat engages in barter with his people?" the woman asked. There was a hint of scorn in her tone. "You do this and that, according to what the priests dictate, and Aravat grants you favors in return?"

Not understanding her meaning, the wife continued to beg. "Please save my husband, for he suffers grievously. It pains me to see him in this condition."

"You may have followed Aravat, but your husband has eaten much flesh, engaged in war, and has spent many nights in the beds of other women. What help will the Living Light be able to provide at this late hour?"

The wife began to weep and fell on her knees. "He's seen his errors, and has asked Aravat to forgive him his debts. Surly Aravat is merciful and will grant peace to a sinner who has asked for mercy?"

Up to this point, the man had not said a word. "Who is it that you are addressing on my behalf?" he asked, breaking his silence.

"Are you so ill that you cannot see? I'm seeking help from these two ladies."

The man looked first at his wife, and then at Hannah. "The stress of the journey and the bright morning sun is affecting your eyes. Besides us, there's only one other person here."

The wife ignored him. "If there is to be no relief from the pain at least let him die knowing that Aravat has forgiven him his numerous sins."

Moved by the wife's sincere words, the woman took pity and raised her eyes to the sky. "The Living Light only visits with sickness those it loves the most." She looked back to the wife. "There is still time and hope. His sickness is painful, but curable. Go to Jericho and seek out the woman who sells baskets by the old city gate. She will tell you where to find a healer. His cure will demand much fasting and many prayers. Men have more of the dark nature in them than women. It will not be easy." She then looked at the man. "After his sickness has been sent away he must not taste flesh, nor engage in war or fighting, and be faithful to both you and Aravat."

The wife bowed in gratitude and praised Aravat for her husband's hopeful deliverance. "Why do you travel openly without protection?" she asked. "Don't you know there is much evil lurking about these days? Women should not be out wandering alone. You had better turn back."

As soon as the couple departed, Hannah and Selith resumed their journey under the glaring midmorning sun.

Selith could tell Hannah's wanted to ask something." Go ahead, what are your questions?"

Hannah laughed to herself. "It is hard keeping company with angelic beings who can read your every thought. Why did you hesitate to help the woman at first?"

Selith kept her eyes on the road, as if watching for something. "Faith is the connecting link between the human mind and the Light, the stronger the faith, the better the connection."

"Why was not the man able to see you when his wife could?"

"You had better get used to it, to some we reveal ourselves, and to others we do not. Pay no attention if you are the only one able to see. There may even be times when you are not able to either. It is of little matter though, as I am always with you. It is a trick of the senses. Humans are never really alone."

They spotted a man sitting on a boulder made of worn sandstone. It was near a bend in the road next to a creek that had run dry. He held his head in his hands as if deep in thought. The two of them were intending to pass without disturbing him when suddenly he opened his eyes. "Peace be with you! I have been waiting for three days. It seems you have had some sort of delay along the way."

The salutation surprised Hannah. "Peace be with you, too!"

The man stood up. His spotless white robe made him stand out from the other travelers along the road. He reached out his hand in a sign of friendship. "My name is Yaakov. I am able to see by the color of your glow that you must be the one I am waiting for."

With a slight twinkle in her eyes, Hannah scrutinized this unusual man. "You have many gifts, indeed, if you are able to see the color of another's ethereal body. Your own glow reveals much about you, too."

A wide smile came across his face. "I was sent by the senior elder, Bilshan, who is also my teacher, to bring you safely to the gathering. It is in a deserted place some distance from here. Would you prefer to rest before proceeding? The days are long and hot, and do not make for easy traveling."

Hannah gazed up at the sun now partly hidden by a few small clouds. "Yes, there is much danger in the air. I think it best however, if we go now, that is if you are willing."

Yaakov was also eager to leave. As they walked, Hannah realized he could not see Selith.

"What is the name of this place we are going?" Hannah asked.

Yaakov glanced around to make certain no one was in hearing distance. "We call it Damascus, although it is not in Syria. It is a place not far from Jerusalem. Long ago, the Great Teacher called it that to fool the False Priest Jonathan and his spies."

"Is its location still unknown to the present day kings?"

Yaakov lowered his voice to a near whisper. "Yes. When the Great Teacher learned that Jonathan had issued an order for his arrest, he went to Jerusalem and surrendered to protect the others. The Teacher took the secret of its location to his grave."

Hannah wondered whom this teacher was, but decided not to ask too many questions. They had just met, and knew little about each other. Considering the times, precaution took precedence over curiosity. After walking for some time without incident, they saw not far away a checkpoint manned by soldiers of the king inspecting travelers. They stopped before getting too near.

Hannah observed Yaakov becoming sad. "They are turning back refugees to prevent them from going into Jerusalem," he said. "There are too many of the poor, sick, and homeless walking about. Most end up begging or in jail. They say that these women will first sell their children, and after that their own bodies. Even with the Greek Seleucids now gone from Judea, the king continues fighting. They draft all the young men, tax those who are not able to fight, and take advantage of any woman between the ages of fourteen and forty."

"Let us go by some other route then," Hannah said as she considered the situation. "It is best if we do not reveal ourselves. They may be looking for more than the obvious." She covered her face with her hood and followed Yaakov as he led her on to one of the lesser-used paths.

Well past midday, they came to a pleasant spot that provided lots of shade. Feeling tired and hungry, Yaakov and Hannah sat down to rest and eat some fruit they found growing nearby among the bushes. Hannah stretched her legs as she sipped some wine from Yaakov's flask. She overcame her initial hesitation, and began to ask Yaakov questions. "I am curious to learn more about this group you belong to."

Somehow, Yaakov trusted her enough to answer. He was normally a cautious man. "There have been many groups, or schools, throughout the history of our people," he said while sitting back against a tree, "comprised of those wishing to live a life based on the teachings of a particular prophet. Our school traces its linage to the time of the exile in Babylon. While in the Babylonian city of Sippar, a great Angel of power who called herself Metatron provided certain revelations concerning Enoch to a group of pious Jews. Afterwards, these Jewish exiles decided to live according to these teachings. With their return to Israel they were detested by the orthodox priesthood in Jerusalem, so these Enochian Jews fled under persecution into the desert."

Hearing him mention both Metatron and Enoch surprised Hannah. "So what happened then?" Hannah asked as she gently touched the pouch that lay hidden inside her robe.

Yaakov paused for a moment. Maybe he was revealing too much. After all, she was a stranger. However, Yaakov felt compelled to finish the tale. It was as if there was some invisible power forcing him. "Just prior to the Maccabee revolt," he continued while scratching his beard, surprised at his own loose tongue, "the high priest Simeon, who was opposed to the Hellenization policy of the Greek speaking Seleucids rulers, had a dream in which an Angel instructed him to hide his youngest son, whose name was Yeshua. Thinking it concerned the child's safety, Simeon took this son to live in a commune of these Enochian Jews. During the time when Yeshua was growing up, the Maccabee revolt broke out. Some of Yeshua's elder brothers deserted the cause of their Zadok forefathers for that of the Hellenizers, while others allied themselves with the Maccabees. Those siding with the rebellion did not know that the Maccabees were searching for some legendary crystals buried deep in secret vaults beneath the temple." Yaakov took the flask back from Hannah and gulped down some wine. He was surprised at himself for being this frank. Perhaps it was because Hannah was so pretty.

"And then? What happened next?" Hannah asked while looking into his large brown eyes.

Yaakov couldn't refuse her. "Many years passed. With all his brothers either dead or in exile, the Maccabees discovered Yeshua's whereabouts and forced him to return to Jerusalem to serve as high priest. Although he was the last remaining member of the senior Zadok linage still in Israel, the Maccabees believed they could control him because he lacked a support base within the Sanhedrin. Eventually, the Maccabees desired to unite the throne and the office of high priest under themselves, so they deposed both the princes of David and the sons of Zadok from their traditional positions within the religious and secular hierarchy. When Yeshua opposed this, they declared him an enemy and forced him too into exile."

After Yaakov finished talking, he became sleepy. He needed to rest. The sudden change in behavior was too much. Could it be that he felt something for this woman? He knew of other cases of people falling in love at first sight but never believed in it. Yaakov closed his eyes. A good many minutes passed as they sat there resting against the old apple tree whose crooked branches hung down next to them, almost touching the ground.

Hannah suddenly noticed that the sky was turning dark and hazy. The air became still and all sounds of nature stopped. Hannah was about to get up when she saw, coming over a hill, a small group of soldiers walking towards them. She roused Yaakov with a shove, and they both stood to greet them.

The soldiers stopped just a few paces away. A rather fat one ran his fingers over his rough unshaven face with a sly grin. "Now, what do we have here?" he asked while jabbing at his companions, "a beautiful young woman in the wild, accompanied by an unarmed weakling."

"We are simple travelers and mean no harm," Yaakov replied. His tone suggested that he was nervous.

"Why, of course, of course you mean no harm, and neither do we. If you hand over the money and your woman, we'll let you go without any hard feelings. If you don't, we'll kill you and take the money and the woman anyway. It's up to you." The soldiers let out loud laughs.

Yaakov became anxious. "We will give you the little money we have, but please leave the lady alone." He couldn't stand the thought of these rough soldiers having their way with Hannah.

A second soldier placed his sword up against Yaakov's throat. "I don't think you are in a position to bargain, worm."

The fat one ordered the others to search them for anything valuable. Then he went over to Hannah and began fondling her breasts. "We've not had any fun for many nights. The officers keep the women all to themselves. We don't need to return to our camp for a few days, so we can at least have that much fun before handing you over. You are quite a beauty, too. I can't wait to start!"

The fat one pointed to some nearby trees. "I'm taking her over there. I'll be back in a little while, and then you can take turns. Send him on his way."

As the fat soldier tried to push Hannah towards the trees, he accidently touched her necklace. His arm suddenly jerked back in pain. "That's strange. I've never had any problem with this arm before. It's my sword arm, and has sent many to their graves."

His breathing began coming in uneven gasps, and he perspired profusely. The fat soldier plopped down on to the ground and rubbed his head in bewilderment.

"You haven't even started, and are done in already," one of the others said with a laugh. "I guess she is too pretty and you are over-excited. I'll take her first while you sit here and relax."

Just as the soldier finished saying this, the wind began blowing, throwing up lots of dust and dirt. The soldiers choked and used their cloaks to protect their mouths and eyes. Looking for a place to take cover, they ran back in the direction they had come, dragging their fat comrade with them. Hannah grabbed Yaakov's arm and ran away in the opposite direction.

To Yaakov's surprise, even though they were only a few paces away, there wasn't the slightest hint of any wind.

"You should be more careful Hannah. Your life force is very strong, like a firefly in the night. Even those who are slaves to the darkness are drawn to it." It was Selith.

Yaakov took a step backwards. "Who are you?" he asked, pointing to Selith.

Hannah was surprised the Angel was showing herself to him.

"She is an Angel," Hannah answered. "Her name is Selith."

Yaakov scratched his head in bewilderment. He didn't know what to make of it all. He was standing face to face with an Angel. And she could talk! Although the community he belonged to had a strong belief in Angels, this was beyond his expectations.

Selith placed her hand on Yaakov's shoulder. A sense of calm came over him.

"Which way is it Yaakov?" Selith asked.

Yaakov nodded his head towards the east. "It is not far from here. We should reach it before nightfall."

The three of them set off. Yaakov walked a little behind the other two. "Was the Yeshua that Yaakov spoke about my great-grandfather?" Hannah asked Selith.

"Yes, Hannah, he was," Selith replied. "Yeshua returned to the community in the desert that raised him, taking the crystals with him. Utilizing an angelic system revealed to him by the crystals, his spiritual powers greatly increased. He became a charismatic leader, going out among the people to preach the coming of a new age, causing many to follow him, both priests and common people. As his popularity spread, his disciples began calling him the Teacher of Righteousness. Fearing this challenge from a real Zadok, and suspecting he was about to proclaim himself a Messiah, the Maccabee False Priest ordered his arrest and execution. Before his capture, however, his only son managed to flee."

Yaakov caught up to Hannah. "You are a descendant of the Great Teacher?" Hannah seemed irritated by his question. She wanted to hear the rest of the story. "That is what Selith just said, was it not?" She turned her attention back to Selith. "What happened to his son?"

Yaakov tugged at Hannah's sleeve. "My own teacher was the student of this Teacher of Righteousness. Perhaps he knows. However, if he does, he has not spoken about it with me."

Hannah's mouth opened in astonishment. "Then your teacher must be very old."

"He passed one hundred years a long time ago."

Hannah stopped and looked at Yaakov. Her eyes turned soft again. "All right, Yaakov," Hannah said while gently patting his hand, "pray tell, what happened to this teacher's community?"

Yaakov stood there for a few seconds, amazed by Hannah's beauty in both body and spirit. "They were pursued by the Maccabees and forced into hiding," he finally answered. "Soon after the death of the Teacher of Righteousness, his disciples wrote down onto scrolls his high-level teachings and waited in longing anticipation for his triumphant return from the dead, as he promised. As time passed, and the original followers began dying off, his community elected new leaders and began accepting members from outside the community to ensure that the teacher's message about the New Covenant would not disappear. The majority of the original members are dead now. Most are new, like me. We enter the New Covenant after following a period of study and carry the title of Initiate."

Hannah remembered once Selith calling her own father an initiate. "If you are still living together as community, how can it be safe?"

"The Maccabees still fear us," Yaakov replied with a shake of the head, coming back to his senses, "as do the traitors in the Sanhedrin who continue to follow the false priests in the temple. Because of this, we no longer have a commune. It is too dangerous. In secret though, we still observe the teachings of Enoch in our private lives. Only occasionally do we gather, and then for only special purposes. We dream of the day when we can once more live together, free to practice our unique way of life."

"This man speaks the truth," Selith said. She could feel Yaakov's growing attachment to Hannah and was a little surprised by it.

Hannah now regretted her earlier irritation. She began to like Yaakov. He knew so much. Hannah followed an impulse and slipped her hand into his as they began to walk again. A smile came across Yaakov's face and his cheeks became red.

Selith urged him not to reveal to anyone what had taken place until an appropriate time, which he readily agreed to out of fear the others might doubt his sanity. Silence reigned for the remainder of the trip. Close to sunset, they arrived at the door of his master's house.

# SCROLL 11

*91-89 BCE*

א

# THE LAST
# GATHERING OF THE INITIATES

O ut of the stream of Light rose the early giants of mysticism, such as Elijah, Isaiah, Ezekiel, and Jeremiah. They drew their strength from it. Deep in caves, or in royal palaces, they foretold with prophetic visions the deaths of kings, the fall of kingdoms, and the punishments to be visited on Israel. They preached their scorn of empty ritualistic worship and blood sacrifices, and sought after the purification of the spirit and the practice of love.

The tradition of prophecy among the people of Israel began with Enoch and Moses, with its formal institution first appearing during the time of Samuel, who in the face of a rising royalty and degenerative priesthood, established the fraternities of Nabiim as schools of prophets. They called themselves Initiates, because this is what their first father Enoch's name signified in the Hebrew language. Samuel made them austere guardians of the esoteric tradition of Moses against the kings and high priests who sought to dominate through the law instead of the spirit. In the eyes of these Initiates, the blind worship of tradition, unbending orthodoxy, and

stale ritual are always opposed to the spirit of prophecy. Ritual was
the dark side of true prayer, and formalistic religion, the dark side
of spirituality.

Throughout the history of the Nabiim, many took Nazarite
vows, consecrating themselves solely to Aravat, practicing extreme
austerity, and living apart from the common people. There rose
among some of these Nabiim the terrible and exciting call to serve
as a prophet, taking on the yoke of speaking publicly. For these
Initiates, when a person answered the divine call of prophecy, a new
life was created. One no longer felt alone, but instead lived in total
communion with the Living Light and all truth, ready to proceed
eternally from one moment to another in the power of the spirit.
In this new life, their thoughts became one with the Divine Will,
possessing a clear grasp of the present, and having a solid faith in
the final success of their divine mission. That superior force that
wrenched the truth from their souls, at times with heart-breaking
anguish, constituted the prophetic element. It was the same prophetic manifestation that throughout human history has been the
thunderbolts and lightning flashes of truth.

* * *

They gathered as a group in this holy place and were in the
power of the prophets of old. The twelve elders sat on stools
arranged in a small semi-circle that faced the rest. These elders carried the title of the Keepers of the Law, serving as advisors to
this order of Nabiim founded by the Teacher of Righteousness
before his execution by the Maccabees many years before. Selected
by the entire community because of their learning, gifts, and age,
the elders would serve the order until death.

Sitting inside the circle of elders on an elevated platform was
Bilshan of the tribe of Gad, and the other two members of the
Council of Three, the body that oversaw the affairs of the order.
Elected by an assembly of the entire community every three years,

the council nominated the elders and received new members into the order. Similar to Bilshan, the other two members of the Council, Yoav of Judah and Machala of the tribe of Levi, had both crossed their one hundred year marks. In addition to being on the council, Bilshan served as Maskil, the Master of the order. The Initiates surrounded the elders and the Council of Three in a circle, representing the never-ending nature of all creation.

The people of Palestine referred to this community of Initiates by the Aramaic name Natsarraya, which meant Keepers of the Law. Educated Judeans and Seleucid officials, both preferring to use Greek instead of Aramaic, called them Nazarenes. As many had also taken a Nazarite vow, the name seemed appropriate.

These Initiates had promised when entering the community not to imprison the Living Light in word, creed, or religion. They treasured, read, and re-read the old sacred writings, and the scrolls of the prophets who had proved to be right. Fostering the gift of prophecy among themselves, they were receptors of that stream of spiritual power that had been opened to their people, desiring no more than to nurture and sustain the mystical love of the Light. Through centuries of mystic cultivation, they held the lines of spiritual communication open in spite of the failings of those who were nominally in charge of doing so for the Jewish nation.

Many were absent that day, either imprisoned or dead at the hands of Maccabee King Alexander Jannaeus and his Sadducee allies. Because of the recent wave of persecution unleashed against their order, a sense of dread and apprehension filled the hall. Only the elders and council members that had survived earlier persecutions had experienced anything akin to the present trials.

As was the custom at the beginning of each gathering, they lit lamps filled with oil made from olives that grew on a hill overlooking the ancient city of Jerusalem. The fragrance was sweet and penetrating, and had a calming effect on those who smelled it. King

David planted the olive trees on the hill himself when he was old and near death. Fearful of the impending Day of Judgment, he promised that one of his descendants would atone for his sins by watering the trees with tears wept for the sins of all humanity.

Some were sitting quietly chatting among themselves, while still others just sat, waiting. With the cares and concerns of the outside world put aside, a peaceful silence spread gently over the assembled body. All eyes closed as they sought to touch the Light.

Moving into the Stream of Living Light felt like entering a fast flowing river of water. It was a living invisible steam of spirituality, in existence since the beginning of time. It was now for the Initiates to touch and be touched by this stream that connected them with all creation.

If, during this time, the spirit of prophecy poured into one of the Initiates, that chosen messenger of the spirit would rise and address the gathered meeting. There was no effort to curtail any leading of the spirit, as it was a sacred sign of the Light.

Bilshan was famous in his younger days for his often-dramatic movement of the spirit during gatherings. Since most of the Initiates from that period had already transited back into the Light, only legends remained about his renowned gifts of prophecy. The order maintained written records of Bilshan's predictions made while he was still a teen, over one hundred years ago. Reading them now, many discovered that he accurately foretold the events that had taken place during the previous seventy-five years.

After a while, Yael of the tribe of Dan, one of the youngest members, rose to address the gathering. At first, she played nervously with her hands, as if trying to get enough courage to speak. After a few tortured seconds of standing in front of everyone, she was at last able to say something in a low voice, as if almost talking to herself. "We should not fear to be living receptacles for the Living Light, instead let us be its worthy channels. There is no other way for the Light to reveal its Divine Will, other than through its prophets. The Living Light may choose to speak to us in various ways not always easily understood. Nevertheless, it is not for us to demand the method, it is only for us to listen, to discern the meaning, and carry out the Divine Will, whatever it is." With that, she sat back down and closed her eyes.

A few minutes after Yael's prophecy, a couple of short remarks followed, some concerning the evil times they lived in, still others about the need to stay centered during prayer. Then out of nowhere, an Initiate fell out of his chair and onto the hard floor, trembling and speaking words no one could understand. This was followed by a great surge of life force, as if a switch had been turned on, flowing through the chamber with the strength of lightning. The entire group began shaking and moving, with many Initiates driven out of their seats. The Shekhinah had arrived.

Lasting a good while, it ceased as quickly as it had begun. Calm returned once more to the assembled gathering. Nobody gave much notice to the radical changes as they continued concentrating on the moment. Yoav the Scribe, of the tribe of Issachar, reached for one of the scrolls rolled up near his seat and read aloud a verse from the Book of Enoch. It was a short piece and he gave no commentary. Following this came more silence and meditation.

Milka of the tribe of Reuben, serving that day as chair of the gathering, rose from her stool. "Since we cannot know you, we are only able to love you," she said in a solemn voice, in an expression of her reverence to the Living Light.

Milka turned to the elders and greeted them. After they returned her salutation, she faced the gathered assembly of Initiates. "Welcome, and be glad! For the Living Light, the prophets Enoch and Isaiah, and all the prophets are here with us as we meet. Be ever mindful of our pledge to serve the Living Light."

Milka walked over to a long stone table situated in the middle of the human circle of Initiates. A number of ancient-looking scrolls were lying on its surface, along with various other artifacts used for healing and divination. She then proceeded to sit on a chair made of polished brass. Inlaid in delicate patterns along its side were numerous quartz crystals. Chiseled near the top of the chair was an inscription in an ancient form of their language, no longer understandable. Legend had it that those entering the Promised Land after the forty years of wandering had crafted it according to instructions given to Moses following a prayer session in the Ark.

After the construction of the first temple in Jerusalem, the high priests placed the chair in a secret chamber known only to them. Towards the end of his reign, King Saul learned about it through one of his spies and had it removed to a room next to the throne chamber. Soon after, his rule ended, and the chair passed on to David, who, sensing its power, did not use it As a chosen instrument of the Living Light, he was already in its power, and could communicate directly with the Light without the use of a medium. After Solomon ascended the throne, he discovered that, while sitting in the chair, many things opened up to him. Thus, he desired it for his use when sitting in judgment.

In the following centuries, the fame of this chair spread far, reaching even the priests of Nebuchadnezzar. When the Babylonians invaded Jerusalem, their general, Nebuzar-adan, ordered the chair removed from the palace before its destruction, intending to present it to his king as a gift. However, before his army reached the gates of the city, Jeremiah hid the chair. The very thought of Nebuchadnezzar using it terrified the prophet. Returning from exile, a new order of Nabiim, dedicated to living according to the writings of Enoch, recovered it, and now kept it for safekeeping to prevent the wicked Maccabees from utilizing its power for their own evil purposes.

Now sitting in the chair with her head resting firmly against its back, Milka addressed the assembled Initiates. "Let us seek the guidance of the Shekhinah. Dark times have fallen upon the land." A short pause followed her words. "I bring you sad tidings." She was fighting tears and speaking with difficulty. "We have just learned that the Maccabee Lion of Wrath, Alexander Jannaeus, executed 800 supporters of the Greek speaking Jews and their Pharisee allies. As if his darkness was not deep enough, he slit the throats of their wives and children before the condemned men's eyes as he ate with his concubines. Did his Sadducee supporters beg him to spare these people's lives? No, they were more than happy to weaken their opponent's hands as they are more interested in power than mercy."

Machala stood and looked over to Milka. "It is obvious that the evil one seeks to increase his power through violence. We should respond with a similar increase of love. The evil of violence will beat against the shield of peaceful resistance until it becomes like the softest of rains. Our peaceful resistance will protect us while we are together, and sustain us when we are alone. If this evil is instead answered with hatred, anger, or fear, the balance between Light and dark will be tipped in favor of the darkness."

Milka nodded her head in approval. "Machala's point is well taken. I think we can all agree on this, can we not?"

A male Initiate rose. "These are wise words indeed. If we do nothing however, our order may not survive this wave of persecution. Our numbers are shrinking rapidly, and few these days willingly risk their lives to learn our ways, let alone seek to enter the New Covenant."

Machala was quick to reply. "It is in times as these that we must be firmly rooted in our faith. The living Shekhinah often provides these challenges as a way to strengthen our dependence on it. And what better opportunity is there to convert those whose hearts have not yet turned, then through our own persecution. If we love all, including our tormentors in the midst of persecution, there is always hope."

A period of silence followed as the Initiates tried to sense how these words felt, for they trusted the Shekhinah above all else. Its eye is always clear.

Yaakov stood up to address the Initiates. "It is true that in times such as these the Light may grow stronger than before. However, if in the end there are no more like us to silently serve as guardians of the law, what then? Will the Light have been served if we vanish into the lost books of history?"

Several Initiates rose, all talking at the same time. Milka beckoned with her hands. "Do not be hasty in your judgments or thoughts. Let the Light work through us in order that we may discover its will. One at a time, please."

Uzia of the tribe of Benjamin, an Initiate who had lost his parents recently to the wickedness of the Maccabees got up. "Yaakov's point speaks to my heart. I, too, fear for our order. If forced by the circumstance into peacefully resisting in the name of the Light, so be it. We should not be afraid to forfeit our lives, for at the end this will be taken from us in any case. Nevertheless, why go looking for trouble? There is enough in these dark days without having to seek it out."

Several of the male Initiates nodded their heads in agreement.

Yael stood up again. "The weapons of our warfare are not carnal ones. We will use spiritual means to achieve spiritual ends. All those who live by the Light and confess to it will choose to use spiritual weapons. Those wrestling with flesh and blood have thrown away their spiritual weapons."

Listening with patience, Bilshan waited as his thoughts cleared. With his legs no longer strong, and unable to stand for any length of time, he motioned that he wanted to say something.

"Many days ago an Angel of Light came to me in a dream," he said with an air of authority, "revealing that a maiden would assist us and our people in this time of great peril. The Angel foretold she would bear a message. Upon awakening, I instructed Yaakov to find and bring her here. He accomplished his task, and she arrived last night. We talked into the early hours of the morning. I have learned much."

There was a stir in the hall as nobody was expecting this. It was a complete surprise. "The young woman claims to be the heir of our esteemed founder, the Teacher of Righteousness. She carries the Record Keeper of Enoch, and says she is here at the request of holy Angels. I have no reason to doubt her, but you can judge for yourselves. Divine message or not, it is still for us to discern with our spiritual eyes which paths to take."

With this, he turned to a corner of the room partially hidden by a long curtain. There, standing unnoticed was Hannah, dressed in a light blue cotton robe, holding a staff in one hand and a crystal in the other. Bilshan beckoned her to come forward and show herself. For a moment, Hannah hesitated. Not only was she not used to speaking in front of people, she was also afraid that her lack of a formal education might belittle the importance of her appointed task. Selith gave her a slight push however, forcing her out into the open. Hannah grabbed tightly her staff to give her a sense of security and coughed nervously to clear her throat. "I bring you tidings from the Living Light!" Her voice quivered a bit.

"Hannah of Galilee, please find a seat among the Initiates," Bilshan replied. "Although you are not one of us, your mother and father both belonged to our order before their tragic betrayal to the wicked Maccabee king. I knew them well. You shall at least, this day, be their spiritual representative."

Hannah did not waste time to locate a place to stand next to Yaakov. "Once more I bid you welcome," Yaakov said with a smile while extending his hand in a sign if friendship. He felt a chill when she shook it. He wanted to look at her more, but was afraid of showing his feelings. "I have heard that your mother and father were well respected within these halls," he said.

His warm greeting made Hannah feel somewhat calmer. More herself, she briefly scanned the hall. "I notice many empty stools. Is it your custom for members to not attend gatherings called by the elders?"

Yaakov looked around sadly. "Alas, they would be here if it was possible, but I am afraid they cannot unless they can return from Sheol at will. The Maccabees hunt us down because we refuse to recognize them as either kings or high priests. The Sadducees despise us because we know they betrayed the Sons of Zadok in return for personal gain. And the Pharisees consider us heretics for not acknowledging their version of the law and them as its interpreters. All three wish to see us finished off. What is stranger," he added, changing his tone to a whisper, "is that they seem to know our every move, even though we carry on with the upmost secrecy."

Chalchalya the elder spoke to Bilshan while looking over at Hannah. "I've never heard that any remaining heirs of the Teacher still lived. From what we know, they murdered the child along with her mother. What proof is this girl able to bring forth to substantiate her claim?"

Hearing this, Hannah became angry. "If I speak falsely," she said boldly, regaining her courage, "let the Light strike me down dead in your presence. I cannot bring my dear mother and father back to this life to testify on my behalf. Those who have lost their spiritual sight because of the dirt in their eye cannot see many things. If the Light is to continue shining, it is best if we all know who our master is."

Hannah was at a loss to know where her words came from. They certainly were not hers. Hannah noticed however, that the

Teacher Crystal was so hot, that it slightly burnt her skin from inside its pouch.

Hannah startled the Initiates. Chalchalya was visibly angry and pounded the arm of his stool. "How dare this uncouth and uneducated peasant from Galilee address a scribe and an elder in such a manner? I reached my enlightenment long before she was born, and have written acknowledgements of it given by this very order. People travel long distances to hear me speak, and I've quite a following among the priests. I ask again, what evidence can she provide? One gem and a fancy staff is not enough. I say throw her out. Take the crystal from her. Her mission will then be finished!"

Selith stood behind Hannah and whispered in her ear. "Depend on the staff. Rely on it to guide you."

Hannah rubbed her hand over the staff. "What proof do I need to produce, lover of smooth things? I do not need to listen to the foul words of one such as you. I know who you serve, and so shall all the rest soon enough." Hannah gazed around at the surprised faces of the Initiates and nervously raised her staff. "For the Light!" she cried out in a loud voice.

Chalchalya changed his tone and became very friendly. He began rubbing his hands together. "Let's not get too overly excited. We're all under a lot of stress these days. I'm sorry if I lost my temper. You are a newcomer and are unfamiliar with our ways. I sincerely apologize to you. We can discuss these issues later over a nice hot meal. I'm certain that everything will be cleared up to your satisfaction."

Bilshan raised the Rod of the Maskil, the outward symbol of his authority as master of the order. "Let us not quarrel, but ask for the peace of the Light to enlighten our minds. Hannah, it would be better if you at least showed some respect to the elders. I am sure your parents would agree with me if they were here." He turned to address the elders once more. "The crystal she holds is a Record

Keeper. The instructions were for the elders to listen to what it has to say."

Bilshan asked Yaakov to help him walk over to where Hannah was standing, as those not in the Covenant could not enter the inner circle of the elders. The other elders grabbed some torches and joined him. Yoav the scribe seemed the most eager to see the crystal, putting his face close to it.

"What is your hurry, my friend?" Bilshan asked. "Do you think there is a special message for your eyes only?"

Yoav was unhappy at Bilshan's comment. "You're not a scribe Bilshan, unless you think that by your long years you have gained that ability through time and mediation."

Bilshan was not one to mince words. "It is not through the physical, but the spiritual eyes that one learns the truth. Learning and knowledge, while important, are just things we cling to. Will you take your learning with you into the life to come? If you are going to travel far Yoav, you had better pack lightly."

Not heeding Bilshan's words, Yoav tried grabbing the crystal from Hannah's hands. As he did, Hannah turned her hands away to prevent him from touching it. "You can only peer into it," Hannah said.

Frustrated, but not willing to take it from her by force, Yoav proceeded to look into the inner recesses of the crystal. As he did, he discovered that inside were strange markings he was unable to read.

Chalchalya also looked at the strange markings. "It looks like some form of devilish. Is this a ruse? Maybe it's some trickery of the Maccabees. Do you know for certain who this young woman is, Bilshan?"

Bilshan shuddered as he glanced around at the other elders. "We must get to the bottom of this right away. If there is indeed some deception, we are in trouble. However, I do not think the

Maccabees are the deceivers. They do not have the power to fool our eyes. Only the dark ones are capable of it, making it all the more serious. We could be facing an enemy who has grown in power."

Chalchalya ordered Yaakov to accompany Hannah to the large stone table. A stern look appeared on Chalchalya's face. "Who really sent you? Yes, it might have been Angels, but what kind of Angels, dark or Light?"

A deadly silence descended over the room. As she stood there under everyone's gaze, Hannah felt that the Angels chose the wrong person. If she were unable to deal with these men, how would it go in any contest with even stronger foes, such as the Watchers? Hannah suddenly felt Selith's hand on her shoulder. She remembered that the Angel could read her thoughts.

Chalchalya noticed her necklace. "What additional proof do we need that she's a spy for Beelzebub? The necklace is engraved with the same devilish script as inside the stone."

He reached over to touch it. As his hand got close, a bolt of electricity surged out, burning his hand. "It's true," he cried out, holding it in pain, "she's a slave of the dark ones. Yaakov, grab her, tie her up before she does any more harm."

Yaakov didn't know what to do. He could sense that Hannah was looking for a way out. Maybe he would flee with her. They could return to her old home in Galilee and get married. She would need a man. Machala intervened before his plan could take shape. "Hannah, you need not fear us," she said. "We mean you no harm."

Hannah paused for a moment. Machala's words and the tone of her voice were remarkably similar to those of Rikbiela. Hannah looked into Machala's kind eyes. She sensed a gentle energy reaching out to her, urging more patience.

Machala faced the elders. "Sometimes I am surprised at your own stupidity. Men will never be able to completely rid themselves of their dark inheritance." Machala walked at a slow pace over to

Hannah and with her hands touched the necklace. Nothing happened. Through this, Machala demonstrated that the necklace was not evil. Taking Hannah by the hand, Machala led her back into the center of the room. The other elders, feeling a twinge of embarrassment at their previous actions, made way for the two of them.

"If you compare this script to that which is inscribed on the chair Milka is sitting on," Machala said, arriving back at the altar, "you will notice the similarities. It is not devilish, but Angelic Script. If Hannah is able to read it, what more evidence do we require that she is sent from the Light?"

Machala took a step back from Hannah. "Hannah, read to us the message in the Record Keeper."

Hannah paused for a moment, but saw Selith nod to her to obey. She put the crystal against the space between her eyes for several moments, taking the image of it into her mind. As Hannah merged into its life force and became one with it, the crystal glowed a soft white, revealing specific letters on its surface, while sounds similar to, yet different from music, emitted mysteriously from its core.

Hannah fell into a trance, with her mind gone into another dimension. In a voice no longer hers, she began talking in a slow and deliberate manner. "The Record Keeper tells of a terrible struggle long ago between the Angels of Light who protect the earth, and Beliar the dark angel. Beliar has instructed his slave, Bechira, and the false oracle to find and kill Isaiah." She then paused and returned to this world. "It is silent again."

"What a marvel! She can see where others are blind," Yaakov proclaimed in a loud voice. He wanted everyone, especially Hannah, to know he supported her claims.

Hannah could sense Yaakov's feelings about her. She had to struggle to attune herself back to the cosmic frequency of the crystal.

"Samael, the lord of all evil," Hannah said in a solemn way as she returned the crystal to her heavenly eye, "seeks victory over the Light he has sworn to extinguish. When our sun enters its point of maximum debilitation in relation to its own sun, the galactic sun, and the dark age of men begins, Samael will rearm men with the knowledge they need to destroy the earth. When you see these signs, you will know that this time has come. Kings of men will shake their fists at the mount of the daughters of Zion, the hill of Jerusalem. They will go up from the Valley of Acco to fight against Philistia, and even up to the boundaries of Jerusalem."

"When these dark days arrive, do not lose heart," Hannah continued. "Before time, before the creation of the sun and the moon, before the creation of the stars, a sacred sound sprang forth from the Living Light. From this was born a Child of the Light, one held in mystery and kept near the Light until the need of the Children of Light was greatest. At their time of great need, the Children of Light shall summon all the forces of the Light, all the saints from on high and all the Angels of the Light, who shall raise their voices to open anew the Gate of Light, closed since the fall of the Watchers. Then the kings of men will be afraid and prostrate themselves with terror when they see the Daughter of Wisdom seated on the throne of glory as the Child of Light passes through the open gate."

Hannah finished and put the crystal back into her pouch. She then took out one of the grounding stones Selith had given her, and held it tightly in her left hand. Machala touched Hannah's shoulder. "Thank you, sweet child. Your task, at least for the moment, is fulfilled."

Overwhelmed by what he had just heard, Bilshan looked upward and raised his arms. "My ears have heard the voice of the Living Light. Let the Divine Will be done!"

Hannah realized she was witnessing the passing of the Age of the Prophets. Their time was waning against the rising tide of darkness. What powers did they still possess to combat these evil forces? The words of Record Keeper provided a small glimmer of hope, to open anew a gate through which a Mashiakh could enter. She wondered if these Nabiim were up to such an arduous task.

The elders returned to their chairs. As they did, Yoav stopped Machala. "I am able to understand why only Hannah could read the crystal, as she had been entrusted with its delivery. It was a safer way, given the present evil times. However, I am confused as to why Chalchalya was not able to touch her necklace, yet you could? Is it because all males are prohibited from touching it?"

Machala turned to him. "Being male or female has nothing to do with it. I am familiar with this necklace. It has a long and noble heritage. It was originally in the possession of Moses' Median wife, Zipporah, who found it lying on a bed of gems in the desert as she and her sisters tended their father's sheep. Taking it for themselves, they found quite by accident that it had the power to cure all manner of illnesses, and bring its owner peace of mind and happiness. It never however, brought wealth or victory in battles. Hence, they considered it something more for women than for men.

Thinking that Moses was always taking great risks by grazing his sheep close to their sacred mountain, Mount Karkom, Zipporah insisted he wear it for protection. As a result, Moses was wearing it on the day when he spoke with Aravat on the summit of that mountain, imparting to it even greater power to protect the wearer against evil. Moses was able to wear it, and he was a man, was he not? No, there must be some other reason. I think we are about to discover something concerning Chalchalya."

Yoav opened his eyes wide in amazement and shot a glance over to Chalchalya, who was sitting in his high stool chatting with one of the other elders. Using her hand, Machala motioned for Yoav to remain silent as she accompanied him back to his stool.

The Initiates once more waited as silence filled the hall. It was clear from the looks on their faces that an intense feeling of anticipation was weighing on them as a bigger power worked in their midst.

Finally, Bilshan rose to address the gathered. "We have heard the message from the crystal. As is our tradition, when there are promptings of the spirit, we should follow them to share with the others. The rest of us must test that prompting to see if it has any significance to our situation."

After a brief pause, Chalchalya got up and began walking around. He paid particular attention to some of the male Initiates that always supported his positions, to make certain they were ready for the debate that was about to begin.

"Yes, yes. This magic stone does indeed reveal much," he said. "But it asks as many questions as it answers. How do we even know these are the times spoken about? How do we build this force of Light? And who is this Daughter of Wisdom? It's too confusing. It would be better to take some time to think it over. Maybe the next time we gather, those of us that have a more proven record in discerning these types of higher level mysteries may have some additional insight."

His followers, seeing his point, nodded their heads in agreement. Machala got up. "Discernment is not limited to those who claim to have special talent in this regard, or have high levels of education. We should continue discussing it now."

Large divisions soon became apparent between those who agreed with Machala, and those siding with Chalchalya. Milka asked for both Machala and Chalchalya to return to their seats.

The entire time, Bilshan had been examining Hannah with great interest, barely taking his eyes off her. "Having lived these one hundred and twenty-five years," he said after giving it all some thought, "I can attest that these are the days that the Record Keeper speaks about. Ever since the Wicked Priest Jonathan, that Spreader of Lies, killed our Teacher of Righteousness, I knew that dark times were on the horizon, even though I knew nothing of this crystal. After his arrest, I visited our Teacher as he awaited execution in Jerusalem. Being that day, they allowed us to talk in private before they took him away to the place of execution. It was then he foretold much of what we learned today. One additional thing was that he promised was to bodily return to lead us during the dark times. I cannot say for certain, but it is possible that he figured out how to put his spiritual energy into the Record Keeper, and it is he who is guiding us now!"

Chalchalya stood up and pounded his large staff in anger on the floor. "Nonsense!" he shouted. "We've no proof that the great teacher is speaking through this stone. For all we know, it's just some cheap conjurer's trick. Where is our beloved Teacher of Righteousness now? He has not returned as he promised, and for good reason. He is dead now for some seventy years. It's unlawful to dig into his grave, but I can promise that nobody has moved his bones. They're still there. The priests in the temple have forbidden any talk about this resurrection fantasy. It is heresy and not supported by the scriptures. Even if he is speaking through the stone these are not the evil days it foretells. We've at last a king who only wants peace, and to rid our land of the hated Greek speakers, whether Jew or Gentile. Is this such a bad thing?"

"How would the priests know anything about the true law, those who now monopolize its teachings?" Bilshan asked in return as he waved his rod in the air. "They have betrayed the people of Israel by siding with the usurpers in return for the privileges of the offices bestowed on them. Our kings are not of David and the high priests no longer the Sons of Zadok. The Maccabees seek to rid the country of any who oppose them and considers traitors those who do not assist in doing so."

Chalchalya turned around to face Bilshan with an air of authority. "I demand proof that these are the times spoken of by the stone, real proof and not just wild ramblings from an old man past his prime."

Bilshan showed him the Rod of the Maskil. "You forget Chalchalya, that I am the master of this order and not you. You have no right to demand anything!"

Chalchalya turned his head away from Bilshan and sneered.

Bilshan was old and not used to these kinds of heated exchanges, but continued anyway. "What more proof do you need? Armies are on the march; new empires are in the making. Everywhere there is warfare, starvation, and suffering. Even here in our own land, Alexander Jannaeus, who has now become the Lion of Wrath, is in league with the Seekers-After-Smooth-Things, the Sadducees, to turn our land and people away from the True Law."

Chalchalya tried to interrupt, but Bilshan stopped him with a wave of his hand. "I am not finished. Is it always your habit to stop the spirit from flowing where it wants to go?"

Chalchalya held his tongue.

Bilshan got up and walked over to Chalchalya. He spoke directly into this face. "What other proof do we need? Listen again to the words. He has shaken his fist at the mount of the daughters of Zion, the hill of Jerusalem, and has gone up from the Valley of Acco to fight against Philistia, and even up to the boundaries of Jerusalem. This verse is encoded. For those with eyes to see and ears to hear, it is easy to decipher. We need say no more about the time of the dark prince's return. It is now."

Bilshan sat down back down, visibly exhausted.

Chalchalya, sensing his opponent was weakening, rose and reverently bowed to Bilshan. "You're still the best at interpreting prophecies," he said in a softer tone, "we all acknowledge that. I'll concede the point and say no more about the time. However, it still leaves unanswered how to build up the Light to open the gate, and who this Daughter of Wisdom is. I again urge the gathering that we not reach hasty conclusions while under so much stress. Things of great importance need time to ponder over."

Chalchalya stood there, waiting for someone to challenge him. A few moments passed and nobody did. "You see, most here agree with me," he said with a smile on his face, revealing his glee at achieving victory. "I suggest we end now. Some of my friends have brought new wine stored in Grecian urns. In addition, there is a great assortment of dried salted meats and breads of all sorts. This is a real treat given the severity of the times."

Many of his supporters had already gotten up from their seats and were heading for the refreshments when Yael stood up. "If you please, I have something to add to this discussion."

Chalchalya's followers rolled their eyes and chuckled. Taken only recently into the order by Machala, Yael was considered a novice when it came to prophecy, as most times she just said what was on her mind without giving it much thought. Because of this, Chalchalya's followers never took her seriously.

The majority of the Initiates ignored her this time, too, as Chalchalya and his followers wanted to finish things here. Some even began speaking all the louder to drown her out.

Pounding her staff on the table, Milka ordered the Initiates back to their seats to hear what Yael had to say. Yael spoke in a loud voice. "It will be the Daughter of Wisdom who will show us the way! We must find her first, and after finding her, she will teach us the Angelic sounds referred to in the scroll that will open the gate."

"The spirit is quickening today," Yoav said, standing up. "Yael is right in saying this."

Hearing it, Yael returned to her feet. "Who is to say there is not to be more than one Daughter of Wisdom?"

Machala now also rose. "This is true, as the Daughter of Wisdom was also how our father Enoch referred to a Mashiakh."

At the utterance of the word Mashiakh, the entire hall became still. This most sacred and holy of words was not one said lightly, for it contained within it all the energy of the universe. The Teacher of Righteousness in the early days had taught his followers the power of it.

"I don't believe it," Chalchalya scoffed. "How can the one that is supposed to teach us to open the gate, be at the same time, the one to come though it? You see, it only gets more confusing the more we discuss it. That's why we must give this some time. It's a difficult riddle to solve."

Yael appeared nervous. In spite of this, she gathered up enough courage to defend her point. "It is not too difficult, if the eye has been opened."

Chalchalya dismissed her comment with a wave of the hand. "Our young Yael has come a long way it seems. It's a shame that she's been an Initiate for so few years. Otherwise, we could consider what she has said in a more serious way. As an elder, if I can offer a small piece of constructive criticism to our young member. You'd better not try to solve issues over your head and have more respect for those whose eyes are clearer than yours."

A roar of laughter erupted from his followers, to the great embarrassment of Yael.

Machala was visibly angry. She stared Chalchalya in the face. "How dare you mock prophecy offered by an Initiate?" Machala turned to Bilshan. "I demand that Chalchalya be Eldered for this breach. He has no excuse for his rude behavior, other than being a man."

Milka stood up. "I agree with Machala. Chalchalya should be Eldered."

Chalchalya laughed. "What's this, the women are ganging up on the men? Why is it that I'm not surprised that Milka is taking sides." Chalchalya walked over to Milka and stared at her breasts for a moment. "Milka does not like me, or any man for that matter," he said with a snicker. "You shouldn't keep your feelings bottled up inside. Give them a free hand. Express yourself. Come on, show your anger."

Machala placed herself between Milka and Chalchalya. "Leave her alone, Chalchalya. Do not encourage her pain to resurface. The burden she carries is heavy enough."

"I'm only trying to help in her voyage of self-discovery. In any event, this request for Eldering must come from Yael, if she feels insulted. However, I'll say to the women present, this is work for men. This will rule out any woman qualifying as the Daughter of Wisdom. They're too weak to fight with the dark powers."

Chalchalya looked over to Hannah, who had been keenly observing the proceedings. He was about to say something when suddenly Machala walked back to the center of the room. "The answer to this so-called riddle is right here in our vey midst." Machala placed her hand on Hannah. "It should easy for anyone with the power to judge a person by the glow about their bodies to see this girl is no ordinary person. She has been anointed with angelic oil." Machala looked back at Chalchalya. "Why not tell us what the glow about her body says? You noticed it the minute she walked into the room. In addition, you can certainly see the companion that stands behind her stool, even if the others cannot. Tell us what your clear eyes see now?"

Chalchalya strutted over to his chair. Using his staff, he swiped at one of the lamps lit with David's oil, extinguishing its flame. "I'm able to see with a clear eye all right. I didn't want to hurt the feelings of our esteemed elder, Bilshan, who brought her here, so I kept my mouth shut. Now, forced by your rudeness, I'll tell everyone here the truth. This woman is a witch! She's a spy of the dark one and a daughter of Beelzebub!"

A great uproar rose from among the Initiates and elders, with loud shouts ringing out from Chalchalya's supporters of, "Seize her! Bind her!"

Machala raised her hand. "He lies!" she cried out in the righteous voice of one about to reveal a truth. "She has the glow of an Angel! It is as clear as day that the Holy Shekhinah has descended upon her. She is its holy bride and divine indwelling. As the glory that emanates from the Light, she is to be a teacher that guides the way to the Tree of Life that stands in the Eternal Sea. She is not a witch at all, but one of the three Daughters of Wisdom who will open the gate. You know I speak the truth, Chalchalya!"

In a sign of support, Bilshan went over and stood next to Machala. "It is as you say, Machala. Moreover, I believe that the Teacher of Righteousness is guiding us through her, and the crystal. There can be no mistake about it. The years have only sharpened my spiritual eyes, not dimmed them."

Chalchalya stood and threw his cloak back, revealing a long black sword. He pulled it out of its scabbard and raised it high. "We shall see who is right!"

As he lunged at Hannah, Selith called out to her, "Hannah, use your staff."

Chalchalya came down hard with his sword, wanting to kill her with a single blow. Hannah however, picked up a stool to block it, sending sparks flying everywhere, and knocking her down from the impact. Seeing that Chalchalya was getting ready to strike again, Hannah used her hands to scoot along the floor to get away.

"Get up Hannah, be quick," Selith shouted.

Hannah attempted to do as Selith said, but it was too late. He took another swipe at her. Seeing it coming, Hannah rolled on the ground, causing the blade to miss its mark.

"The staff Hannah; use the staff," Selith called out.

Chalchalya laughed. "What, your Angel friend is unable to save you? Her energy is waning with the weakening sun."

Seeing Hannah lying helpless on the floor, Chalchalya prepared to finish her off. Raising his sword high, he let it fall with all the force he could muster. Hannah held out her staff, the same used by Moses in Egypt and David against the Giant Goliath. When the sword made contact with the holy object, a bolt of white lightening shot out, illuminating the entire hall in a blaze of a bright light.

Chalchalya's appearance suddenly changed. In his place now stood a warrior fully decked in black armor. Matted hair hung down to his shoulders and a large earring pierced his left earlobe. Hannah recognized him at once. It was Kasdaya.

Hannah moved back a few paces in fear. As she did, she noticed by the look on their faces that only Machala, Bilshan, Yael, and Milka, were aware of the transformation. The other Initiates still only saw Chalchalya.

Selith pulled out her staff. "Kasdaya, for too long have you labored here among these Initiates, leading many into the dark pit. You have been a snake in the grass betraying a great many to the king. This is the real reason why you had them leave their hiding places and come here today, in order to make it easy for the king to finish them off. Even as we speak, a troop of his soldiers is on their way here to arrest the entire gathering. With the last of the prophets out of the way, the Watchers' return will be all that easier. What say you to this, son of the serpent?"

The Watcher laughed as he spit on the floor in contempt. "Your power is spent Light slut. The days when you could order us around are gone, in case you haven't already noticed."

Kasdaya looked Hannah over from head to toe. "You won't escape me this time. Our children will be worthy of their sire."

Kasdaya reached for Hannah. Selith blocked him though with her staff. Angered, the fallen Angel was about to strike Selith with his large curved sword, when Hannah hit his legs with her own staff. The Watcher let out a cry as black blood flowed profusely from the wound. Backing up some as he tried to stop the bleeding, Kasdaya curled his lip while looking at Hannah.

"You're a fool to fall for their lies," the Watcher sneered. "In that wild state of nature these stupid Angels always hearken back to; men's lives were nasty, brutish, and short. What was there other than bloody competition, diffidence, and the pursuit of glory? Men constantly fought for gain and reputation."

The Watcher was starting to fade. "We're creating offspring who are not ugly giants as before, but are good looking, educated and cultured. Our sons will teach men how to establish efficient governments to increase the brutality of their rule. Men will willingly cede their natural rights in return for what they desire most, power, position, wealth and women."

Kasdaya barred his yellow teeth. "This war is just beginning. I'll get you in the end, White Witch. You can't defeat us. We'll kill everyone one of these weaklings stupid enough to follow you."

Laughing, he disappeared into a cloud of black smoke.

Silence filled the hall. A small group of male Initiates scrambled out the back door.

Hannah was still lying on the floor. They almost ran over her.

Yaakov shook his fist at them. "There go the followers of Chalchalya. I say good riddance to them!"

Machala had observed it too. "We should not be so harsh on them. They did not know he deceived them."

She stooped down to inspect a small pile of grey ashes; all that remained of Chalchalya. "Now everything is clear."

Hannah got up and straightened up her robe. "What is clear?"

Machala stood there closely looking at Hannah. Tears came to her eyes. "Now we know. It was he who betrayed your parents to the Maccabee king."

Hannah shook her head in silence. "How could this be?"

"Your grandfather, the son of our founder, brought Chalchalya into the order. He was his best pupil and passed on to him many secrets of the esoteric arts. As Chalchalya's abilities grew, so did his ambition. After the death of his master, he wanted to marry your mother and claim the title of Teacher of Righteousness. She feared that his main objective however was to take the crystals for himself. To thwart his plans, she married another Initiate. Chalchalya never forgave her. It must have been him who told Hycranus where they were hiding, hoping after her death to take the crystals."

Machala looked over at Selith. "He did not find them on her though. His anger and desire for revenge was the door that Kasdaya used to take possession of Chalchalya's body and soul."

Bilshan nodded his head in agreement. "There is much to learn from Chalchalya's desire for revenge and lust for power."

Bilshan was Maskil of the order. Its ultimate fate was in his hands, even in its final moments. "The elders will stay behind," he said in a voice still full of determination. "Our part in this is about to end. Chalchalya has betrayed us."

Taking the Rod of the Maskil, Bilshan smashed it hard against the stone alter, shattering it into many pieces. "We will not give the false priest-kings the pleasure of victory. We will take another form. This order is now dissolved and no more, but another rises to take its place. The Teacher of Righteousness still lives!"

Machala went over to the stone alter to gather up the sacred objects. "There is no time to waste. The younger Initiates must flee. The future belongs to them now. The righteous must live by their faithfulness so they can be saved on account of their fidelity to the Righteous Teacher."

Yael and Milka helped Machala put the order's most valuable items into cloth satchels. Hannah started doing the same, working alongside the two Initiates. Machala stopped her and held her hand. "You will walk a lonely path. But in the life to come you will sit next to the Tree of Life and enjoy its fruits."

Bilshan urged them towards the door. "Quick now, the younger Initiates must set out right away. The soldiers may arrive at any moment. We will let them arrest us, leading them to believe they have caught us all. They will not discover until it is too late that some have escaped. We can expect no mercy from the Maccabees. We will suffer the same fate as our great teacher did those many years ago."

"I agree," Machala said. "Hannah, you must get to Galilee in safety. The Maccabees dare not pursue you there, for that land is not fully under their control. They will not readily give cause to the Seleucid's to start a new war until they have consolidated their gains in Judea and Samaria. In fact, the Seleucids may secretly assist you, since they are still smarting over their loss of Judea."

Bilshan raised his hands in a final blessing. "Go forth and spread the Light. All hope now rests on you!"

The other young Initiates departed. Hannah and Yaakov were the last to go. Hannah however refused to budge. "I am not ready to lead such an important mission. Machala must go with us."

Machala smiled at Hannah's innocence. "No Hannah, I cannot, although I would like to. I am long in years and not far from death. I would only be a burden."

Hannah turned to Selith. "She must go with us," she insisted. "Please make her agree."

The Angel put her hand on Machala's shoulder in a sign of friendship. "Hannah is right. They will need someone with experience to guide them, at least at the start."

Machala was tired and shook her head. "I am too old for such a quest. Hannah has you and the crystals."

Selith kept her hand on Machala's shoulders. "Depend on the Light, it will give you strength."

Yaakov grabbed Hannah by the arm. He viewed this as the perfect opportunity to make his move. "We can take charge of things," Yaakov said. "I have been an Initiate for many years already. I am ready to lead."

Hannah placed her hand on his and smiled. Yaakov took this as a sign of her consent.

Selith didn't pay any attention to Yaakov. She stood there, still waiting for Machala's answer.

"We will meet up on the Mount of Olives at midnight," Machala finally said, after thinking it over. How could she argue with an Angel? "It will be dark, as there will be no moon tonight. From there we will travel north. Inform the others."

Yaakov was clearly unhappy. Nevertheless, he took Hannah and led her out. Machala was old. He would just have to wait. His time would come.

Selith bid Bilshan farewell and escorted Machala to a safe place, hence brining to an end the order of Nabiim founded by the Teacher of Righteousness.

# ב

# CHILDREN OF LIGHT

The small group of young Nabiim met on top of Mount Ha Zeitim, the Mount of Olives. It was a ridge made up of three peaks running from north to south. Olive groves covered its slopes, providing security from the prying eyes of soldiers patrolling the city walls. The night being cool, Yaakov placed a woolen shawl over Hannah's shoulders. Not willing yet to openly acknowledge it, Hannah was happy for his kind attention.

"It is written in our sacred books," Machala said to the youthful Initiates, as she pointed down at the city, "that the glory of the Light went up from the midst of Jerusalem, and stood on this mountain. We will carry forward the glory of that Light."

Machala was visibly fatigued. It had been a long day. "Our priests rule by outward laws and rituals," she continued, using much of her remaining strength to communicate this important point, "and the temple is the visible sign of it. They wrongly believe the Covenant with the people of Israel is one of forms. The kings and high priests defend this covenant with carnal weapons, and outward armor. The tribe of Levi, made themselves by the law of a carnal commandment, offer up outward blood offerings and sacrifices, and make use of empty rituals that serve to give them power. They go looking for the Light in buildings and books, instead of in the hearts of people, and in nature. Forgotten they have, that the Light enlightens everyone. It enlightened Moses, the prophets, and especially the Nabiim, whose love of the Light is like the twilight before the dawn."

Finished, Machala leaned against a tree to rest for a spell. Moved by Machala's words, Hannah took the elder initiate's hand and looked her in the eye. "Soon there will be daylight though, when the sun rises to mark the beginning of a new day." Hannah was not one easily provoked to speak, but there was a fire burning inside that compelled her to open to the flow of the life force bubbling up inside of her. "The Mashiakh will be this sun, created before the six days of creation. We are the elect, the children of the True Covenant of Israel, who must now prepare the way for the Mashiakh to come, in our time, to our land."

They didn't know if it was the place or the words just spoken, but the Initiates felt too a sudden surge of the life force. They sat in it for a few moments to pray in silence for the success of the journey. Unfortunately, time was not on their side. They soon left the city, taking the road that led from Jerusalem to Jericho, as it was the fastest way to the Jordan River. Because of the heavy caravan traffic, it was easy to blend in with the crowds of moving people. At night, they camped by themselves to avoid the distractions of caravan life.

They did not enter Jericho proper, choosing instead to travel along the roads going north that were sandwiched between the river and the eastern foothills of Mounts Gerizin and Ebal. Their food was running low, and many were tired and hungry from the journey.

Halting for the night, Hannah assisted Yael in filling everyone's cups with plain water from a nearby well. "Do not be despondent," Hannah said as she went from person to person. "It may seem impossible that such a poor band will be able to stem the rising tide of darkness. We must not give in to these feelings however, for Samael implants them in your hearts, although you recognize it not. Instead, let us have faith that the Light will make us grow into a very great number, who will someday send our message to the ends of the world and throughout the ages."

Hannah felt a little uneasy speaking out in this manner. She knew her new companions enjoyed the advantage of years of study and training while she was barely literate. She disregarded her feelings though, speaking directly from the heart.

Machala seemed pleased that Hannah was trying her best. Some of the men however, appeared agitated. Not only was she not an Initiate, but she was female. Although they were used to having women serve as elders, never did one take the position of Maskil. Yael and Milka were standing nearby, and felt sorry for Hannah. "Do not pay any attention to them," Milka said while leading Hannah away. "Men always think they are the most capable. It is only because they are willing to resort to violence if you disagree."

"We should not let our personal feelings blur our vision," Yael added, looking at Milka. "They are still our brothers in spirit and a good bunch. The old order is dead. It will take some time for them to adjust to the new situation."

"You have more faith in them than I do. We cannot wait forever. If Hannah's Record Keeper is correct, time is not on our side."

Hannah smiled, amused by her new friends. Yael was the shorter of the two and chubby, while Milka appeared robust and very strong. Men would consider them both beautiful in face and body. "I am not too worried," Hannah said as she took Yael and Milka by the arms. "Circumstances are fast changing for everybody, including me. We should cross the stream by feeling for the stones, one step at a time."

"We will soon enter Galilee," Milka said as she turned her gaze northward. "I have been to that place before. The people of that land suffer much."

"We will bring to them the Living Light," Yael said with feeling, "in the form of healing and prayers. Unlike those who offer their prayers up for the people in exchange for money, we will not take anything from the needy in return for our services, instead depending on the Light and nature for our substance."

The three of them said their goodnights. It was late and everyone was preparing for bed. Yaakov went over to Hannah's simple blanket that served as her bed. "When should we speak to Machala," he said in a hushed tone. He didn't want the others to hear him. "We will be entering Galilee any day now. We should get her blessing and make it known to the community."

Hannah appeared confused. "Get her blessing for what?"

"Why, for our marriage of course."

Hannah stepped back in surprise. "We do not need to rush things. There are important matters to take care of first. How about we discuss it again after we are more settled?"

Yaakov felt disappointed. He was hoping to begin their new life together soon. He could barely get anything done, with his thoughts constantly on Hannah. She was so beautiful.

She reached over and kissed his cheek. "Now get some sleep, Yaakov. We have a long day in front of us tomorrow. Machala is getting weaker and weaker. The trip is too much for her. Maybe you and the other men can construct a make-shift stretcher to carry her on."

Placated by the kiss, Yaakov prepared to go. "I will see what we can do. Goodnight Hannah." With that, he left.

"What are your plans?" It was Selith.

"Concerning what?" Hannah replied as she prepared her bed.

"Do not play games with me. You cannot satisfy his desires. It is best to tell him now, no need to lead him on. Otherwise it may cause trouble later."

"But I like him. I never promised to remain single my entire life."

"You did however promise to lead this sacred task. If you become his wife, that is over. He will want to assume that role. He is a man."

Deep down, Hannah knew Selith was right, but she was too tired to think about it. Hannah lay down on her thin blanket and closed her eyes. There were sharp stones sticking up from the hard ground, jabbing at her. Ignoring them, she fell fast asleep.

They arrived in Galilee some weeks after their departure from Jerusalem. Stepping onto its lush plains, the small group gave thanks for their safe arrival. Here, the false priest-king in Jerusalem would not be able to harm them, for the Syrian Greek speakers still controlled this part of Palestine. Taking advantage of their new freedom from the religious hierarchy in Jerusalem, they instantly began going about the towns and villages healing the sick and preaching peace, sobriety, and abstinence from flesh. Most important of all, they brought to all the good news about the coming of the Mashiakh.

ג

# GROWING PAINS

They had set up camp and were resting after a hard day's work. Machala was asleep, tucked away underneath some sprawling apple trees. Suddenly a shout rang out that somebody was approaching. It was a lone woman, not much older than they were. Yael was the first to speak. "Peace be with you, and welcome!" she said with her hand raised in greeting. "Although we have little ourselves, whatever we have we will be glad to share."

The woman appeared quite pleased. "Thank you for your hearty welcome," she replied while glancing around at all the smiling faces that surrounded her. "By the sound and looks of it, maybe I have found those I am searching for."

"And who may that be, sister?" Yael asked. "Have we met before?"

"I am looking for those called the Children of Light."

The members of the small group exchanged looks with each other on hearing this name.

"We have no particular name," Yael said, "at least none that we have given ourselves."

Yaakov walked up to the stranger. Hannah had left in search for some wild fruit. As a result, he regarded himself as their leader in her absence. "It seems that we are short on manners this night," he said in a tone that displayed authority. "Please come in and have a seat. These are only some old logs, but they do make for nice chairs when there is nothing else."

The stranger sat and continued examining them as she sipped some water they had provided. "They say you are a brilliant star shining forth in the darkness of night," she said, "and that a new light is beaming throughout Galilee. Many are offering thanksgiving and praise for the shattering of the widespread darkness that fills our land. Is it true that you despise all earthly things, loving all the creatures, including even the beasts of burden, and that you own everything in common? I see that you each wear only a simple white robe that is tied with a cord instead of a belt."

Yaakov was suspicious of someone wandering into their camp uninvited asking lots of questions about their way of life right away. Instead of answering, he kept filling her glass with water and smiling.

"I can see that you have no fear of the dangers that lurk in the night," the stranger said. She then scanned the community's meager setting. "Since you have no tents, what do you do when it rains?"

"If the weather it bad, we sleep in grottos and caves, as did the prophets of old," Yael answered as she looked at Yaakov. At least this question was simple enough, and the answer did not reveal much.

"I have heard in the villages that many of the people eagerly listen to the teachings of the Children of Light. And that some even undergo a baptism of water after selling their belongings and giving the proceeds for the good of the community."

Encouraged by these words, Yael was eager to speak. She was talkative by nature. "Yes, they crossed over into the New Covenant. Once we establish our new home, they will come and join us."

Yaakov was clearly unhappy with Yael opening up to the stranger without knowing more about her first. "Many in Galilee are afraid of this new light," he said with a hint of unhappiness in his voice. "The priests loyal to Jerusalem will certainly send out spies to find out more about our work and plans. They will suffer no threats to their positions as lords. We have already seen the first small signs of hostility. Yesterday, on entering a village close to the border of Judea to offer healing in exchange for food and water, we were met with sticks, stones, and were even spat at, by the local ruffians."

"Yes, you were very angry about this brother Yaakov," Yael added, interrupting him. "Instead of offering resistance or cursing our abusers though, we bore it courageously, singing songs of praise and thanksgiving. By doing so, we showed to any of the villagers whose hearts were open, that these ruffians were acting under the power of the dark one." To Yaakov's obvious displeasure, Yael continued talking. "We strive above all for peace and kindness, including with those who do not like us." Glancing over at Yaakov's sour face, she added, "We conduct ourselves with great modesty and peacefulness, avoiding any hint of scandal. We speak only when necessary, and carry out our assigned tasks with disciplined actions. We strive most of all to keep our eyes focused on the earth, while our minds soar to the Light."

The stranger noticed the interaction between Yaakov and Yael with some amusement. "Yes, I have heard that there is not a trace of malice, abusive speech, or arguments among these Children of Light. Maybe I was mistaken in thinking that you were this group." As she spoke, she moved her head back and forth between Yael and Yaakov.

A hint of embarrassment showed clearly on their faces. As Yaakov reached over to pour more water into her glass, Hannah returned and saw the stranger sitting there. "Sobe," she cried out with excitement. "How on heaven did you find us?"

The woman got off her seat and gave Hannah a big hug. "It was not difficult. Everyone has heard of you and your little band by now."

"I am sorry that I have had no time to visit you since your parent's death." A look of sadness came across her face as she recalled the deaths of her aunt and uncle. "There is much to tell you." Hannah rested in Sobe's warm embrace. Remembering that they were not alone, Hannah turned the visitor around to face the group. "I am sorry. This is my cousin, Sobe. I hope you made her feel welcome."

"They made me feel right at home," Sobe said before anyone was able to answer, "as if I were already a member of the family. In fact, it seems that they are already acting just as any family would."

Everybody laughed at hearing this. Yaakov, however, felt a little embarrassed. He hoped that Hannah's cousin didn't have a bad impression of him. Someday they would be relatives. He would make things up with her later.

The Children of Light continued going about doing good works and prophesying, begging for any necessary food in return. With whatever meager scraps they accumulated in the villages, they returned to share with the others, to eat in a spirit of joy and thankfulness. If any small crumbs remained, they fed them to the birds and insects.

# ל

# MEN ARE IN WARS AND STRIFE

They arrived near Nian, nestled in the lush valley between Mounts Tabor and Carmel, coming back late after helping some poor farmers, and discovered they were completely out of food. Uzia reminisced about his earlier life when he was able to eat as much as he wanted, whenever he wanted.

Yael walked over and patted him on the back in a sign of friendship. "There is no better spiritual exercise than to endure suffering for the Light. It grinds away at the earthly ego, while at the same time empowering our spirits. At first, it seems painful, but afterwards it becomes much easier. At least, that is what I have been discovering. Look at Hannah over there. Nothing is bothering her. Food or no food, she is always trusting in the Light. We should strive to imitate her. She is always deep in prayer, whenever the chance allows, and so should we be."

Uzia rolled his eyes, and sunk his head deeper into his hands as he continued thinking about food.

Yael still felt sorry for him, and started massaging his shoulders to make him feel better. As she did, Uzia spotted an old woman walking up the hill towards them.

"Who is that?" he asked. "Where did she come from?" Yael and Uzia were both surprised at what they saw. In her rough, worn hands, the old woman carried a large cloth bag. She stopped right in front of Yael and Uzia, and plopped the bag on to the ground with a thud. "You look like a couple of starved sparrows. Give thanks and partake in the fruits of the land!" After saying this, she scurried away into the coolness of the fading day.

Yael peered into the bag to discover it was full of fresh picked fruit. Calling the others together, she retold to them the story.

"It must be a miracle," Milka volunteered with wide-open eyes. "You mean to tell us that an old woman carried this heavy bag, all by herself, up the steep hill? Maybe you could not see that there were others helping her, because it was getting dark."

"We do not swear oaths, but I promise you, no others were with her," Uzia replied, as he stuffed a huge piece of apple into his mouth. "Yael can attest to it too. She came out of nowhere and left in the same manner. I agree. It was truly a miracle."

Having finished most of the fruit, they noticed a troop of armed horsemen approaching from the direction of the river. They were riding at a fast pace, and at first seemed content to pass the camp without bothering it. At least until one of the soldiers towards the back spotted Milka. He brought his horse to a halt.

"What do we have here?" he asked with a grin on his face. "How about going for a little pleasure ride on my horse?"

Milka ignored him.

"What, not even the common decency to say a friendly hello," the soldier said gruffly. "What manner of people are you anyway? Where are you from?"

By this time, the entire troop was gathering about, curious as to what was happening. A very tall rider, dressed more regally than the rest, rode over to inquire about the situation. The soldier saluted him. "Just investigating a bit, sir. Some road tramps by the look of it, and obviously not on any commercial business."

Noticing that some of the other women were joining Milka, the officer addressed them. "Who's the leader here?"

"We are a law abiding group," Yael answered with a polite nod, "wandering healers of the sick. We mean no harm and wish you peace."

Her reply surprised him. He got off his horse to have a closer look. "Healers? Who sent you out to do this work?"

"We are a spiritual community," Yael replied. She kept her eyes lowered.

"A spiritual community, is it? What priest gave you permission to do this? Under whose authority do you work? Where are the men?"

"The men are over there. We will fetch them."

The men became apprehensive as soon as they saw the soldiers. Yaakov took the lead. "Peace be with you! How can we be of service?"

The officer's tone was curt. "What do you mean by offering me peace? I don't want peace, but the blood of the hated Seleucids! Where are you from?"

Yaakov's hands begin to tremble. He remembered the encounter with the soldiers while escorting Hannah to the gathering. "We are from numerous places. But we are all Jews."

The officer got close to Yaakov's face. "Then why haven't you answered the summons for all able bodied men to join the army? Perhaps you support the Seleucid dogs, although, you don't seem to be Hellenized Jews."

"We are not Greeks, and we do not support the Seleucids. We are followers of the same Aravat as you."

"Then why aren't you serving in the army?" the officer scoffed. "Do you want to leave it to others to fight your battles for you? Have you no shame?"

Uzia observed that Yaakov was having a difficult time. "It is against our beliefs to shed blood," he answered for his friend.

"I've never heard of such a thing. You can't be of the same religion as me, as my Aravat is terrible and vengeful. Come now, and tell me the truth. Why haven't you joined?"

Machala and Hannah had moved, unnoticed, within earshot of the interrogation. Machala took hold of Hannah's arm. "You must not get involved. It is too dangerous. They are too many."

Hannah struggled to get free of her grip. "I will do what I must."

Selith held Hannah's other arm. "Do not speak so loudly and listen to Machala. Wait until we see how things develop. They must learn to stand on their own feet."

Hannah stopped struggling.

Many of the mounted men had gotten off their horses to inspect the women.

"Where are you from?" one of the soldiers asked Milka.

"I was born in Hebron."

"Where's your husband?"

"I am unmarried."

"Widowed? I'm sorry to hear that."

Milka did not want to pursue the conversation any longer. She would not tell a falsehood, so she gave no reply.

"You must get pretty lonely at night without a man. I'm free tonight. How about it?" The soldier swatted her backside.

Yaakov walked over to be next to Milka. "We are a peaceful group who serve Aravat. Why do you make trouble for us?"

The soldier grabbed Yaakov's tunic so tightly that it interfered with his breathing. "I wasn't talking to you, now was I? If you don't want to fight, I can do what I please with the merchandise." He threw Yaakov on to the ground with so much force that his nose began to bleed.

A large bearded soldier strutted over to where Yael was standing and began fondling her. His companions began to laugh.

"Give him the slightest encouragement, and off he goes," one of his comrades said with a laugh. "He must be the father of half of Galilee."

Uzia ran over to protect Yael. The bearded soldier put his two large hands on his hips and smiled. "So you want to fight over the woman? Ok, I'll put one arm behind my back. Whoever knocks the other over first gets her. Agreed?"

A few of his friends formed a circle to jeer them on. "You cannot do these things," Uzia said to his opponent. "Let her go in peace."

The soldiers began pushing Uzia inside the circle from one to the other until he fell down. Then they began to kick him. Yael pulled at their arms, begging the soldiers to stop. This only made them kick harder.

Grinning, the bearded soldier went over and began squeezing her breasts as if they were a toy. "You want to save him? I'll give you the chance." He pushed her in the direction of the woods. She fell to the ground and folded her arms in front of her chest in an attempt to ward off his hands, but two of the other soldiers ran over to pick her up and held her arms back, allowing him to do as he pleased.

The bearded soldier looked over to Uzia who was lying on the ground. "Okay, it's finished. Since you refuse to fight for her, she belongs to me. Take her into the woods. Let's not waste time."

Yael looked over at Uzia. "Do not give in to their evil and fight. I do not care if I die." Uzia dropped his head in shame.

The leader turned to his troops. "Looks like a gang of thieves to me. Take these men as conscripts. Execute any who refuse to wield a sword. The women will come to our camp." A loud cheer rang out, with many pounding their spears on the ground in glee.

Machala chose this moment to appear in front of the officer. Hannah stood next to her, supporting Machala with her arm. He fell back a few steps, as he had never seen a woman such as this before. Although very old, her long flowing hair and noble features took him by surprise. He could tell that she was different from the rest.

She walked straight up to him. "Does that include me, too?"

"Of what concern is it to you who I take and what I do with them. Are you their leader?"

"The one that we follow is not of this world. One that you dare not fight against, unless you are more foolish than you seem."

Surprised by her answer, he examined her closer. "Who are you?"

"It does not matter. However, I am able to tell you this much—he that seeks you is not far away. You should not be wasting your time here with the likes of these people if you wish to save you and your men from an untimely end."

The officer looked around. He could not believe what he had heard. He suspected that Machala had the gift of sight and wanted to test her. "Where was my place of birth?"

Machala looked him directly in the eyes. "Although you are of high rank now, it was not always so. You were born to your father's servant in the back of a small dirty hut in the town of Adasa. Much is noble about you, but you will never be able to satisfy the deep insecurity that you labor under by taking the lives of your fellows. There is only one path that is able to give you peace, if you are willing to follow it."

Upon hearing this, he mounted his large steed and raised his hand, ordering his men to do the same. He looked down at Machala. "What you said has truth to it, I know. However, it is something that must wait until later. I have not the time now."

The armed horsemen left as suddenly as they had appeared. "It is a shame you did not begin now," Machala said to herself when they had vanished over the darkening hills, "for you will have no tomorrow."

Machala turned to the others. "You were right not to resist in anger or turn to the dark power. Wars and fighting are the way of the world. We must love those who inflict us with insults and injury. Samael seeks converts, and if you return hate with hate, he has won and your heart belongs to him. Instead, pray and be joyful in your trials so that perhaps the hearts of those who hate have some chance of turning to the Light before it is too late."

Yaakov and a few of the others began putting things back into order while giving thanks for their deliverance. That night after prayers, they gathered to discuss the renewed fighting between the Seleucids and Maccabees.

Yaakov had a concerned look on his face. "The Lion of Wrath is extending his reach into Galilee. It explains the presence of the Judean soldiers today. They normally would not dare ride this far north. It is probably not the best time to be wandering about the countryside."

Machala gazed into the starless night. She was also worried. "Yes, I too have felt the change. Our prayers are a shield protecting us, but as the power of the dark ones increase, it becomes harder."

"Then, we must increase the strength of our life force to match their power," Hannah said.

Machala nodded her head in agreement. "This however, will take time, many years, and the dark ones will not leave you in peace while you are building it up. They desire nothing more, then to prevent you from opening the Light Gate. You are most vulnerable now, at the start of the work."

Hannah saw that Machala was sleepy. "It has been a long day."

Machala patted Hannah on the shoulder. "Yes, I am tired. I have seen too many winters. I will retire to bed now."

Hannah escorted their spiritual mother to a secluded place where she could lay down and put a blanket over her. Machala was soon asleep. Unnoticed by the others, Hannah watched as Selith put her hands on Machala's head. "I am worried about her health," Hannah said. "She has been coughing blood recently in spite of the herbs I give her."

"It is the natural course of things," the Angel answered. "She must make way so that you can lead." The Angel's answer didn't please Hannah. She felt unready for such a task.

Hannah walked back to the campfire where the others were waiting. As she sat back down, Hannah noticed the look of concern on their faces as they contemplated life without Machala.

Yaakov put some more sticks into the fire. "We have been wandering about Galilee for some time now," he said. "We should find a home."

They sat there prayerfully, thinking about it. After a while, Yael suddenly stood up with excitement. "There is a way!"

Both Uzia and Yaakov glanced at each other with a look of resignation. Yael was always the first to say something. Nevertheless, Hannah was eager to hear what she had to say. "Yes, go on Yael."

"We should settle on Mount Carmel," she said with a broad smile beaming across her face.

"Go to Mount Carmel?" Yaakov asked indignantly, while shaking his head in disbelief. "We all are aware that this is forbidden, and would be condemned by the entire nation of Israel. What nonsense."

"Like all men, you exercise judgment too quickly Yaakov," Milka replied in Yael's defense. "Is there more you wish to say?"

Yael was unsure if she should go on. Perhaps her idea was foolish after all. She put her fingers into her mouth and moved the loose dirt around with her foot. Looking over to Milka, as if asking for permission, she answered, "If given the chance, yes."

"Feel free to speak," Milka replied sternly. "Do not be intimidated by those who are not able to see as clearly as you. There are always people who wish to put out the spark of the spirit with the cold water of doubt." Milka gave Yaakov a hard stare.

Being familiar with her temperament, neither Yaakov nor Uzia were willing to challenge Milka openly. They stared unhappily at the ground below their feet.

Yael stood up straight and kept her eyes fixed on Milka to avoid looking at the others. "We should proceed to the very summit of Mount Carmel where the force of the sacred life force is strongest."

The more Yael spoke, the more confidence she felt. "It will not only provide us with large amounts of the life force that we will be able to draw on to open the gate with, but it may also help keep us hidden from any evil eyes searching for us. No dark prince can keep his sight focused for any length of time on such a sacred site."

Hannah stood up next to Yael. "Mount Carmel is one of the three energy vortexes," she said. "While the Foundation Stone at the Great Temple in Jerusalem is activated, the vortexes are able to shield us from evil." This was one of the many things Hannah had learned this from the Teacher Crystal.

Yaakov continued to shake his head. "You still have not solved the problem of how to get around the prohibition against building permanent structures there. Are we to live like animals among the trees?"

"We will build tents on the summit," Yael replied. "It is within the law. We can build our homes someplace close to the base of the mountain."

Hannah smiled. She was happy to be in the company of such spiritually gifted people. "Yael has spoken well," Hannah said. "Mount Carmel was sacred to the prophet Elijah. The Seleucids dare not disturb us that near to the sacred mountain, out of fear of provoking the people."

Sobe was sitting nearby, observing everything. "This is indeed wondrous," she said, "to see the invisible hand of Aravat, our creator, working among his chosen people. When learning that I was about to set out in search of you, a man from the village of my husband's family, requested to speak with me. A person of considerable wealth and position, he was miraculously cured from a serious illness after undergoing baptism in one of the towns you visited soon after your arrival in Galilee. This man told me that he owned land not far away from Mount Carmel and wanted to donate it to you, if you desired to have it."

After hearing Sobe's revelation, a feeling of happiness sprang up among the group. Milka clapped her hands. "The Light has spoken. Mount Carmel will be our new home."

* * *

After a few days' journey, they reached the foot of Mount Carmel. Seeing its peak rise up from the plains of Galilee, their hearts jumped for joy. Machala was no longer able to walk, so they carried her on a stretcher.

"Lift me up so I can see the mountain," she asked them.

Yaakov and Uzia did as she bid. Seeing it, her eyes sparkled.

She beckoned Hannah to come closer. "I am leaving," she said in a barely audible whisper. "Do not be sad. All things are subject to decay and death, this is an unchanging law. The body must die so that we can be reborn into the eternal Light."

Machala closed her eyes. Hannah shook her head in disbelief. Taking hold of Machala's hand, tears rolled down her face. "No, no! I will not let you leave us. Please do not go, not now! Our work has just started."

Machala opened her eyes once more to gaze upon Hannah. The tone of the voice revealed her weariness. "The fallen angels are more powerful than before, things are changing faster than we anticipated." Stroking Hannah's face with her hands, she continued. "You are a blessed girl, just as your mother was. I have completed my task, and now you must carry on where I left off."

Hannah was fighting hard not to sob. "I still have so much to learn, how am I to lead?"

"Follow the Light. It will be your teacher."

Hannah noticed Selith come over. Machala saw her too. "Greetings good friend," Machala said as she held out her hand. "Have you come to assist me on my last journey?"

Selith gently touched Machala on the head. "I am sorry, but I must remain behind," the Angel said in sweet sounding tones. It sounded more like singing than speech. Angels often used this method of communication when humans needed special comforting or reassurance. "There is still work for me to do. There are others coming to escort you into the Light. We will meet again."

Selith bent down and kissed Machala on the cheek in a sign of friendship. "Peace be with you."

Uzia had a surprised look on his face. "Who is Machala talking to? Maybe she is hallucinating."

Having met an Angel already but still unwilling to admit it publically, Yaakov guessed what was happening. "Quiet, let her pass in peace."

Selith told Hannah to unfold the blanket they were using to cover Machala and spread it on the ground. Yael and Milka helped remove Machala's robe, laying their teacher gently on the blanket so that she faced the sun. As they did, a couple birds landed nearby and began singing a wonderful song.

Suddenly the wind ceased blowing. Machala raised her hands and spoke. "I return to the Angel of Earth my body" She then fixed her gaze upon the sky. "Come now, Angel of Eternal Life, and escort my life force into the radiant bliss of the Living Light. Take me home, I am now ready."

Machala closed her eyes. Her life force began its transition back into the realm of Light from whence it came. She had passed from this transient life into the life eternal.

Machala's face had a warm and gentle smile on it. As the life force departed her body, all signs of old age vanished. Her body changed to that of a young girl, without a single wrinkle or blemish. Machala's hair turned black, and from her body emitted the sweet fragrance of freshly cut flowers.

Hannah and the others looked on in blessed amazement as Machala's body began to glow and turn transparent. Hannah recalled the legends that Selith had told her about the deaths of the great prophets. Because of their great purity and connection with the divine life force, their bodies showed no signs of death or disease at the time of their transition. Now Hannah had witnessed it herself, and felt blessed to be in the presence of a saint. A soft breeze made the nearby wild grass wave back and forth. Stricken with grief, Hannah began singing softly the lamentation hymns of her people.

They sought out some locals from a nearby village to assist them and buried Machala's body beneath a large tree next to a path that led up to the mountain's peak. One by one, each paid their respects to the last of the Nabiim while Yael and Milka wept for the passing of their teacher. Machala had brought both of them into the old order.

Hannah sat some distance from the others, at a loss of what to do next.

"Have you forgotten the promise you made to Metatron and the other Angels?"

Hannah raised her head to see Selith standing there. "Of course not, but how am I supposed to accomplish it? I am too young and untested to take on the Watchers myself."

"You are never alone, Hannah. Besides, you have the Teacher Crystal. It will guide you."

Hannah put her head in her hands. "Will they follow me? Why should they? At least they studied under a teacher for many years and can read and write. I am unworthy to buckle their sandal straps, let alone lead."

Selith grew in size and began to glow brighter than the midday sun. Hannah covered her eyes. "Never doubt the Divine Will," the Angel said. "The blood of Zadok flows through your veins. You were destined to lead from the moment of your birth. Both your parents and your aunt and uncle gave their lives to save you and prevent the crystals from falling into the hands of the dark ones. Were their deaths in vain?"

Selith regained her normal appearance and put her arm on Hannah's shoulder. "As for your lack of education, have you already forgotten that David was as unschooled as you were, as were most of the great prophets? It did not prevent them from answering the call to lead."

Hannah realized that there was no other way. She could at least try. Perhaps it would be best to marry Yaakov, after all. He was educated and seemed capable enough to lead them.

Hannah got up and stretched her legs. Taking out her staff, she began walking back to where the others were sitting. Hannah turned around, wishing to thank Selith, but discovered she was no longer there.

Hannah scratched her head. "I wish I could learn that trick."

"As any magician will tell you," a voice replied out of nowhere, "everything is an illusion."

Hannah smiled.

# SCROLL 111

*77-76 BCE*

א

# NAZARETH

Over the years, the community blossomed. Quite a few had married, and families began to crop up like wild flowers after a spring rain. That is, except for Yaakov and Hannah. Establishing the new community proved to be an arduous task, one requiring their full attention. They kept thinking that things would eventually settle down enough for them to do the same. However, time waits for neither man nor woman.

Not able to live on Mount Carmel, they had established their community not far from the base of its northern side, next to the ruins of Nazara, an ancient sacred site. In honor of this holy ground, they called their village Nazareth. It was also similar enough in sound to Nazarene. Although Bilshan had officially ended the old order of Nazarene Nabiim founded by the Teacher of Righteousness many years ago, the community nevertheless, continued using the name to refer to themselves.

Hannah taught these Nazarenes the Ishim way of life. They ate only fresh and uncooked foods taken from the table of nature. They daily performed special exercise to increase the quantity and quality of their bodily life force, supplemented with frequent prayer and meditation. As the life force of Nazareth increased through these practices, people from neighboring villages made visits to feel and benefit from it. Many burdened with sickness and other troubles came amid the numerous reports of miraculous healings. Left at the entrance to Nazareth in thanksgiving, were crutches, bandages, and other objects associated with their illnesses. Pilgrims, traveling from all parts of Palestine to visit the holy mountain, returned home with many tales of the miracles they witnessed. As the word spread, Nazareth quickly became too small to house all the visitors. Therefore, the community constructed a two story wooden building for guests outside the wall of the village to serve as both a lodge, and hospice for the sick.

Along with the fame of Nazareth came stories about Hannah. Afraid of exposing the community to Nergal, the Eye of Beelzebub, Hannah seldom ventured far. She preferred instead a life of solitude and prayer to increase the life force they were building. She spent more and more time on Mount Carmel, and experienced the sweet consolations of divine mediation.

Using the Teacher Crystal, the Light revealed to her not only present and future things, but also the secret thoughts of both friend and foe alike. Yaakov and the others often saw Hannah so consumed in prayer that her body floated above the ground. People in nearby villages, would sometime tell how, in the middle of the night, there would be great surges of light from on top of the mountain, and tales began to spread about seeing Hannah conversing with Angelic beings near its peak.

Hannah built a tabernacle on top of Mount Carmel. Because of the prohibition against building permanent structures, they placed it in a large tent especially constructed to house the Shekhinah. Being the most sacred mountain along the eastern coast of the Great Sea, Mount Carmel was well suited for their purpose, as it was unlawful to spill blood on it and to disturb nature. To increase the powerful spiritual life force of the mountain, they planted gardens of fruit and vegetables around its base.

After they had erected the tabernacle, Hannah brought them together on top of the holy mountain to dedicate it to the Living Light. She raised her hands in prayer. "We have established the Light's abode on the top of this sacred mountain. It is now the most exalted among the hills, and the peoples' spiritual life force shall flow to it, so that the living Light can be the peoples' path to the Tree of Life in the Eternal Sea. The Tabernacle of Light is with the people, and it will dwell in them, and they shall be its people."

* * *

The moon was full in the sign of Shor, and the air was crisp and clear. Hannah and Selith sat together next to the tabernacle on Mount Carmel. Hannah held the Teacher Crystal in her hand as she spoke. "It is time to instruct the others on how to use the sound keys given by Ariel to Enoch when he walked the sky. It has been years already. The community has been preparing the life force of their bodies through our special exercises and diets and can now serve as channels of the Shekinah."

"Yes, I know. They will arrive soon."

Hannah turned to the Angel with a look of surprise on her face. "I did not tell you about it." Then Hannah smiled. She realized that Selith had read her mind.

Selith refilled Hannah's cup with a special herbal wine that she made herself. "They will need to practice for a long time before there is sufficient life force to open the Light Gate. They must be diligent in the face of great odds."

"I have informed them so already."

Selith get up. "You had better prepare. They are almost here."

Soon the summit of the mountain overflowed with the adult members of the community. After sitting in the silence for a while, the Shekinah began to move among them. Hannah had them rise and face the moon, raising their arms with their palms turned outward, while focusing on the clear white rays encircling it. Using their minds to absorb the life force emanating from the full moon, they felt a pressure in their chests, forcing some to take a few steps backwards involuntarily.

Hannah felt her own life force merge with that of the moon. Moved by this powerful surge, Hannah addressed the Nazarenes as they stood there. "To open anew the Gate of Light, we must build a force field strong enough to do so with the sacred sound keys. We must build it here on Mount Carmel, so that when the stars are auspicious, and the field is strong enough, we can pry open the gate to allow through it the Mashiakh."

A long pause followed as everyone began feeling an unseen power moving in their midst. As it reached its peak, Hannah spoke in a soft but steady voice.

"We must come into the mysteries of mysteries, using three sound keys. We will turn these keys inside their locks to open the doors to the Holy Streams of Life, Sound, and Light. Have faith, and all will be accomplished, for fear and doubt are the dark one's weapons. In the hours when the sun begins its ascent, just as life breathes into the awakening earth, you will enter the Holy Stream of Life, as this stream releases the power of the first key. With your back to Brother Sun and your feet at the root of Sister Tree, place one hand on the tree and the other at your side, palm down." She showed them how to do it.

"As you embrace the tree," she continued, "the power of the Holy Stream of Life will fill your body and you will tremble with its power. Inhale deeply. Feel the power of the life force. As you exhale, say the word *life*." Hannah had them repeat it many times after her, to get a sense of the power contained within.

"Do not be fooled by the simplicity of this word, for it is a powerful sound key. You and the word will become one. Repeat this exercise until you feel the life force flowing through your body. As your skills increase, you will gradually merge with the Tree of Life that sinks its roots deep into the Holy Stream of Life springing from life eternal."

Hannah paused to allow the life force to flow freely through their bodies.

"When the sun is in mid-heaven, when all creatures and plants are still and seek for the silence, meditate on the Holy Stream of Sound for it is only heard in the silence of the mind. When we enter into this world at birth, it is with the sound of the Holy Stream of Sound in our ears as it moves through the stars and crosses into the endless realms. In the beginning of creation, there was nothing but the Sound, the Sound was with the Light, and the Sound was the Light. It was the sacred sounds that brought down the walls of Jericho in times of old, and that will open anew the Gate of Light."

"Meditate on the sound of water rushing by or of streams that are full after a spring rain; for these are the sounds of the Light, although few recognize it. Place your mind into this Holy Stream of Sound. Let it fill your entire body. Become the sound itself, so that the Holy Steam of Sound can take you to the endless realm of the Living Light where the currents of the world rise and fall."

Many were now listening with the ears of the spirit.

"When the day ends and darkness covers the earth, you shall follow the law of nature and rest. In the moment before falling asleep, place your mind in the bright and far away stars, for your thoughts before you sleep are like the bow of a skilled archer, which send the arrow directly to its target. Join your mind before sleep with the stars, for they are Light. When you enter this Holy Stream of Light, the chains of death lose their grip, and breaking free from these shackles, you will ascend into the endless realm of the Living Light."

"Use your spiritual eye and soar to the farthest reaches of the sky, where thousands of suns are afire. In the beginning of time, there was only the Living Light. Place your mind in this Light. Become one with it until it fills your entire body. Say in silence *Light,* merging into the Light itself. Then the Holy Stream of Light will carry you to the endless Ocean of Light, which gave birth to all creation and you will become one with it."

# ב

# DEEP MYSTERIOUS THINGS

It rained almost every day. Only occasionally did the sun make its appearance through the dark brooding clouds. Yael had climbed to the top of the sacred mountain, carrying a small bag stuffed full of dried fruit that she wanted to give Hannah. It has been weeks since anyone had set eyes on her, and the community felt that someone should pay Hannah a visit to make certain she was all right. Yael reached the summit and found a dry piece of ground on which to place the bag while she went looking for their teacher. After a short while, she spotted Hannah sitting with her eyes closed underneath the sprawling branches of an ancient-looking tree. Yael was not able to decide if she should disturb her, as she herself knew what it was like to pierce the cloud of unknowing during meditation.

Yael mulled it over for a minute or two, and thought that perhaps the Light had provided her with this moment as an opportunity to pray. She had been too busy recently with the affairs of the community to take time to enter into the deeper states of spiritual life.

Yael found a comfortable place not far from Hannah and closed her eyes. The next thing she knew, someone was gently shaking her.

"Sister Yael, it is time to return now. You had better take something to eat and drink."

Yael opened her eyes and saw Hannah holding some fresh fruit in her hands. Yael stretched her arms out. "So, you came back into this world," she said with a smile. "It is about time, I was getting worried about you."

Hannah laughed while helping Yael to her feet. "Waiting for me? You have been sitting here for a week!"

"You mean to tell me that I have been out that long? Why, it seems just like a few minutes ago. Maybe I fell asleep."

"You were not asleep, but were resting in the arms of the eternal. Maybe you are catching up for lost time. You should make certain that your work in the community never extinguishes your desire and need for meditation and prayer." As Hannah admonished Yael, she handed her some dates. "Here, take some. We can go and pick some wild berries on the side of the mountain after you are done, after your body becomes used to being back in this dimension."

Yael ate the dates and was about to take a few sips of honey wine to wash it down when she dropped the wooden goblet on to the ground. Yael pointed to a place behind where Hannah stood. "Hannah, look! There is someone here with us. Do you know her?"

Hannah smiled and bid her to come forward and show herself more clearly. "This is my friend and teacher Selith. She is also my Guardian Angel."

Yael rubbed her eyes in total amazement. "I have never seen an Angel before. When did she arrive?"

"I have always been with Hannah," Selith answered back, "although, not even she was aware of it for the longest time."

"She talks, too! Oh my, what will the others think after I tell them about this? They already consider me odd. They will write me off for good."

Hannah motioned for them all to sit down. "There is no need to tell anyone about Selith. Those whose eyes are open will see her. For the others, they are exactly at the level where they are supposed to be in their spiritual evolution. It is not possible for all of us to be at the same stage spiritually."

Yael was not able to take her eyes off Selith. The Angel however, appeared undisturbed by the attention.

"I am glad that you came to visit me, Yael," Hannah said, as she poured her a new glass of wine. "There are some things on my mind that I want to discuss with you."

"Are you going to scold me for not being diligent enough in my prayer life? I promise I will do better in the future. The problem is that there are too many demands from the community. They have put me in charge of cleaning the hospice and lodge. I have to sweep the floors, wash all the dishes, change the bedding, and much more. Every day one of the men comes to inspect my work. If one thing is not done up to their standards, they give me a hard time. Where is the time to pray?"

"It is not about your prayer life. I have witnessed your capabilities."

"Then it must be about the community. I am sorry, but I am not in charge. Yaakov is. If you have any problems, you should address them to him."

"Yaakov is doing a fine job. He and the other men are building a wonderful community. No, it is about a much larger problem than that."

Hannah got up and asked Yael to follow her. The three of them went to a high vantage point where they were able to see for long distances in spite of the clouds. Hannah pointed to the sea. "What do you see there?"

Yael gazed out onto the vast blue body of water. "There are a few fishing boats, some larger ships further away, not much else."

Selith pointed out to the sea. "Look again," she said. "This time, use your spiritual eyes."

Yael strained to see more, but was unable to.

"Center down, and do not try too hard. Set your mind free as when you meditate. You are not searching for things, but for a feeling about things." Selith closed her eyes halfway to demonstrate.

Yael did as instructed. She straightened her body so that her spine was erect. She tucked her chin in slightly, with her hands hanging loosely at her side and her feet just a little apart. She let the life force flow freely through its channels in her body. It took a while, but Yael was eventually able to make out a thick black haze that hugged the surface of the water far away to the north. "What is that black smoke? It smells awful."

"It is the approaching darkness," Hannah answered. "It gets closer every day, and will arrive at our shores before too long."

Yael was confused. She kept her eyes fixed on the smoke. "Who is making it? It is not possible that something this foul was made by human hands."

"You are right," Hannah said. The look on her face revealed her anguish. "No human is capable of making a thing this sinister, at least not yet. Wicked angels called Watchers are making it. They were once exiled, but have returned to take the world for Samael's lord lieutenant, Beelzebub."

The very mention of Beelzebub's name made Yael nervous. "What do they intend to do?"

Selith was the one who replied. "They seek to destroy us and everything good. We are the final obstacles to Samael's mastery over the planet. Everywhere else in the world, the prophets have died, and there are no new ones able to replace them because of the galactic sun's spiritual debilitation."

"Perhaps you can now understand the reason why I have recently spent most of my time on this mountain, praying," Hannah added with a slight hint of despair. "A single person's prayers are, however, not strong enough to match their power. Time is running out. Perhaps we started our project too late."

Hannah's tone surprised Yael, as she considered Hannah unbeatable.

"Hannah is right to be concerned," Selith said. "She is only one person, and Beelzebub has not only the Watchers to aid him. The Watchers have bred sons from human women and have taken dark creatures as their teachers. As we speak, these foul offspring are learning the evil art of statecraft. Many men are flocking to their banner with every passing day and look greedily upon Palestine. The battle over its control will soon start. Much blood will flow before it is over." Selith turned to face Yael. "If they ever gain control of the three vortexes, it will greatly aid their cause."

Yael looked at Hannah with a deep feeling of pity. She realized the heavy burden Hannah had been carrying alone. "I wish I could be of help, but as anyone in Nazareth can tell you, I am the least qualified of all. I am just a lowly serving maid. You are revealing this to the wrong person. Perhaps I can go fetch Milka, she might have some ideas."

Hannah took Yael by the hand. "This is where you are wrong. You are indeed the right person. There is nobody else for this job, but you."

Yael was embarrassed to hear Hannah say this about her. "What can I do to stop this darkness, if you and your Angel have no hope?"

"Alone we can do nothing," Hannah replied, "but together we have a chance."

Selith took hold of Yael's other hand. "Only a small glimmer of hope lies between us and the dark power. We must have sufficient time to make enough life force to re-open the Light Gate. The Mashiakh is the last chance for the human. The community's progress is however, too slow. At this rate, the sons of the Watchers will crush us if we are still this weak."

"Of course, I will do my part. I cannot leave it all up to you. You just give the order and I will carry it out, no matter how difficult."

Hannah looked deep into Yael's eyes. "You must understand, Yael, that your task will be difficult. The first step is the most so, that of realizing your own powers. Even if you accomplish this, you must reveal your spiritual gifts to the community, and that will not be easy either. It will be hard for them to accept that you are a chosen one. These many years, the Shekhinah deliberately kept your powers secret to protect you from Nergal, the Eye of Beelzebub. Now you can understand why, against the wishes of the others, Machala chose you as her student. It is also the reason why Chalchalya went out of his way to make you look incompetent. It is that impression that still lingers in the minds of the community, an impression that we did not challenge to protect you." Long ago, the Teacher Crystal had informed Hannah about Yael.

"How was Chalchalya able to know anything about me?" Yael asked.

"Every living and non-living thing is encased in a field of the life force," Selith answered. "Some are born with the gift of seeing these fields, while for others it comes with the opening of their spiritual eyes. By seeing the colors and the intensity of the field, much can be learned."

"Is the path we are suggesting for you acceptable?" Hannah asked.

Yael's answer was immediate. "I accept wholeheartedly whatever you propose."

Selith was relieved, as the challenge was more than Hannah could face alone. "Let us go into the tabernacle and anoint Yael with the sacred oil to fortify her with the loving force of the

Shekhinah. From now on, those who listen to her words will feel its power flowing through her."

With Yael's hands now wrapped with fine linen, they returned from the mountaintop, as they escorted her to the small path that led down to Nazareth.

"Do not delay. Go out into the countryside to establish as many prayer groups as soon as possible," Hannah advised. "Take Milka along with you. You two make a good pair. Instruct these groups how to direct their prayers to the tabernacle here in order to increase the power of its field. Send out others, who are willing, in groups of two to do likewise. Our community will be the spark that sets Galilee ablaze with the Light!"

"Be forewarned, "Selith cautioned. "Beelzebub will stir up against you those with wicked hearts. Hannah and I will remain near the tabernacle to keep it safe from his gaze, and help direct the energy from the prayer groups into it. Keep to the Light and obey it, it will be your teacher. I wish there was more I could do to help, but sadly our age is gone too. The humans must win this battle for themselves."

Hannah smiled. "You are always keen to remind us of this, my dear teacher. Remember Yael, only a few are able to see Selith, so be careful what you say. Moreover, take her word when she says they can be of little help, and what small amount she provides may taste bitter."

Yael made her way back down the mountain alone. Entering Nazareth, she saw a group of people from outside the community listening to a talk about life in the New Covenant. As she got closer, one of the male members of the community came up to her.

"Where have been these last weeks?" he asked curtly. "Yaakov and the others were wondering why you deserted your duties in the lodges. We thought you said you were going to be gone for the afternoon and just look at you now, strolling leisurely back as if you did not have a care in the world. As a result, we had to ask some of the men to do the cleaning. What an embarrassment for them to have to do such menial tasks. You should go and beg their forgiveness right away!"

Yael paid little heed to his scolding. Wanting to listen to what they were telling the visitors, she sat next to a crippled man in some tall fresh-smelling grass. She placed her hand on his lame leg. He nodded to her, and then looked at her hand on his leg. It had been years since he had any feeling in it. He thought however, that he could feel a slight tingling sensation. She motioned for him to listen to the speaker.

"We are a small band that lives a life of righteousness," one of the men from the community was saying, "because it serves as the solid foundation for our practices. Sharing everything, owning all in common, we live a life of holy simplicity, believing that those who seek to obtain the treasures of the material world in abundance destroy in themselves a portion of the Light. To increase our own measure of the Light, we eat only fresh and clean foods, never partaking in the flesh of slain beats. We daily practice breathing exercises and secret physical postures to increase our life force. In addition, we are advocates of the curative effects of fresh air and sunshine, and are well versed in the healing properties of diet, herbs, massage, and precious stones. We study the course of the stars and planets for both prediction and healing. Because of our belief that the Light exists in every individual and in all of nature, we never participate in wars, nor engage in conflicts or disputes."

Yael wanted to add something, but felt a little hesitant to get up in front of all these strangers and the men of the community, who were now doing the talking. She rubbed her newly anointed hands together, remembering the instructions given to her by Hannah and her Guardian Angel, but she remained afraid. Suddenly, the lame man touched her arm. Looking into her eyes, he nodded as if empowering Yael to speak.

Without thinking, Yael got up and entered the inner part of the human circle where the speaker was standing. He greeted Yael.

"Peace be with you sister! This time of the day, you should be busy with your cleaning chores. Why are you here?"

She ignored him, and turned to the crowd. "You now see your life through smoked glass and dark sayings," she said in a loud clear manner, "but I speak to you in the living tongue of the Living Light. All that this brother has said is true about our life, and it will serve as a good example for anyone to follow to find peace and health. However, he has not disclosed the key that unlocks the secrets behind these things. That key is love." She looked around, her gaze pausing on the crippled man for a moment.

One of the men of the community pulled at her arm, trying to get her to leave, but Yael resisted.

"Renunciation must not be just some stern dry asceticism," Yael continued, "it must be mixed with love, engendered by love, sustained, and illuminated by love. We must seek to acquire virtue by love, rather than the laborious attainment of love through virtue. We must love the Light, loving this one thing that gathers our hearts together to the fountain of Light and life, walking in it, and having unity with one another. Since all creation contains a measure of this Light, we must love it all. Because, other than in extreme peaks of mystic vision, it is impossible to experience the Light directly, we must simply love it. Renunciation is not an end in itself. Self-denial that does not lead to love leads instead to pride and the living darkness. Our way of life should not only increase the measure of Light within us, but also provide a strong foundation from which to participate in the more active life of healing and transforming the world."

Yael stared directly at the cripple. "You must first obey the laws of the Earthly Angels. Allow these Angels to clean and renew your bodies. If you believe in the Earthly Angels and obey their laws, your faith will sustain you and you will experience health and long life and the dark one, with all his sins, diseases, and uncleanness, will leave your body. Go, repent, baptizes yourselves with water, so that you can be born again."

Yael turned to the cripple, who was staring at her with wide-open eyes. She went over to him. "Rise and be healed! This day the Light has saved you!"

The man moved his leg, slowly. After bending it back and forth a few times, he tried getting up, but fell down. Yael went over and held out her bandaged hand. "Take it and walk!"

Looking into Yael's determined eyes, he raised his arm and took hold of hers. He pulled himself up. Finding that he was standing, he let out a cry of joy. Yael let go of him and asked him to walk to the center of the circle for all to see. Wobbling, he dutifully followed Yael to the amazement of all. Songs of thanksgiving spontaneously broke out from the crowd and there was much rejoicing. Afterwards, they held a wonderful gathering in the Light, where many of the visitors crossed over into the New Covenant.

ג

# TO WALK AND
# TALK WITH THE ANGELS

Whenever Hannah walked among the numerous gardens of the community, she forgot for a moment the burden she carried, feeling instead a sense of sweet serenity while contemplating the beauty and wisdom of creation. Whether it was looking at the sun or moon, gazing at the stars, or the plants of the earth, great joy filled her heart in praise for the wonder of it all.

Morning had broken, and Hannah was tending a small batch of newly planted Myrrh saplings next to the neat rows of Frankincense trees that were there when the community founded Nazareth. Both would someday be useful in their healing work. As she stood up to stretch her back, Hannah caught sight of a couple of young boys running along the small dirt path that bordered the garden. In the hands of one was a little white rabbit in a makeshift cage.

"What do you have there, little friend?" Hannah asked as they passed by.

"It's a rabbit that I caught," was the boy's reply.

"What do you plan on doing with it?"

"I'm taking it to Japha to sell. It will make someone a good meal, and some fine gloves for winter." He held up the cage to get a better view of his prisoner.

"He is not from Nazareth," his companion volunteered. "His parents are here to visit Mount Carmel."

Hannah looked at the boy with the rabbit. "Maybe this rabbit has a family of its own. Perhaps it would be best if you let it return home."

"But I want to use the money I get from selling it to buy some sweet things to eat."

Hannah thought for a moment. "I have heard that there are giants that roam about looking for little boys to capture. Once they do, they put them in cages."

The two boys opened their eyes wide.

"What do they want to do with the boys?" one of them asked.

"They want to sell them to mean people, so that they can buy something sweet to eat with the money. But sometimes, they just gobble them up."

They two boys swallowed hard as they looked nervously around for any sign of giants.

"Are any of these giants around here?"

"I never tell lies," Hannah answered. "I have seen one of these fiendish creatures myself to the south of here. To this little rabbit, you are a giant wishing to sell it to mean men. If you are not willing to show it mercy, why will the giants show you any?"

Looking at the small rabbit, the boy with the cage immediately dropped it. Then the both of them ran away as fast as their legs could carry them.

Hannah opened the cage. "Sister rabbit, why did you allow yourself to be tricked like this?"

After getting out of its miserable cage, the small rabbit immediately hopped over to Hannah and lay down on her lap. Hannah let it rest for a while before putting it on the ground so it could run free. However, the rabbit refused to leave. As a result, she decided to let it stay in their community and eat from their gardens. Even the cats dared not to bother the little rabbit.

Later that day after the midday meal, Hannah and her cousin Sobe made their way around the nearby gardens to give the food in their stomachs a chance to digest properly. They proceeded at a slow pace while taking in the natural beauty.

"It seems like a long time since we first arrived," Hannah said as they navigated the more challenging ditches and gullies.

Sobe took a deep breath before speaking. No longer young, she was tired from the physical exertion. "The years show clearly on my face, but you still look the same. You are indeed a blessed being Hannah." Hannah often wondered about it too, why the others showed their age, but she didn't. Perhaps it had something to do with the staff, as Moses and David also lived very long lives.

They were getting close to the main thoroughfare leading out of Nazareth. Spotting a worm trying to make it safely across the busy road, Hannah stopped and picked it up, placing it in the grass on the other side, away from the danger of plodding feet or the keen eyes of the birds.

An old pilgrim walking along the path that led from Mount Carmel saw her do this. "Why did you save that lowly insect?" he asked. "Isn't it part of the natural rhythm of life and death for them to serve as food for the birds? I often just hit them with my spade to get them out my way."

Hannah noticed from his clothes that the man was a Judean. "Everything on this earth carries within it the spark of the divine," she replied. "Because of this, all life is precious. Before the fall of the Watchers, all creatures big and small were under the care of the Ishim. They labored daily for the Angel of Earth. If one reads the fifth commandment that Aravat gave Moses on Mount Karkom, it says that one should not kill. That holy and sacred commandment does not only forbid the killing of humans, but all creatures. The priests claim otherwise to cover up for the blood lust of their own sex."

Hannah and Sobe bid the man peace and continued walking. They were just about to turn a corner when Hannah held Sobe back. "Listen, somebody is arguing," Hannah said while she kept her hand on Sobe's arm.

Yaakov was speaking, his voice rising to a high pitch in agitation. "I know you would never tell a falsehood," he said, "but we must have some formal proof of your spiritual achievements if the others are to follow you into the dangers that lurk outside these walls."

Hannah gave a look to Sobe. She knew it would be hard for the others to accept the changes in Yael. Hannah had heard that some of the more senior men were demanding that Yael continue as housekeeper of the guest lodge. Yaakov in particular was suspicious.

"I think the ring is more than enough proof," Milka said to refute Yaakov's disbelief. "Hannah would never give her such a precious gem, if did she not believe Yael was in the power of the Shekhinah." This caused a stir.

"Why is the ring special?" Uzia asked.

Yael held it up for all to see. There, on her first finger, was a brightly polished yellow sapphire imbedded onto a band of fine silver.

Milka answered for her friend, as she was well versed in stone lore. "Yellow sapphire gives its wearer spiritual sight and freedom from fear of the evil ones. Hannah was right in giving this to Yael, in light of the task she placed on her. She will need help with both to be successful."

Yaakov was still not convinced. "I need more proof than a ring."

Yael removed the bandages around her hand that no one had noticed. In the middle on the back of both were Angelic writings. Even though the sun had set, they glowed brightly enough that one could easily read by them.

"Where did you get these markings?" Uzia asked in anger. "You know that it is forbidden to use the sacred oil without permission. Did you rub it on your hands yourself, or did Milka do it for you?"

"Inside the tabernacle, after Hannah and," she paused before saying more, "after Hannah anointed me with the sacred oil."

"We need no further proof," Milka said. "No matter what the men say, she has been anointed for this task."

"I think we must ask Hannah if this is true," Uzia said with a tone of authority. "We have established procedures for this kind of thing. If she indeed did this, it is against the rules. The council must first agree to anoint Yael." He held out a broom to Yael. "This is the sign of your position. You have overstepped your bounds!" He realized that holy oil graced her hands, and pulled back the broom with a jerk, thinking that perhaps Yael should not touch it.

Milka scoffed. "Confused as to which rule is more important Uzia? How easily trapped is the mind by foolish designs of their own making. Have you already forgotten that in our community, the spirit governs, and not rules established by men."

"Without rules, there is anarchy, and anarchy always leads to violence," Uzia replied in a stern manner. He was now an elder, and was keen to ensure that everybody respected his position as such. "Is violence what you and the other women desire?"

"It is only because men are unable to control themselves that they build structures and hierarchy," Milka retorted, angry from this kind of talk.

Yael put herself between Milka and the men. "If you wish to consult Hannah, suit yourselves. Who is stopping you? There are no rules forbidding it, are there? I am taking Milka with me, and leaving. There is no time to waste. The dark power will soon be upon us. We will go out to face it. I have no fear."

Hannah and Sobe stepped out into the clearing. "What would you like to ask me?"

Uzia was not intimidated. "If what they say is true, you have overstepped your bounds. You have no right to anoint people without permission." He looked over to Yaakov for moral support. Uzia knew that Yaakov aspired to follow his former teacher and someday be Maskil of the order. This was the time to show that he had what it took.

In her hands, Hannah held a small clay pot with newly sprouted herbs inside it. She touched their tender leaves as if the plant was a newborn child.

"Rejoice Children of the Light, for you now walk in Truth and the way of eternal life. Look with the eyes of your spirit on the sights and sounds of the Angels of Earth. In the fresh blue sky dwells the Angel of Air, in our ponds the Angel of Water, and with the day's new sun the Angel of Sun. As these three Angels are on the outside, they are the same on the inside of your bodies, in the form of your breath, blood, and bodily warmth. All are one with the Angel of Earth." Hannah held high the pot for all to see.

Everyone's mood instantly changed. "Are you able to see the pot?" Hannah asked. "I put some seeds in it a couple of days ago. These seeds have soaked in water so that the Angel of Water could enter inside them. After this, the Angels of Air and Sun embraced them. These three Angels awoke the Angel of Life within the seed. After this, I put the awakened seed into the soil of the Angel of Earth, and there all the Angels entered into it. Within a few days, the sprout became grass. There is no more powerful miracle in life than this."

Yaakov scratched his head. "What has this to do with Yael and her improper anointment?"

Hannah brushed lightly the tops of the little shoots of grass and closed her eyes. As she did, a glow of soft whitish-blue light surrounded her body, and a wonderful scent of fresh flowers filled the air. "It has everything to do with it. If you are unable to understand the mystery of something as simple as this grass, how can you fathom even deeper mysteries?" Hannah passed the small pot around so that each had the opportunity to touch it and feel its life force. A powerful surge of energy went into their hands, up their arms, and into their bodies.

"Hold the humble plant in order that the power of the Angels may enter your bodies," Hannah continued. "There is a Holy Stream of Life, the Shekhinah, which gave birth to all the Angels. It is invisible to those who eyes have not opened for they are blind to the spirit and walk in darkness. But you will enter the Stream of Life that gave birth to all creation, and it will carry you to everlasting life."

"Where can we find the Angel of Sun in these young shoots?" Hannah asked Uzia.

"Why even the children of the community know the answer," he said with a slight smirk, as if unhappy that she put such an easy question to him. "It is in its bright green color."

"If we crush the leaves of this tender plant, we will feel its water of life," Yaakov volunteered. "This is the blood of the earthly Angels."

Hannah passed around the small pot again. "Put your face close to the grass and feel the Angel of Air as you breathe deeply, for she lives in the grass as in all plants."

Hannah used her fingers to dig into the soil of the pot. "The Angel of Earth nurtures the small seeds just as we were inside our mother's womb. And just as when we were born; when these first shoots of grass force their way upward through the soil, it is a victory over death where the darkness reigns. Life is always a victory over the power of darkness."

Hannah turned back to Uzia. "Which Angel shook your hands with power just now with its life force?"

Uzia hesitated as he thought it over. After a short while, he hung his head, embarrassed that he did not know. Neither did Yaakov. "The Angel of Life," Milka replied.

"Plants are life," Hannah said while touching gently Uzia's hand, in a sign of friendship, "and we are life, and this life flows between the two in a holy bond of love. When we come in physical contact with the plants or with each other, we create a bridge to the Holy Stream of Light that gave birth to all creation. These Streams of Light have no end and crisscross the heavenly kingdoms."

Hannah placed her other hand on to Yaakov's face. "Do you not sense the Angel of Joy?" she asked Yaakov? A big smile came across his face. "This joy is everywhere," Hannah said, happy at Yaakov's response. "It is in the songs of the birds, the smell of newly cut grass, and in the beauty of nature. When we become one with this joy, we truly enter the Living Light."

Then Hannah did something nobody expected. She had each one go and touch Yael's hands on the very place the sacred oil had graced them. "Do you not feel the Angel of Power?" Hannah asked. She then had them do likewise to the grass. They were surprised that both caused their hands to tingle. "The Angel of Power is the shining light that surrounds all living things. So tell me now, if you still think Yael's anointment was improper. What does the glow around her hands tell you?"

They all nodded their heads in acknowledgment. "When we touch the plants with love, don't they return it?" Hannah asked them. "When we truly love somebody, do we not wish only the best for them?" Hannah looked Yaakov in the eyes. It told him everything. "If the simple plants can welcome the Angel of Love, cannot we do the same for Yael? Make this Angel your constant companion, for it is love that calls to us the living life force that will be our guide into everlasting life."

Yaakov and Uzia went over to Yael and shook her hand. "I have been wrong about you all these years," Yaakov said. "We have had an Angel in our midst and I was blind to it." Yael cried as he hugged her.

Uzia felt the worst. Many years ago, at the start of their community, he wanted to marry Yael, but she refused his proposal. It had hurt his feelings and ever since, they grew further apart, almost becoming adversaries. "I banished the Angel of Love from my heart. I owe you an apology," Uzia said to Yael with a head lowered in shame. In response, Yael placed his hands together and kissed them. "Do not blame yourself, Uzia. It was I who refused you."

Tears rolled down his cheek. "All these years we could have spent together."

"The Angel of Wisdom sees all and knows all," Milka said as she pulled Yael away from Uzia. "There is a reason for everything, even if we are unaware of it. Wisdom is the law of the universe and eternal order. It not only governs the seasons, the weather, and the movement of the planets, moon, and the sun, but also people's relationships with each other."

Uzia was not happy with Milka's intercession. He always suspected she had a role in Yael's refusal to marry him. "You fulfill your sacred task," Uzia said to Yael. "That is most important. I cannot argue with the Angels."

Yael smiled at his reply. If Uzia only knew about Selith, he would realize how close he was to the real reason she was leaving Nazareth.

Milka took Yael by the hand. "We shared the same teacher, and are spiritual sisters. Our fates are tied together."

Some of the other women volunteered to go out too, as did a couple of the more spiritually gifted men.

"No, the men must stay here," Hannah insisted. "The community itself must not be put into danger."

"But it is not safe for women to be out traveling alone," Yaakov said as he looked at the poor condition of the women, "especially if there is truth to what Yael claims about the dark forces arriving soon. Women are no match for them."

"Healing and bringing people into the Light is work better suited for women," Milka replied as she prepared to depart.

Uzia embraced Yael. "Come back safe and sound. Do not die before I have a chance to make it up for all the trouble I caused."

"I am not afraid to die," Yael said. There was a look of determination in her eyes. "While I am out there, hold fast to our belief that there is no such thing as death. When our spirits depart from their bodies and enter the Holy Stream of Light, we will rise again to everlasting life."

Milka stared hard at Yael. She never heard her say anything this profound. Maybe there was something about that sacred oil. Hannah escorted her two friends to the gate of the community. She would miss them. Hannah still held the small pot of grass in her hands. "You had better make the Angel of Work your constant companion," she said. "For just like her, you must never be still. Make certain to keep moving from place to place. A moving target is harder to hit."

Yael loved tending the plants in the garden. "Not only does the Angel of Work make certain that the roots of the plant absorb enough water to live, so that it may overcome death," she said, "but when we feel the life force in the plants, we are also feeling the eternal rhythm of the universe."

Milka smiled. It was going to be wonderful traveling with Yael.

Arriving at the gate, Hannah handed Yael the little potted plant. "Peace is a gift of the Light. Just as we greet each other with peace, so do the plants greet each of us. When you touch the plants, you will find the peace of all the Angels."

Hannah bade farewell to Yael and Milka. "Let the humble plants be your guides into the eternal realm of Light," Hannah said as she waved goodbye. "In them are hidden many secrets. Continue working in the garden of mysteries so that the Angels can take you to the Stream of Life. Share what you have learned from the humble plants with the sons of men."

Her two best friends were now gone. Hannah felt a little sad as she turned back towards Mount Carmel. She would return to the tabernacles and spend her days praying for them. She noticed Selith walking next to her. "Everything that you learn, all that is revealed with the eyes and ears of the spirit," the Angel said, "of what use are they if you do not go out as messengers of the Truth and Light; for by its fruit, do we know the value of the tree."

Hannah had a great desire to go into the silence, and seek her teacher, the Light. She would need it now more than ever for strength, to face the coming struggle.

# ך

# THOSE WHO TRUST WILL
# UNDERSTAND THE TRUTH

Dressed in white robes, and carrying no belongings, Yael, Milka, and the other Nazarenes went out in groups of two. They gave hope to all by spreading the good news about the impending Mashiakh. Throughout the towns and villages of Galilee, many began following their example of peace, humility, and love, resulting in the formation of small groups dedicated to their way of life.

They were able to move about freely in places still under the control of the Greek-speaking Seleucids, as no official persecution policy against the Nazarenes existed. This was due, in part, to their empire belonging to a common Greek civilization, spreading from the high mountains of India to the western shores of the Mediterranean, fostering a degree of tolerance towards subject cultures. It was quite different in those areas of Galilee now controlled by the Maccabees. Here, there was little tolerance for dissenting beliefs outside the narrow confines of accepted Jewish orthodoxy.

It was still early morning when they gathered inside the courtyard of the local Nazarene community. Yael and Milka were eager to meet those who now considered themselves part of the New Covenant. The town of Dabaritta had seen lots of fighting between Seleucid and Maccabee forces, with the Maccabees recently wresting control of it from their opponents. A small group, Yael sensed the fear in their hearts over what the Maccabee garrison and their reinstated priestly allies might do to them.

"Peace be with you, Nechemia," Yael said to their elder.

"And with you", he replied with his hand raised in friendship. "I am happy to see you safe. Things are certainly not the same as they were in the early days." He wore a frown on his face.

"Do not give in to despair," Milka returned, with a determined look. "It is a tool the evil ones use to weaken us. Faith is the armor we wear, and the Angels our swords."

"It is hard to have faith with a hostile army camped outside your walls. The former priest of our village was a Pharisee, and did little to disturb us. He has fled, however, and his replacement is a Sadducee with powerful connections in Jerusalem. He came by yesterday, escorted by a contingent of soldiers, and called us heretics. It is strange that those who initially opposed the Maccabees with so much blood and vigor are now their most trusted allies, while their old supporters, the Pharisees, are more open to letting us live in peace."

"The enemy of the enemy has become a friend," Milka replied. "Still, I do not trust the Pharisees either, as much depends on the intrigues at the king's court in Jerusalem. It is an unstable situation that could change at any moment."

Yael looked up at the thick hazy clouds that hovered above their heads. "It has been months since we have seen the sun, and yet it never rains. The darkness is arriving and the battle for Galilee is about to begin. From now on, we will see more than the occasional raid from Judea, as the Maccabees smell the rot of the declining Seleucid Empire. It is only a matter of time until all of Galilee belongs to them. We must be prepared."

Nechemia pointed to a man lying nearby on a mat. "A friend pleaded to allow him to attend our gathering, hoping you might heal him. He was once a skilled craftsman of some fame. Unfortunately, the Seleucids suspected him of being a Maccabee sympathizer. As punishment, they smashed the bones of his arm with sledgehammers. After this, they took his two daughters to serve the soldiers. As if this was not enough, the captain of the Greek troops forced him to watch as they raped his wife. His daughters never returned, and his wife lost her mind. The poor wretch now spends his days begging on the streets."

Yael looked at a woman sitting next to the man. With her hair disheveled, she wore clothes that were close to rags. "Is this his wife?"

"Yes, but she will not answer if you speak to her."

Yael turned her attention back to the man and sensed the living darkness inhabiting his lame arm. "Do you believe there is a higher power that has the means to cure you?" Yael asked him while she touched his arm.

"Yes, I do, but I have yet to find the one able to bring me into this power."

Rubbing his arm up and down, Yael sent into it some of her own life force. "There is no one person who can open that door for you. The power is there for all to access. It is free and needs no gatekeeper. It is your belief that opens the door to healing."

Yael asked him to close his eyes and pray. While he did, Yael saw the color of the life force surrounding his body turn a bright yellow. She continued to massage the places where the life force was stagnant. "Stretch out your arm!" Yael commanded.

It had been years since he had been able to move it, but now, in front of these people and under his own willpower, he did. At first, it was only a small twitch of his fingers, and then the muscles in his hand jumped. Finally, the entire arm began moving up and down.

Seeing that he had the use of his arm once more, the man broke down in tears.

Yael then went over to his wife. She could see with her spiritual eye the living darkness hovering all around her body. It was more similar to a thick putrid haze than the clear, water-like qualities of a healthy life force. The soldiers, in their rage, had transferred their hate and anger to her when she was most vulnerable. Yael stretched out the hand that had Hannah's ring on it. Immediately the woman crouched down, and put her hands in front of her body. "Leave me alone, slave of the witch. You've no real power of your own. Deep down you know you are a nothing but a worthless cleaning girl. Don't put on airs with me." The woman stood up and pulled off her robe with a hard yank. "Anyone who wants this piece of meat can have it," she yelled out, naked.

Yael became confused.

Milka wanted to say something to the woman. "You too, slut?" the woman said in a hissing tone before Milka could speak. "Why not tell everyone what you did with those soldier boys when you were young. You enjoyed it as they stood in line with their stinking meat breath to take turns with you. Admit it. You've nothing over me. We're the same."

The woman let out a shrill laugh, forcing everyone to back away. Yael recovered her courage, and wasted no time. She touched the woman with the ring. The woman screeched, holding the place that had made contact with it. She growled and spit at Yael. "It's not enough. I'm stronger than the silly ring. You're so stupid. The real power does not lie in the sacred object, but in the one who wields it."

The wife of the man took a stick off the ground and began to beat people with it, forcing everyone to scatter. Some ran out the door in fear of their lives. Yael raised her hand to try once more to touch her with it, but the woman struck Yael with the stick, knocking her to the ground.

In the midst of all the commotion, the husband suddenly lunged at his wife. Now that he had use of both of his arms again, he was able to wrestle her down onto the hard earthen floor of the courtyard. His wife bit him, and used her long uncut fingernails to scratch at his eyes, but he wouldn't let go.

"Sarah. I love you. I love you." He said it repeatedly.

His wife shook her head back and forth. "I'm a slut. No one can love me. Have me, take me, I'm only worthless meat to be enjoyed."

Despite this, her husband persisted. "Sarah. I love you. I love you."

The more he said this, the weaker his wife became, until at last she lost consciousness. Lying there, her husband thought she was dead. Yael went over to examine her. "Sarah, Sarah," she called out, "follow the Light. It will lead you back."

The woman opened her eyes after a moment. The first person she saw was her husband. She smiled and grabbed his hand. "I love you too."

Rejoicing erupted. "I have never met a man such as this," Milka said, relieved. "Even though the living darkness lived in his arm all these years, he did not allow it to enter his heart."

Nechemia was even more impressed. "If soldiers did that to my wife, in front of my eyes, I doubt if I could ever love her as before."

Looking at the couple as they embraced, everyone was curious. How was he able to keep the darkness from destroying him and his wife? What was his secret?

"There is no secret," the man said. "I am a humble tradesman with no formal education. Seeing the miseries inflicted upon my poor family, I began praying every day. Whether I was begging, or taking care of my wife, I prayed, never stopping until I went to sleep. Every day, my wife removed her clothes and begged me to have her, but I resisted by praying. When she solicited the men in the village to take her, they often desired to take advantage of her mental condition. However, when they heard me praying, they could not carry it out. There was nothing else, only the power of prayer."

"You forget to mention one other of your secrets," Yael said, "The love for your wife. The prayers were the fuel, but the love was the match that set it on fire."

The news about this soon reached the head of the Maccabee garrison. After consulting with the Sadducee, he issued an order to seize Yael and Milka for questioning. They learned about it and left Dabaritta at once in order not to make trouble for the community. With their hoods pulled over their heads, Yael and Milka snuck through the back alleys until they reached the outskirts of the village. After seeking guidance from the living Shekhinah, they decided to walk in the direction of Sigoph.

ה

# LET THE PURE
# BE YOUR GUIDE

Milka and Yael arrived outside the walls of Sigoph and discovered it, too, had fallen to forces loyal to the Maccabees.
With the Seleucids busy with their own war in the north, they were
unable to take it back. There were no Nazarenes here.

"Our work will be difficult," Milka said as she looked at the
closed gate that barred their way. "The Sadducees consider us heretics, and will have the authorities arrest us on the slightest pretense.
Someone in Dabaritta told me that the Maccabees have promised
a reward for providing information about anyone matching the
description of Hannah."

Yael smiled. "Well, that saves us. Not many are as pretty as she is."

Milka looked at her and frowned. "Now is not the time for
joking. What shall we do? I do not think we will provide much help
in building the life force if they take us into slavery. It is hard to
pray while satisfying the lust of an oafish brute."

Yael rubbed the ring that Hannah gave her. "We must be mindful that the others are looking to us for guidance. We must set a

good example, not only for now, but also for the future generations of those that choose our way of life. What we do will leave a lasting impression."

"If we fail, there will be no future generations to worry about," Milka replied as she put her hands on her hips.

Yael could tell her friend was frustrated. "I say, let the Shekhinah decide. Let us put our total trust in it and see what happens."

Milka was at first hesitant to follow Yael's suggestion, but seeing that it was futile to rely on her own confused thinking, she finally agreed.

The two of them sat down on a small boulder and closed their eyes. Yael thought she was able to see Selith with her mind's eye, sitting there in their midst. After some minutes passed, Milka gave Yael as small nudge. "I think we should go in. We have a task to do. The Angel of Work will be our guide."

Yael realized Milka was right. The darkness was ever nearing. Time was not on their side.

Instead of using the main gate, they walked around the outer perimeter of the wall. They saw a large caravan entering through one of the minor doors, and easily slipped by the guards by walking next to the pack animals. As they proceeded to the main market street, many of the locals noticed that they were only two, both wearing white robes, and carrying no belongings. It did not take long for the word to spread that they were Nazarenes.

Yael and Milka spent a good part of the day under the glaring sun, curing with herbs, precious stones, and prayers. The ill were many.

"It is through love that the Angels know you walk on their paths so that they may come to serve you," Yael said to those seeking healing. "Seeing the Angels, Beelzebub, with all his sins, diseases, and uncleanness, will leave your body. Stop living a sinful life. Repent, and then find clean water with which to wash yourselves, symbolizing your new life."

Resting up against an old wall made of stone, some of the local ruffians heckled her. Many of them had the reputation for being petty thieves and pickpockets.

Milka continued to examine the many women who came for healing. She normally preferred that Yael tend to the men. "None can be happy except those who follow the law," Yael said in a loud voice.

The leader of the ruffians smirked. "But we do obey the laws of Moses, our lawgiver, as they are written in Holy Scriptures." With a wink to his fellows he added, "Well, at least some times we do."

Undeterred, Yael walked straight over to him. "Do not look for the law in your scriptures, for the law is life, whereas the scripture is dead. Moses did not receive his laws from Aravat in writing, but through the living word. The law is the living word of the living Aravat, given to the living prophets for all the living people. In everything that is alive, is the law written. You can find it in the grass, in the trees, in the rivers, in the mountains, in the birds, in the fish, but look for it mainly in yourselves. All living things are nearer to Aravat than scripture. Aravat so made life and all living things that they might, by the everlasting word, teach the laws of the Light."

To the surprise of their leader, some of the ruffians began to pay attention. Yael reached down to pat the grass. "Aravat wrote not these laws in the pages of books, but in your hearts, your spirit and in all of nature. Scripture is the work of man, but life and all its hosts are the work of the Light. Why do you not listen to the words of Aravat written in the works of nature? Why do you study instead, the dead scriptures that are the work of the hands of men?"

Their leader grew afraid that his fellows might give up their evil ways. So he strode up to Yael's face. "You're such a pretty one," he said while looking her over. There was a hint of lust in his eyes. It was clear he wanted to intimidate her. Milka observed it and was about to confront him, but Yael motioned for her to remain sitting. "If you're so smart," he said, "why don't you explain to us how can we know the laws elsewhere than in the scriptures? You say that they are in nature. So where are they? Go ahead and read them to us, that is, if you can." He turned his head away and made a face in a mocking manner.

Yael backed away. He was so close, that his chest nearly touched hers. "You do not understand the words of life, because you are in death. Darkness covers your eyes and your ears are stopped with deafness. It will not help poring over dead scriptures if by your deeds you deny Aravat who has given you the scriptures."

Milka got up and began walking among the ruffians, directly speaking to them. "The Light and its laws are not in gluttony, drunkenness, riotous living, lustfulness, in seeking after ill-gotten riches, nor in hatred of your enemies. These things come from the fallen angels and the lord of all evils." The ruffians became nervous upon hearing this.

Milka kept going, seeing that her words were having some effect. "If you do these things, the Light cannot enter into you because evil and all manner of abominations have their dwelling in your body. Do not defile your body, for it is the temple of the Shekinah, a temple of the Living Light. Purify the temple so that its Lord can live in it and occupy a place that is worthy of it." The leader of the ruffians grew afraid and left. Maybe they were witches.

Milka and Yael left the city that night and found a place to lie down in the grass outside the town walls. They tried to get a good night's sleep. It was not easy for the air was stale and not moving.

They woke the next morning and said their morning prayers. Yael suddenly felt uncomfortable. Milka noticed the change in her. "What is the matter, sister? Perhaps we should rest for a day or so before going on. We have not taken a break since we started out."

"No, it's not that. I am not tired at all," Yael answered. "Something else is bothering me, but I cannot tell what it is. Maybe we should eat our breakfast over there in that patch of woods."

Milka had no objection. After relocating, they sat and enjoyed the warm morning sunshine. All of the sudden, they heard loud voices coming from the field they had just left. Milka peered through the trees that were providing cover.

"Look there," Milka whispered, "it is a group of rough men searching the grounds. They must be looking for us."

The men went around beating the bushes in the field with large crude sticks until they grew tired and returned to town.

"They must be the supporters of the Maccabees," Yael said after it was safe to talk again. "Someone must have told on us."

"I am glad that I found you. I have been looking all over the place." Startled, they turned to see a young woman wearing the simple clothes of a peasant, standing there with a basket in her hands. "My name is Artakifa," she said. "I heard you speak yesterday and wanted to bring you something to eat and drink." She handed them the basket. "There are some seeds and berries, as well as a small flask of wine made from green plums. It is very refreshing."

Milka and Yael looked at each other in disbelief. How did this girl find them while those men could not? With her urging them to take the basket, they put away their fears and ate.

"You must be more careful today," Artakifa said. "The religious leaders have orders for your arrest. They are furious over what you told the people yesterday."

"And what do you think about what we said?" Milka asked. "Do you also consider it a crime?"

"What you said has no fault. It has been said before many times and in many places."

"And how would a young peasant girl know this?" Milka pressed her.

"I have heard it said, that is all," the girl answered humbly.

Yael and Milka continued eating while watching the girl more closely.

"Would you like to come with us?" Yael asked.

"I have no family in the regular way. I would be happy to travel with you. I am anxious to learn more about your beliefs and way of life."

"Where to next?" Yael asked Milka, after they were finished with eating.

"No need to leave this quickly," Artakifa said in reply to Yael. "There is a large crowd that will arrive shortly. They are coming to hear you speak some more."

"How do you know this?" Milka asked, surprised to hear the news. "Are your eyes that good that you can see through trees?"

Artakifa laughed. "I saw them gathering about early this morning near the old well. I overheard one of the say they were going to seek you out."

"Well, how will they find us?" Yael wondered. "Maybe we should go to them."

"I do not think it is safe to move about openly," Artakifa replied. "There are many people looking for you, some are good and some are bad. If you stay here, nestled in the arms of nature, those who are good will find you. If you go out into the world of men, those who are bad will find you."

"You are a wise girl for your age. What do you do for a living?" Yael asked.

"I am a simple shepherd. There is much to learn from watching sheep, especially concerning the ways of wolves."

Moments later a small crowd of women walked into the same place that the men had searched without success. They came, in spite of the official hostility from the local priests. After finding them in the woods, Yael and Milka located a nice clearing where they held a wonderful gathering in the Light.

ו

# SUFFER THE INNOCENTS

After leaving Sigoph, Yael and Milka set out with Artakifa for the towns and villages bordering the western shore of the Sea of Galilee.

A few days later, some of the locals learned that they had come from Nazareth and brought to them the sick and lame. The people witnessed firsthand the cures they performed.

Yael and Milka were eager to talk with those who felt spiritually ready to receive the Light. They stood on a large boulder so all could hear, and Yael began prophesying about the start of the dark age and the coming of the Mashiakh.

Someone asked where their powers of healing came from. "The gift of healing comes from the Living Light that is accessible to all," Yael answered for them. "There is no need for intermediaries. This Light is not found in temples made by the hands of humans, but in our own bodies, which are living temples of the Living Light."

"How can we be these temples?" another asked.

"You must not eat the flesh of slain beasts," Milka answered. "You must also end the superstitious ceremonies that involve blood offerings to appease an angry god for your sins. These are the first steps. Master these and the Angels will open the door to deeper truths for you."

The people were surprised to hear this. "This isn't what the priests teach. They have us go to the temple once a year to give them a blood offering."

Yael replied. "Priests use rituals to assume positions of authority by acting as gatekeepers between Aravat and the people. Never forget, that the real teacher is in your heart, and is free for all."

Yael and Milka noticed that the spiritual eyes of some were now open, and were glad for it. Towards the end, they encouraged all to pray for the Mashiakh to come.

Their unorthodox teachings outraged the local priests, who wanted to send them to Jerusalem for questioning by the Sanhedrin. However, the Judean official in charge of the Maccabee garrison desired to deal with them more harshly. To him, nothing was more threatening to the established religious and secular order than wandering women folk healers spreading heresies.

Soldiers came for them with thick ropes. As they approached, an old woman standing nearby asked, "What crimes have they committed?"

"What's it to you, old fart," one of soldiers replied. He gave the old woman a hard shove to get her out of the way.

They began tying up Yael and Milka. Their leader, who appeared to have seen many battles, gave particular notice to Yael. "Nice and chubby, particularly in the right places," he said with a laugh while he patted her bottom.

"You brute, leave her alone," Milka said in her defense.

The leader went over and squeezed hard Milka's face with his large strong hands. "Who asked for your opinion, bitch?"

The leader motioned for them to get moving. "The captain wants to see them right away. We'll have our chance later."

The soldiers paraded Yael and Milka thought the streets like common thieves. "The Mashiakh will come to end the outward temple and its worship," Milka cried out in a loud voice, seeing some of the townspeople stop and stare, "and build a new one in the hearts of the righteous. He will show the false priests for what they are and end the tithes they force upon you."

A soldier turned around and kicked Milka. "You are a mouthy bitch, aren't you?" Milka fell to her knees. With her hands bound behind her back, the soldier then tore the front of her robe to expose her flesh and began dragging her along the ground with the rope that bound her. Many of the local men standing about struggled to get a glimpse of her body, while mothers shooed their sons away.

They soon arrived at the garrison's headquarters. The commander ordered a trial to take place, but set no date. He hoped that by leaving them in jail for as long as possible without proper nourishment, their resolve would weaken, making it easier to extract a confession. In addition, he promised the chief jailor, a Greek previously employed by the Seleucid government, a reward if the female prisoners became pregnant. What could be better than to have these traveling female healers show up for the trial with their bellies sticking out, without husbands to vouch for them? It would be easy to discredit them in the eyes of the men, who would demand punishment for their sins.

That night, Yael and Milka sat in their unlit cell, alone and hungry. The jailor had not provided them with a single drop of water to drink, or a crumb to eat. To keep their spirits up, they prayed together and sang. Close to midnight, as they were drifting off to sleep, they thought they heard somebody talking to them. Startled, they realized the voice was coming from a small single window situated high above their heads, as it was the only source of air and light from the outside.

"Who is it?" Yael called up to it. "What do you want?"

"It is me, Artakifa. Can you see me?"

Examining the window more closely, they were able to see a small head sticking through the narrow slit. "What are you doing?" Milka asked. "How did you climb up there? There are no trees, just a sharp wall."

"It does not matter. I am small in frame, and my bones still young. I am going to throw you some fruit and a flask with water in it. Here they come, catch them."

A few pieces of fruit flew down from the window, followed by a wooden flask that hit the floor with a bounce. "Did you get them?" Artakifa asked down to them.

"Yes, we got them. How did you buy these things?" Milka asked. "I thought you said you had no money. You did not steal them, did you?"

"Of course I did not steal them. One of the people you healed today requested that I give them to you since you refused any payment."

"Do you bring us news?" Yael asked.

"No good news. Be prepared for the worse. They plan on starving a confession out of you."

"What can we confess to?" Yael retorted. "We have committed no crime."

"That is not all. They plan to make both of you pregnant to discredit the Nazarenes in the eyes of the common people."

"They will stone us for adultery afterwards," Milka said as she lowered her head. "It is clear; this is how they plan to get rid of us."

"I do not agree," Artakifa replied. "They are not priests, and have no concern for the law. They will not miss the opportunity to make some money by selling you into slavery."

"Then you must help us escape," Yael said, There was desperation in her voice.

"I wish I was able to, but there is nothing I can do against so many armed men."

Yael and Milka realized the helplessness of their situation. Thinking it over for a minute, Yael took off her ring. "I am going to throw something up to you. I want you to take it to Nazareth right away. When you get there, ask for Hannah, she is the leader of our community. Give it to her. She will understand what it means."

"I do not want to leave you here alone. At least with me here, I can provide you with food and drink."

"Please do as I ask. Here it comes. Catch it."

Yael threw the ring up, but it missed the narrow slit. "Let me try again. Can you put your hand through the slit?"

They saw her small slender arm reach through the window. Yael tired once more, but again could not throw the ring close enough to Artakifa's hand for her to catch it.

"Let me give it a try," Milka said. "I was considered the best thrower in our village when I was a young girl."

Yael handed the ring to her. Milka looked at Artakifa's hand for a minute, and after taking careful aim, tossed it in the air.

"Got it!" Artakifa cried out.

"Not so loud!" Milka cautioned. "Do you want to wake the guards?"

They once more saw Artakifa's small head peeking through the narrow slit.

"Now, go at once," Yael ordered. "Do not stop until you get to Nazareth. You are a blessed friend indeed. Go in peace!"

Her head disappeared. She was gone. Yael hoped that somehow Hannah and Selith would be able to figure out a way to save them. If only they had enough time.

Yael rested on Milka's shoulder. After a few minutes, Yael turned her eyes towards her friend. "What is it like?"

"What is what like?"

"To have a man force himself on you?"

Milka leaned her head back on to the cold wall and closed her eyes. "I had hoped never to think about it again. It is like dying. In fact, maybe dying is better. The very act of this violence, like all violence, is the personification of the living darkness." She paused and took a deep breath. "I was only twelve years old. After a long siege, the enemy took our village. The soldiers came into our house and after killing my father, took turns all night long with my mother and two sisters. When they grew tired of it, they killed them too. I was not old enough, not yet a woman in body, so the officer in charge spared my life, and took me as a slave." Milka spoke in hushed tones.

"I was tall for my age and became a woman earlier than most. My master was kind, but soon began to have relations with me. After some time, I was sold to satisfy a gambling debt to a company of royal guards. The soldiers would get drunk and take turns with me. Hatred built up in my heart as I lay there nightly, hoping that each one was sober enough to be quickly done with it. No matter how hard I try, I cannot forget. I pray that this time I am better prepared, both physically and spiritually, to face the onslaught of their evil."

"We should not talk about it. The darkness will be here soon enough, why invite it any earlier?" Yael regretted causing Milka further pain.

"They will first humiliate you. It is how the darkness prepares you for its entrance. They will touch you everywhere, and then it happens. Since they are in the heat of violence, it will not take them long once they begin. That is, unless they are too drunk. Then it takes what seems like forever."

Yael was no longer able to hold back her tears. "I am so scared. I never thought things would end this way. How can these soldiers be so mean? Do they not have families of their own?"

"When men become soldiers they go mad with the smell of blood in their nostrils. They revert to their original dark nature. Even the priests bless the soldiers, for they too are men and share in their darkness. Wherever there is war, there is rape and violence against women. They are twins. Men are nasty brutes. The world would be a better place without them."

"When do you think will they begin?"

"It is difficult to say, but they will not delay for long. We have to be pregnant by many months before they can parade us in front of the people, and who knows how many times it will take before we get pregnant."

Yael wiped her tears away. With a damp palm, she grabbed Milka's hand and began to pray.

The next day, the chief jailor bought some jugs of wine, and invited the guards to drink with him. Yael and Milka could hear them getting drunk as they began telling lewd stories to each other. After a while, the guards burst into their cell. Some held leather wine goblets and others large hunks of roasted meat in their hands.

Slobbering and barely able to speak, the chief jailor came over to Yael. He spoke with a loud, coarse voice. "Get up and take off your clothes. They want to see the goods I'm selling today."

Yael did not respond, but continued to sit there, terrified. The jailor went over and grabbed a whip. He began hitting her. One of the other guards pulled it out his hand to stop him. "Don't put any marks on her if you want the full price."

The guards went over and pulled Yael up against her will. She tried with all her might to keep them away, but it was useless. They pulled off her robe and a wild yell went out as Yael struggled to get free of their grasp. Two held her arms behind her back while the others came over to take turns touching her. As they did, Yael began to sob. "Remember your mothers, sisters, daughters, and your wives." This only made them angrier and they began to curse her.

They took her over to a bed and tied her on to it. Yael was able to see Milka sitting with her eyes closed. A couple of the other guards went over to Milka and violently ripped off her white robe. They tied her on to one of the long tables close to the door.

"Leave her alone, you know the deal," the jailor said. "The big one is mine. You get the chubby one." He staggered over to the table that held Milka. A few of the guards complained, but soon realized there was nothing they could do about it.

The jailor started right away. Yael did not want to look, but could hear the sound of it. The guards soon began with her. Although the pain and the humiliation were terrible, Yael was glad that Milka only had to satisfy one. She prayed for these men and their families. Resolved not to let the living darkness enter her friend's life force, she prayed most for Milka.

ז

# IN SIN MY
# MOTHER CONCEIVED ME

Both Yael and Milka were pregnant. It had been a while since the guards showed any interest in harassing them, although occasionally if they had too much wine to drink, the soldiers would come in to curse and grope them. They passed the time praying, and waiting for the time of their transfer to the slave markets.

Since becoming pregnant, the jailor began feeding them more regularly in the hopes they would fetch more money if they looked healthier. After getting drunk one night, he told them that the Judeans in charge were afraid, now that the Seleucids were once more sending soldiers into Galilee. As the garrison was too small in number to offer any effective defense, they began discussing when and how to dispose of the two women before returning to Judea. With time short, they would have to be content selling them to wholesalers, who would in-turn take them to the large slave markets in Damascus for resale.

Yael and Milka huddled together to keep warm as the evening chill bit into their bones. Forced into wearing unwashed and ragged robes, they felt deserted and alone. They often talked about Nazareth, and wondered how the others were faring.

It was close to midnight, yet they were having difficulty falling asleep. Startled by the sound of the door to their cell opening, Milka clenched the front of her torn robe to cover herself. It was the chief jailer. Normally if he came in at this hour, he was up to no good. Instead, even though it was dark, they could see that he was carrying something in his arms. Kneeling down in front them, they saw his burden was a small still girl.

"This is my only child. She just passed her twelfth year," he said as he stroked his daughter's head. "Three days ago she came down with the fever and today lost consciousness. I can barely hear her breathing."

"This is a sign from your God," he said, remorseful and full of tears, "and is my just punishment. One of the children in your bellies is mine, and he wishes to take a life for it in exchange. Please, pray for the child. He can take my life as payment, but not the life of one who is innocent."

"What do you care about innocent girls?" Milka asked scornfully. She carried his child inside her womb and felt little pity. "What crime were we guilty of, other than healing the sick? If she lives, she will only grow up and have to face the likes of you. It would be better that she died."

He held his unconsciousness daughter in his arms, and continued to cry, as he rocked her back and forth. "It's your miserable father's fault. He has sinned, and now you must die for it. Please don't leave me, my little jewel. Please don't die."

Yael put her hand on the child's forehead. Looking at the dying child, she felt sorry. She told the jailer that if he wanted to save his daughter, he would have to repent for his sins and begin a new life. He readily agreed.

Yael could feel the life force slipping away from the girl. "What did you do with that small cloth pouch of gems we had when we were arrested?" she asked the jailor.

"I put it outside, as the guards complained about its odor."

"Of course, it smells like fresh flowers," Milka said as she curled her lips. "What would a man know about it?"

Yael gave Milka a hard look, as if to remind her not to let hatred worm its way into her heart. "Can you still find it?" Yael asked.

The jailor then did something that surprised them both. He put his daughter onto Milka's lap as he went out to search for the little bag. Milka stared into the girl's face, and as she did, her heart felt a sense of relief as she let go of some of the bitterness that had built over the last few months.

In a few minutes, the jailor retuned with the pouch, now worn looking from its long exposure to the elements. Yael opened it and took out a few small healing stones.

She held up a creamy-white gem with a waxy surface. "This is Serpentine, from the deep mines of Khatoon in the land of the Persians. Quick now, go bring me some boiled water."

Using the hard handle of the blade that they used to cut their fruit, Yael pounded a small piece of the stone into a fine powder. After the jailor retuned with the water, she took her bowl and mixed the water and powder together to make a paste. Yael put the paste into the girl's mouth using her little finger.

"Hand me a big Carnelian stone," Yael said to Milka.

Using her free hand, as she did not want the girl to fall off her lap, Milka took out a bright brown quartz stone and gave it to her. Yael began rubbing the soles of the girl's feet with it from heel to toe to absorb the excessive body heat. When she finished, she took the stone and put it on the girl's forehead. "This will weaken the hold of the evil life force that has taken over her body. Have any of the soldiers touched her?"

The jailer began to sob once more.

Yael shook her head in sorrow. "There is an old woman who lives in the forest outside of town, famous for her healing skills. Do you know who I mean?"

"You mean the witch of the meadows? Is she also one of your kind?"

"No, she is not a Nazarene," Yael replied. "Her tradition dates back to the time before the first prophets, only a few still remain. She is well versed in the healing arts of many lands. Go ask her to make a broth made from the roots of Petasites and Ziggiberis, and the leaves of Kalaminthe and Peristereon. You must bring it to us while it is still hot, and do not use any bowls or flasks made from hides. Do you understand? In addition, bring us many blankets. We must bring your daughter to crisis through sweating. The battle between the evil and good has begun, and we must provide a way out of her body for the evil life force to leave. Now, go at once. The hour is late and time is not on our side."

As soon as he left, Milka and Yael laid hands on her and began praying. As they did, the girl began gurgling and thrashing her head back and forth. The more they prayed, the more violent the girl's reaction.

Milka held the girl close to her body. "When will men learn the consequences of their evil actions? They must have done something terrible to this little girl. It is no ordinary fever she has."

"If we are going to win this battle with the dark life force," Yael said in reply, "you must let go of all that anger. It is feeding it, and making it stronger."

Milka thought it over for a minute. She closed her eyes in prayer, and took the child's hand, placing it on her belly. "This is your sister. She wants you to live, for she loves you very much. And I love you, too."

Yael began to cry. "How do you know it is a girl that you carry?"

"I just know."


Shortly before dawn, the jailor returned with the broth. With much effort, as the girl resisted fiercely, they forced her to drink it. They covered her in blankets, and continued praying as the sweat poured profusely out of her small pores.

The jailor watched intently while his daughter fought for her life. He pulled something out of his leather satchel. "I almost forgot to give you this. The old witch said it might be of some use."

He handed it to Yael. It was an old-looking, small piece of scroll. On it was the Hebrew letter caph, in the form of an opened hand.

"What does it mean?" the jailor asked Yael, still trying to avoid talking to Milka.

"I do not know. I am not familiar with it. You will need to ask her," she said, pointing to Milka.

Milka took the tattered piece of parchment, and placed in near the heart of the little girl. "The open hand means to seize and hold," she said, talking more to Yael than to the jailor. "The dark life force has seized the girl, and we are holding her against its wishes. The twenty-two letters of the Hebrew alphabet form the twenty-two paths to the Tree of Life. The Tree of Life has four elements—Fire, Air, Water, and Earth. According to this mystery tradition, the life force corresponds to the letter caph, the number twenty-two, and the element of fire. When did your daughter lose consciousness?"

"It was yesterday, sometime around mid-morning."

"When twenty-two hours have passed, it will be the time when her life force has its greatest chance of fighting off this evil that has entered her through a foul deed. The evil will be defeated through fire. We have cooked the herbs, and she drank it hot. You see, the evil flees with the sweat."

"This means our course of action was correct?" Yael asked.

"Yes, it was. She will live."

"Since you are familiar with this mystery tradition, why did you not say so earlier? You could have saved the poor father much anxiety."

"Why does he deserve any mercy?"

Yael did not reply, but instead prayed silently for her friend's wounded heart.

Just as the sun was rising, the little girl opened her eyes. "Daddy, I want my daddy!"

Milka gladly handed her over to the father, who gave thanks to Aravat for saving his child.

When news about this reached the Judean guards, they accused the jailor of treason for forsaking his former dark ways, forcing him to flee with his family. In a hurry, as the Seleucid soldiers would arrive soon, they bound Yael and Milka with strong ropes, and paraded them in front of the men of the village who accused them of many sins.

They marched Yael and Milka over to the priests who gave the guards permission to sell them out of fear of retribution if they refused. Slavers were waiting outside the village square, who in exchange for the women gave the soldiers a few silver Seleucid coins.

Now in chains, the slavers hauled Yael and Milka out of town. The slavers rode on mules while they walked behind. As they left, a few of the townspeople watched. The men cursed them, but those healed by these Nazarenes hid their faces as they wept.

It was a scorching hot day. Yael and Milka struggled to keep up. They soon became weary and began to fall down. They begged for a sip of water but the slavers only laughed at them. Tired, hungry, and with lips cracked from lack of water and the blistering heat, they struggled to keep up with the caravan as it plodded along the well-beaten road to Damascus.

Members of other caravans often stared at them, wondering what crime deserved such punishment. If by chance they saw that they were with child, many of the men assumed the worse and spat at them.

As the day wore on, a man riding in an adjacent caravan who appeared to be a Syrian began eyeing Yael. Seeing that she was pregnant, he asked the head slaver the reason for their chains. The slaver looked back and laughed.

"They're a couple of whores. We're taking them to Damascus for sale to the houses of prostitution. If you see one you like, I'm willing to sell her cheap to save me the trouble of taking her all the way there."

The man expressed some interest, and rode back to inspect Yael more closely. The slaver stopped to allow him more time to decide. Addressing her in Aramaic, the slaver called Yael foul names as he rudely pulled off her robe. He pointed to her breasts. "Even with a swollen belly, it looks like some good meat to me, wouldn't you say?"

"I lost my wife last year during a siege when those hated Judeans overran our village," the Syrian replied. His eyes remained fixed on her large breasts. "She was raped repeatedly before they took her life. It's fitting that a Jewish slave replaces my wife. I'll not be kind to her. It's justice, one of theirs for mine. How much do you want?"

"It's a good deal, these Jews." The slaver spat on the ground. "Hard workers and plenty clean too. In addition, you get the child. If it's a girl, you'll be able to bed her along with the mother, as soon she is old enough. If it's a boy, you can sell him to one of the armies. They're always looking for fighters."

After agreeing on a price, the slaver yanked the chain holding Yael, throwing her down at the feet of her new master. "Here's your slut. If you want the child, you'd better not do much to her until it's born."

He got back on to his mule and the caravan slowly continued its way forward. It had happened so quickly. Yael realized that she and Milka might never see each other again. Once more struggling to keep up with the mules, Milka glanced back towards Yael. The slaver pulled hard on Milka's chains, forcing her head forward.

Yael was unable to give it much thought, as her new master was even crueler than the slavers, forcing her to walk at a faster pace behind the pack animals. "Come on whore," he scolded her in broken Aramaic. "We've some distance to travel before making camp. I'm looking forward to you cooking my meal. When the fires are out, we'll see what we can do together. It's been a long year and I doubt if I can restrain myself. There's more than one way to please me." He laughed as he yanked on her chains.

Close to nightfall, as the caravan taking Milka to Damascus stopped to make camp, a man traveling with his family appeared on the same road. Hailing the traders, he asked if he could accompany them to Damascus, as he was in the service of the Seleucid governor and needed to go there on official business. Happy to have an official traveling with them, they readily agreed.

The next morning as they all set off, the man looked at Milka securely bound behind the mules. He informed the slavers that the Seleucid king was eager to gain the loyalty of his Galilean subjects, and requested that they allow the woman to ride with his wife and daughter in their cart, as she was with child. Reluctant, but not wishing to displease one of the king's officials, they agreed.

Milka got in the cart, and a woman and young girl removed her chains and gave her something to drink. They took out some salve and began applying it to the places where the chains had rubbed the skin raw. Milka felt immense gratitude for their kindness.

Wiping the dust from her swollen eyes, Milka began seeing things more clearly. As she looked at her new hosts in more detail, it seemed as if she knew these people from somewhere. She grabbed the woman's hand. "Have we met before?"

The daughter provided Milka with some more water. "We have met," the woman replied in a pleasant voice. "Perhaps you don't remember since your life has been terrible these last few months, but you saved my daughter's life."

It dawned on Milka who these people were, the jailor's wife and her daughter. The woman put a pillow under Milka to help support the weight of her body. "Upon discovering who you were last night, I insisted that we help you. We're thankful for giving us back our daughter. My husband has seen the errors of his ways and agreed, although he's embarrassed, since you carry his child. We will borrow some money once we get to Damascus to purchase you, as our children share a common father. You will live with us."

Milka began to cry. She cried for herself, for this woman, for these two children, both born and unborn, but most of all for the jailor.

"My husband talked to the slavers and found out what happened to your companion," the mother said to Milka. "We're sorry that we arrived too late to save her. You're a good woman, and we can learn much from you. Fate has blessed my family, although we deserve it not." Reaching over to sort through her own belongings, she handed Milka one of her robes. "Change into this and rid yourself of those filthy rags." It was beautifully dyed multi-colored linen. Milka put it next to her face, savoring the feel of its softness.

As she undressed, both mother and the daughter saw how close she was to giving birth.

The cart, ever so slowly, made its way forward on the road to Damascus. Soon, the other two were lulled into a deep sleep by its slow rocking motion. Milka too felt tired. Before falling asleep, she thought, "Yes, there is much to share with these people. I will teach them the daily communions with the Angels. It is a good place to start."

ח

# THE END OF THE AGE

Yaakov and the elders of the community climbed to the summit of Mount Carmel where they found Hannah deep in prayer. Seldom eating or sleeping, she put all of her efforts into increasing the strength of the life force on Mount Carmel.

Sensing their arrival, Hannah opened her eyes. The elders wasted no time in getting to the point. "The community is in grave danger," Uzia said with much agitation. "Those who have gone out have not returned." Hannah could see the anguish in his face. She knew he was worried about Yael. "What is even more trouble-some," he continued, "raids by Judean soldiers are getting closer to our gates every day. Nobody from the outside visits anymore. Even pilgrimages to this sacred mountain have stopped. Fear of war has stricken the land."

"People are calling for your return," Yaakov added. "It is not right to ignore their pleas." Yaakov used his hands to emphasize his point while Hannah sat there in silence, listening.

A few moments passed when nobody said anything. Finally, Hannah stood up. She walked a few times around the Tabernacle, deep in thought. "It is important for me to remain here," she said, almost as if talking to herself. "Nazareth benefits by what I am doing, even if they do not fully understand how."

Yaakov's expression changed. He was losing patience. "Of course, it is of great value. No one denies it. However, you are missing my point. Circumstances are fast changing. People are scared. You have a duty to lead and take on the challenges from the increased threats on the outside. If you take no action and just sit up here, any harm done will be your responsibility. The members of the community are the sheep and you their Shepard."

Hannah placed her hands together, as in prayer. "Such an important matter should not be decided through human reasoning alone. We must ask the Shekhinah to guide us."

Hannah took a small yarrow stalk out of her medicine pouch. She then broke the dried twig into two uneven pieces. "The Angel of Earth will tell us what to do."

Yaakov put the two uneven pieces into his closed fist. "The shorter of the two will indicate your return to Nazareth, to lead your people."

Hannah continued to pray as she pulled one of the Yarrow twigs out of his hand.

It was the longer piece. The elders became angry. Hannah had never before seen them this way.

"All the years of hard work, and for what?" Uzia said as he looked away. "To have our fate decided by a draw of chance."

The elders stomped away. Yaakov stayed behind. He looked Hannah in the eye. "What about us? I have waited all these years."

"What else am I to do? I must put my duty first. I made a promise." Hannah hung her head. "I should have released you long ago," she said, "so you could have found somebody else. It is my fault."

Yaakov turned to leave. Hannah grabbed his robe. There were tears rolling down her cheeks. "I am sorry Yaakov."

Yaakov pulled free of her grasp with a strong jerk and left. He didn't even look back.

Hannah fell to her knees and cried. "You were wrong to allow him to harbor false hopes." It was Selith.

"How would you know anything about this kind of love? You are not a human." There was a hint of frustration in Hannah's tone.

"Yes, I sometimes wonder what it would be like, to feel things as humans do."

Hannah looked up at Selith in surprise. Could it be that the Angel was sad? Perhaps Angels could develop human-like feelings.

"I am tired," Hannah said as she got up. "The burden grows heavier with the approaching darkness. Rome grows daily in strength and the sons of the Watchers are already arriving. They are truly sons of darkness. So many lives will be lost. They and their Roman allies will stop at nothing short of conquest of the surrounding lands and the total destruction of Israel. We are no match for their dark power."

"You cannot fight fire with fire," Selith replied. "Only the cooling waters of love can extinguish the flames of hate. But you are correct. In the age to come, many will forfeit their lives for their loyalty to Aravat and the Light."

Hannah felt confused. She wandered about the summit until coming to her favorite tree. Hannah sat down next to it, resting her head against its smooth bark, thinking things over. Artakifa had already informed Hannah and Selith about her two friend's fate. In fact, most who had gone out had suffered greatly, as the Maccabees now controlled much of Galilee. However, Hannah had not shared with the community the more ominous threats facing them. Nergal, the Eye of Beelzebub, was ever seeking to penetrate their protective veil. They were not strong enough to defend themselves against the forces of evil if ever he discovered their mission. This was another reason Hannah spent so much of her time next to the Tabernacle in prayer on Mount Carmel, waging a daily spiritual battle with the evil eye. Nor did the community know about the Watchers and their Roman allies. Could the Mashiakh really save them and the world, she wondered? How could his Light be strong enough to overcome the ever-increasing darkness? Surely, men would figure out a way to put it out. It had been this way in the past. Why would this time be any different?

"You should not think such things," Selith said as she handed Hannah some fresh picked grapes.

Hannah laid them on the ground. She wasn't hungry in the least. "I do not know if I am up to the task you have put on my shoulders."

"It will be faith that wins this war with the Watchers."

Hannah sat looking out across the deep water of the Great Sea. She pulled her outer robe closer to keep warm as a strong wind blew thick black clouds towards the shoreline. Selith stood at the edge of the cliff, peering with her sharp Angelic eyes at the long boats from distant lands that sailed into the nearby harbors. They were coarse looking vessels filled with mean soldiers anxious to ply their trade.

Feeling weary, Hannah closed her eyes. She recalled a passage from scrolls written by the first followers of her great-grandfather, the Teacher of Righteousness. Some said they were his own words. Perhaps he saw her predicament in the crystals and wrote them for her. "There arose the Men of Scoffing, who dropped on Israel waters of deceitfulness, causing them to wander in the wilderness where there was no path to them down from the everlasting heights, turning them away from the ways of righteousness. Unfaithful and forsaking the Light, they hid their face from Israel and its Sanctuary, and were delivered up to the sword. But, remembering the Covenant of the forefathers, the Light left a remnant in Israel and did not deliver it up to be destroyed in the age of wrath."

"You did not finish," Selith said. "There is more. Do you want me to complete it for you? The Light will cause a root to spring up from Israel to inherit the land and to prosper on the good things of the earth. They will perceive their iniquity and recognize that they are guilty, yet still for many years they will be like the blind groping for a way. And the Light will observe their deeds, that they sought it with a whole heart, and it will raise for them a Teacher of Righteousness to guide them."

Hearing this, Hannah realized that the Teacher of Righteousness must have known too about the Mashiakh. Perhaps that is why he was so desperate to prevent the Maccabees from getting the crystals, as they were intent on uniting the offices of both king and high priest. With the crystals in their possession, what would prevent them from using their power to proclaim one of their own House to be the long awaited Messiah of their people. Hannah felt that the Teacher of Righteousness was still guiding them, right down to the present moment. Did not Bilshan say that the Teacher had discovered a way to put his life force into the crystals?

There was now complete silence in the stillness. Lost in their own prayers, only the sound of the distant water hitting the rocks of the shore made them aware they were still in this world. The sun had set and a sinister haze hid the moon from view. Selith glanced up and let out an audible sigh. Hannah, too, felt the change as the night suddenly tuned cold and damp.

With an eerie grey foul smelling fog now hugging close to the sea, Hannah said in a sad and melodious tone, "They have banished me from my land, like a bird from its nest. All my friends and sisters are driven far from me."

Below the mountain, the Nazarenes waited for the End of the Age. The world they once knew was dying. The Age of the Angels was now only legend, and the Age of the Prophets in its final hours. Now began the Age of Men. The Children of Light prayed in expectation for a Mashiakh who would save those who believed at the end time, until the return of the sun to its full spiritual power, the Second Coming.

# APPENDIX

# CHRONICLE OF YEARS

## 312 BCE

Founding of the Seleucid Syrian Kingdom from the eastern remnant of the former Macedonian Empire of Alexander the Great. The Seleucid Kingdom is a Hellenistic empire centered in the Near East.

Now part of the Greek empire, Jewish government in Jerusalem changes from rule by the priests (theocracy) to a secular Hellenized polis (commonwealth). A Prince of David who presides over the governing council called the Sanhedrin heads the Jerusalem Patriarchate. These princes are of the line of King David through his descendant Zerubabbel's third wife, Esthra, who is Jewish. Zerubabbel's descendants from his first two non-Jewish wives are ostracized and considered illegitimate. They are also unable to enjoy the elevated status as a Prince of David and hold the title of prince patriarch. This policy continues until the time of King Herod. Five distinct lineages will develop over time: two legitimate and three illegitimate.

Serving underneath the prince patriarch is the Levitical high priest. Since the exile, there has been no king of Israel, only the high priest. According to Jewish halakhic law, the high priest must be a direct descendant of Zadok, the high priest of King David. Throughout the second temple era, the House of Zadok in effect serves as stewards until a legitimate heir of David can re-take the throne. It also supplies the higher priesthood. This continues into the era of Macedonian conquest, when Judaea became a vassal state to whichever was the stronger of the two Macedonian kingdoms of Egypt and Seleucid Syria.

## 305 BCE

Founding of Ptolemaic dynasty, a Greek royal family that will rule Egypt during the Hellenistic period for 275 years.

## 198 BCE

Syrian Seleucid Antiochus III wrests control of Palestine from the Egyptian Ptolemies at the Battle of Panium. Seleucid rule results in the rise of Hellenistic cultural and religious practices. Hellenization divides Jewish society between those favoring Hellenization and those opposing it. There are also divided allegiance to the Hellenizing Ptolemies in Egypt and the Seleucids in Syria.

## 175 BCE

Antiochus IV becomes Seleucid King. Antiochus considers Judaism a primitive superstition. Encouraged by leading Hellenizing Jews, Antiochus pursues Hellenization with zeal. He attacks Jerusalem and pillages the temple, taking captive many women and children. Antiochus effectively bans traditional Jewish religious practice.

High Priest Simon II dies, resulting in conflicts between supporters of his son Onias III who opposes Hellenization and favors the Egyptian Ptolemies and his other son Yeson who favors Hellenization and the Seleucids. This results in civil war. Yeson, who has adopted the Greek name Jason, bribes Seleucid Antiochus to make him high priest. Another Hellenized Jew Menelaus pays a higher bribe to Antiochus and is appointed high priest causing a major shock among conservative Jewry because Menelaus is not a Zadok. As a result, the House of Zadok loses its ancient royal and high priestly prerogative. Menelaus has Onias assassinated and his brother Lysimachus steals holy vessels from the temple in Jerusalem, causing riots and the thief's death at the hands of the rioters. Menelaus is arrested and arraigned before Antiochus, but bribes his way free.

## 170 BCE

Davidic Prince Yosef of the legitimate Tobaidite line (decedents of King David from his Jewish wives) made prince patriarch.

## 168 BCE

Antiochus IV again sacks Jerusalem removing the sacred objects from the Temple and slaughtering many of the city's inhabitants. He establishes a fortress in Jerusalem called the Acra for the protection of the Hellenized Jews who are the best educated and wealthiest of its citizens.

## 167 BCE

Jewish sacrifices, Sabbaths and feasts are banned and circumcision outlawed by the Seleucids. Altars to Greek gods are set up and animals prohibited to Jews sacrificed on them. The Olympian Zeus is placed on the main altar of the temple in Jerusalem. This compels Mattathias Maccabee, a Levite priest, to start a rebellion against the Syrian Seleucid rulers and their Hellenized Jewish supporters. His five sons, the Maccabee brothers Judas, Jonathan, Simon, John and Eleazar and a large number of religious Jews called the Hasidim join him.

## 166 BCE

Mattathias dies and his son Judas 'the Hammer' takes his place as leader of the rebellion. Lacking a real army to confront the Seleucids, they engage in guerilla warfare directed at Hellenized Jews and Seleucid collaborators of whom there are many. The Maccabees destroy pagan altars in the villages, circumcise children, and force many Jews into outlawry.

## 164 BCE

Death of Antiochus IV leads to a political compromise restoring religious freedom to Judea. The Maccabees enter Jerusalem in triumph and ritually cleanse the temple, reestablishing traditional Jewish worship. Iinternal conflicts soon after break out in Jerusalem between the conservative Hasidim party led by Judah and the Hellenized Jews.

## 162 BCE

Hellenizing High Priest Menelaus is removed from office and executed but the Hasidim are unable to put their own man in. The Seleucid king who is still the nominal ruler appoints as his successor the Hellenizer Alcimus who is a descendant of the second son of the last high priest in Solomon's temple during the exile.

Alcimus executes sixty priests because they oppose him and his Hellenized Jewish allies, putting himself in open conflict with the Maccabees. Alcimus flees Jerusalem to complain about the persecution of the Hellenist in Judea to the Roman backed Seleucid pretender Demetrius I. Demetrius grants Alcimus's request to be confirmed as high priest under the protection of his army.

The Maccabees continue the revolt to conquer other lands with Jewish populations or to convert their people. This policy exacerbates the divide between the Pharisees and Sadducees factions within the Hasidim who take opposing sides on the issue. The Pharisees are opposed to the wars of expansion and conversions and advocate for the restoration of the House of David to the throne.

Murder of eleven-year-old Antiochus V by his cousin Demetrius who ascends the Seleucid throne as Demetrius I.

## 160 BCE

A Seleucid army that includes the high priest Alcimus, defeats and kills Judah Maccabee at the Battle of Elasa. His brother Jonathan Maccabee takes over leadership of the rebel forces. The Hellenists become once more rulers upon Judah's death. Alcimus does not long enjoy his triumph, as he dies soon after while pulling down the wall of the temple that divides the court of the Gentiles from that of the Jews.

## Circa BCE 159-153

The last surviving member of the senior Zadok linage serves as high priest, an unnamed person later to be known as the Teacher of Righteousness.

## 153 BCE

Demetrius is challenged by the Roman backed Alexander Balas, a usurper. Both parties seek an alliance with Jonathan Maccabee, with Alexander outbidding Demetrius by offering Jonathan the high priest-hood. Jonathan accepts the position of high priest to the despair of the Zadok leaders. Although the Maccabees are of the Zadok family of priests, they are not members of the appointed senior lineage. By taking the high priesthood, the Maccabees usurp the office of the high priest. Many Zadokites decide not to oppose Jonathan in order to keep their senior and privileged positions as higher priests of the temple.

Within the Sadducee party, there is a sharp division between supporters and opponents of the Maccabees serving as high priests. The majority retain their privileged status by turning their backs on the Zadok leadership and declaring their loyalty to the new high priest Jonathan. Many senior Zadokites however, refuse and go into self-imposed exile into the desert in fear of Jonathan. Their members include the charismatic deposed Zadok high priest who makes a New Testament for the Sons of Zadok. This Teacher of Righteousness is eventually apprehended by Jonathan and put to death; eliminating his greatest rival for the high priesthood. Absent this Teacher, the Zadok community continues to exist in the desert, holding fast to his precepts in the belief that at the End of Days he will return to teach righteousness. This community over time becomes a secretive religious faction in Palestine alongside the more numerous followers of the Pharisees and Sadducees. They will be known by names such as the Essenes, Hassidim, Nazarenes, and the Children of Light. The various communities will be scattered about the ancient Mideast, but will share common practices and beliefs, such as owning of property in common, wearing white robes, not eating meat or fish, pacifism, often going out in pairs to heal the world, rejection of the Maccabees as king-priests, a well-developed Angelology, and Messianism, among other things.

## 150 BCE

Davidic Prince Shetah, a revered sage of Judah, becomes the 40th Tobaidite prince patriarch of Jerusalem. His youngest sister will later marry Alexander Jannaeus, the son of future Maccabee King Hyrcanus.

## 147 BCE

Jonathan assaults, captures, and burns many towns in Judea held by the Seleucids and Hellenist Jews.

## 145 BCE

Jonathan, owing no allegiance to the new Seleucid King Demetrius II, lays siege to the Acra, the symbol of Hellenized Jews and Seleucid control over Judea.

## 142 BCE

Jonathan is assassinated by a pretender to the Seleucid throne and is succeeded by Simon Maccabee, the last remaining son of Mattathias. Simon conquers more territory from the Seleucids and Hellenists Jews and expels the Seleucid garrison from the Acra in Jerusalem.

## 141 BCE

The Maccabee Dynasty is founded by a resolution adopted at a large assembly of priests, people, and elders. Simon becomes both ethnarch (rulers of the nation), replacing the traditional Davidic rulers of royal descent and high priest, replacing the legally appointed lineage of Zadok, until there should arise a faithful prophet in Israel.

## 139 BCE

The Roman Senate recognizes the new Maccabee dynasty. Palestine becomes semi-independent of the Seleucid Empire.

## 135 BCE

Simon is assassinated at the instigation of his son-in-law Ptolemy, son of Abubus. His third son, John, takes the throne. His two elder brothers Mattathias and Judah are murdered alongside their father. John Hyrcanus inherits both the offices of high priest and ethnarch, although some Jews never accept the Maccabees as legitimate kings since they are not lineal descendants of David. He takes the Greek regal name of Hyrcanus I in a significant political and cultural step away from the intransigent opposition to and rejection of Hellenistic culture that characterized the Maccabee rebellion. All subsequent Maccabee rulers follow suit by adopting Greek names and using Greek as a language of court and government. Criticism of Hyrcanus' roles as both high priest and king by the Pharisees leads to a falling out, elevating the status of their opponents the Hellenist Sadducees within the royal circle.

## 135 BCE

Seleucid Antiochus VII marches into Judea, pillages the countryside, and lays a yearlong siege on Jerusalem creating mass starvation within the city. In the end, Hyrcanus I negotiates a truce with

Antiochus where Judea once again recognizes Seleucid control and pays a large tribute. Unable to pay, Hyrcanus loots the tomb of David violating his obligations as high priest and offending the religious conservatives led by the Pharisees. High taxes levied on the population by the Seleucids and the constant warfare on their soil causes great hardship to the people of Judea.

## 129 BCE

Hyrcanus I disregards the ethnarch title and usurps the throne of David, proclaiming himself King of the Jews, becoming the first Maccabee Priest-King. They are Levite priests and therefore not Princes of David. In doing so, he intensifies the conflict with the Pharisees who back the messianic claims to the continuous rule of the Princes of David.

## 128 BCE

Antiochus VII dies in battle against Persia resulting in the breakup of the Seleucid Kingdom allowing Hyrcanus to re-assert Judean independence and conquer new territories. Because the Jewish population is still recovering from the attacks by Antiochus, they cannot provide enough able men for a Hyrcanus-led army forcing him to raise a mercenary army.

## 125 BCE

Davidic Prince Simon becomes 41st Tobaidite prince patriarch of Jerusalem. He is dispossessed of all his property during a Maccabee persecution against the Davidic princes after which he supports his family with a small linen goods store. He is the father of Jose II who is killed as a Davidic claimant to the throne in 88 BCE. Simon is the father of Yeshua Bar-Panthera and grandfather of Princess Sara, who becomes King Herod's 1st wife, known as Doris of Jerusalem, and Jude III, the grandfather of Shammai and great grandfather of Simon V of Perea, the last Dravidic prince of the official Tobaidite and Onaidite Lineages, who is murdered by the Romans in 4 BCE.

## 128-110 BCE

Hyrcanus I continues to engage in wars of conquest including an invasion of the Transjordan and laying a six months siege on Medeba causing mass starvation. He reduces the city of Schechem to ashes and destroys the Samaritan temple on Mount Gerizim. Hyrcanus initiates a military campaign against the Idumeans in the Negev instituting forced conversions, an unprecedented move for a Judean ruler. Hyrcanus begins an extensive military campaign against Samaria placing his sons Antigonus and Aristobulos in charge. Although the siege lasts for a long, difficult year causing many innocent deaths, Hyrcanus is unwilling to give up. Ultimately, Samaria is overrun and destroyed, with the inhabitants sold into slavery.

## 106 BCE

Birth of Gnaeus Pompeius Magnus also known as Pompey or Pompey the Great.

## 104 BCE

Hyrcanus I dies. His will separates the office of high priesthood from secular authority, giving his widow civil authority and appointing his son Aristobulos I high priest. Aristobulos wants the throne, bringing him into direct conflict with the Pharisees. He casts his mother into prison and starves her to death. He imprisons his brother Alexander Jannaeus and murders his other two brothers. He is the first Maccabee to use openly the title of king since according to the Hebrew Scriptures, only descendants of the House of David, are qualified to be kings of Israel. He is hostile to the Pharisees pursuing them with ruthlessness. King Aristobulos has only one child, a daughter, Princess Salome, given to be the wife of three different Davidic princes and birthing three half-brothers, all Davidic princes, Matthias, Mattathiah, and Mattan, who represent three different lineages of the Dravidian dynasty.

## 103 BCE

Aristobulos dies from a painful illness one year after ascending the throne and is succeeded by his brother Antigonus I, who reigns only a few months before dying under mysterious circumstances. His widow, Queen Shlamtzion who now goes by the Hellenized reign name of Salome-Alexandra, releases Alexander Jannaeus from prison. After Alexander Jannaeus ascends the throne, he divorces his first wife, Salome, the sister of former Davidic Prince Patriarch Shetah and aunt of the current prince patriarch and head of the Pharisee faction in the Sanhedrin Simon. He then marries Queen Salome Alexandra, his brother's wife in a levirate marriage. Salome Alexandra is the sister of Simon. During the twenty-seven year reign of Alexander Jannaeus, he is almost constantly involved in military conflicts. Through the course of his nearly thirty-year reign, Alexander Jannaeus conquers the entire coastal plain, topples Western Samaria, and begins the slow conquest of Galilee and the Northern Transjordan.

## 100 BCE

Birth of Gaius Julius Caesar

## 97 BCE

A strong rift exists between the Pharisees and Alexander Jannaeus as the rival Sadducees are avid supporters of Alexander with the king openly adopting the Sadducees rites in the Temple. These disputes culminate in the first civil war between the Pharisees led by Davidic Prince Judah III, the son of Simon II (and nephew to Queen Alexandra) and Alexander Jannaeus' and his Sadducee allies. The war will cost 50,000 people their lives.

## 91 BCE

Alexander Jannaeus brings 800 rebels to Jerusalem and has them crucified; slitting the throats of the rebel's wives and children before their eyes as he eats with his concubines.

## 88 BCE

A new Pharisee backed Davidic rebellion breaks out. Davidic Prince Jose II, son of Simon and nephew of the Maccabee king's wife Alexandra is captured and executed. Jose's own nephew and rival Davidic claimant to the throne Yeshua Bar-Panthera flees to Egypt. Yeshua is the illegitimate son of Davidic Prince Panthera, legitimized by the Sadducees in the Sanhedrin. However, the Pharisees prevent him from taking the office of Patriarch of Jerusalem, forcing him into a war with the Maccabees.

## 83 BCE

Birth of Mark Antony

## 75 BCE

Salome Alexandra, the wife of Alexander Jannaeus, becomes queen regent at her husband's death. He leaves two sons, Hycranus II and Aristobulos II. With the queen regent's rise to power, the Pharisees become the new ruling faction within the Sanhedrin. Alexandra installs her eldest son, Hyrcanus II, strongly supported by the Pharisees, as high priest. The Sanhedrin is reorganized by the Pharisees; changing it from a powerless body into a high court for the administration of justice and religious matters under their control. The Sadducees are forced to leave Jerusalem. There are no wars during her reign, the first peace since the Maccabees took power.

## 67 BCE

Queen Salome Alexandra dies. Upon her death, she names Hyrcanus II as successor to the kingship. He is already high priest but since he shares his mother's religious views sympathetic to the Pharisees, they still support him in spite of their usual opposition to the same person holding both positions. As a result, his younger brother Aristobulos II becomes the favorite of the out of power Sadducees. Encouraged by the Sadducees, Aristobulos rebels against Hyrcanus just three months into his reign. The brothers meet in battle near Jericho where many of Hyrcanus' soldiers go over to Aristobulos to give him victory. Hyrcanus renounces the throne. The Sadducees return to Jerusalem to resume their traditional role as the ruling elites and the Pharisees are once more suppressed.

## 64 BCE

Under the influence of his Idumean advisor Antipater, who because of his ancestor's forced conversion to Judaism, is not recognized as Jewish by the religious conservative Pharisees, Hyrcanus II takes refuge with Aretas III, King of the Nabataeans. This king has been bribed by Antipater into espousing the cause of Hyrcanus by the promise of returning Arabian towns taken by the Maccabees. The Nabataeans advanced toward Jerusalem with an army of 50,000 and besiege the city for several months.

The Romans defeat the Seleucids in Syria, ending their empire.

## 63 BCE

Roman General Pompey enters the Judean civil war on the side of Hyrcanus II. His forces besiege and capture Jerusalem, badly damaging the city and temple. Pompey earns the hatred of the Jews by entering and thus desecrating the temple in Jerusalem. Rome annexes Palestine. Rome takes Aristobulos with his two sons Alexander and Aristobulos as prisoner and Hyrcanus is restored to the position of high priest. The Romans make the Hellenized Antipater head of affairs of state representing Rome's interest. The Pharisees return to power in Jerusalem.

Davidic Prince Yeshua Bar-Panthera, now returned from Egypt, organizes Zealots to oppose the Roman occupation of Jerusalem. He is captured by the Romans and crucified

## 57 BCE

Prince Alexander Maccabee, eldest son of Aristobulos II, marries his cousin Alexandra, daughter of his uncle Hyrcanus II, who has divorced her first husband a Davidic Prince. Alexander escapes from Rome and raises an army of Maccabee loyalists opposed to Roman rule. He is soundly defeated in a battle fought near Jerusalem by a large Roman force but is allowed to go free after the surrender of his army.

Orodes II murders his father to assume the throne of the Persian (Parthian) Empire. He is assisted in the murder by his brother Mithridates

## 56 BCE

Prince Alexander returns to Palestine and raises a new army of Maccabee loyalists, massacring all Romans who fell in his way. The Romans defeat Alexander near Mount Tabor. 10,000 Jews will fall in this battle.

## 53 BCE

Prince Alexander again rallies the Judean nobles but is thwarted by the Roman general Cassius a year later in 52 BC.

Persians and Romans begin a series of wars over territories in the Near East.

## 51 BCE

The young son and favorite of Persian King Orodes, Pacorus, launches an invasion of Syria but is repulsed by the Roman general Cassius.

## 49 BCE

Civil War begins between the Pompey and Julius Caesar. Pompey's army captures Alexander and beheads him.

## 48 BCE

Pompey murdered in Egypt by allies of Julius Caesar. His former allies, Hyrcanus and Antipater switch sides and come to Caesar's aid in Egypt.

## 47 BCE

In gratitude for their assistance, Julius Caesar restores some political authority to Hyrcanus by appointing him high priest and ethnarch, having little practical effect, since Hyrcanus yields to Antipater in everything. Antipater is granted Roman citizenship and made procurator of Judea with the right to collect taxes. Antipater makes his sons Phasael military governor of Jerusalem and Herod military governor of Galilee. Herod captures and executes Ezekias the Jewish rebel and his supporters, earning the respect and admiration of the Romans and the hatred of the Jews. The pro-Roman politics of Antipater leads to his increasing unpopularity among the conservative non-Hellenized Jews.

## 44 BCE

Julius Caesar is murdered in Rome causing a new civil war to break out. Roman General Cassius demands financial support from Judea. Herod is the first to meet his financial goal, selling into slavery the inhabitants of four Judean towns that did not raise the required amount.

## 43 BCE

Antipater is poisoned in Jerusalem at a banquet of Judean nobles under orders of anti-Roman Maccabee loyalist Malichus. The Romans later kill Malichus in revenge.

## 42 BCE

Antipater's sons Phasael and Herod along with Hyrcanus II who had supported Cassius in the Roman civil war switch loyalty to Mark Antony upon the death of Cassius. Herod and Phasael suppress many anti-Roman revolts in Judea, including an attempted coup by Maccabee Prince Antigonus II, the second son of Aristobulos II, and the brother of Alexander. He marries his brother widow Alexandra and receives the backing of Egyptian King Ptolemy. Hyrcanus II supports Herod, because Herod is engaged to his granddaughter Mariamne. A delegation of Jewish nobles complains to Mark Anthony about Herod.

## 41 BCE

While Mark Anthony is in Egypt with Cleopatra, another delegation of Jewish nobles travel there demanding Herod's removal. Anthony orders them executed.

Herod appoints his brother Joseph as Patriarch of Jerusalem, a position normally held by a Davidic Prince, to the anger of the Pharisees and many Jews.

## 40 BCE

Persian prince Pacorus invades Syria and Palestine in alliance with the Roman rebel Quintus Labienus. Antigonus II joins the Persians and seizes Jerusalem. The Persians send his uncle Hyrcanus II to Babylon in chains after cutting off his ears to make him ineligible for the office of high priest. Antipater's son Phasael after being tricked along with Hyrcanus into attending peace talks kills himself in order not to be used as a hostage. Antigonus becomes

King of Judea with Persian support. Antigonus II is to be the last Maccabee King of Judea.

Herod escapes to Masada and then goes to Rome where the Senate declares him King of the Jews.

## 39 BCE

Rome counterattacks in Judea killing Labienus in a battle. Antigonus besieges Herod's family and supporters at Masada, now led by Joseph, Herod's brother. Herod violently subdues a rebellion in Galilee, culminating with the battle of Mount Arbel.

## 38 BCE

Pacorus returns to Syria and is killed in battle with the Romans. Orodes, who is deeply afflicted by the death of his gallant son, appoints his other son Phraates IV as successor, but is soon afterwards killed by the same son. Herod subdues all resistance to him in Galilee but soon after, Maccabee loyalists re-take Galilee forcing Herod to reinvade it with much force to subdue the population. In Judea, Antigonus defeats Herod's brother Joseph and his Roman guards near Jericho leaving no survivors. Antigonus defiles Joseph's body by cutting off the head. Herod swears an oath to destroy the House of Maccabee in revenge. Shortly after, Galilee rebels once more rise in support of Antigonus, as does parts of Judea. Herod escapes an assassination attempt in a bathhouse. Towards the end of the year, Herod engages Antigonus in battle defeating him to retake most of Palestine.

With the death of his brother Joseph, Herod appoints his brother's son Joseph as prince patriarch of Jerusalem.

## 37 BCE

Herod restores the Zadoks to the office of high priest by bringing back from exile in Egypt Boethius, a Sadducee. Many consider this branch of the Zadoks illegitimate due to their establishing a copy of the temple in Jerusalem near Alexandria, Egypt and for serving the pharaohs as generals. Herod restores the Zadoks to the office of high priest to prevent the Maccabees from ever reclaiming that office again.

Herod takes back Jerusalem with Roman support. The Roman soldiers and Jews loyal to Herod massacre the population. Antigonus surrenders. Fearing Antigonus might convince the Roman senate that Herod is not the legitimate king, Herod turns Antigonus over to Mark Antony who beheads him, thus ending the Maccabee dynasty and the old order of priest-kings of neither Zadok nor Davidic blood. Herod marries Maccabee princes and daughter of Alexandra, Mariamne.

The Sanhedrin officially recognizes the formerly non-legitimate Jewish-Persian Abiudite lineage of Davidic princes when it became apparent that the Tobaite and the Onaidite lines of the legitimate Meshullamite dynasty are dying off. Herod agrees since his first wife belongs to the Abiudite line and this will make their son eligible to be a prince patriarch. The Sanhedrin also makes eligible for princely status the formally illegitimate Rhesaite Line.

## 36 BCE

Aristobulos III, son of Queen Alexandra and former King Alexander, and Herod's brother-in-law is drowned on orders by Herod.

## 32 BCE

Shammai, a Davidic prince and the last of the legitimate Tobaidite princes to rule, becomes prince patriarch for one year.

## 31 BCE

Yaakov ben Matthan, an Abuidite (formerly non-legitimate) Davidic prince, becomes prince patriarch.

## 30 BCE

Herod Executes Hyrcanus II, former king, ethnarc, and high priest.

## 29 BCE

After divorcing her the year before to marry someone else, Herod executes his former queen, Marianne Maccabee, daughter of former queen, Alexandra.

Birth of Davidic Prince Yosef 'the carpenter' to reigning Prince patriarch Yaakov ben Matthan.

## 28 BCE

Herod executes his brother-in-law Kostobar.

## 24 BCE

Millions starve to death in Palestine during the Great Shmittah Year Famine, named so because it occurs during the seventh Shmittah year of the Sabbatical Week of Years that was also the Year of Jubilees. Because of this, the land was not cultivated and remained fallow. The entire Jewish population was expecting the freedom to be resting and studying the Torah while using the extra-bountiful harvests that evoked the blessings of YHWH. The presence of a great famine, in the seventh year of a Sabbatical week of years, shows to the common people the extreme displeasure of YHWH at the kingship of Herod. The time of Jacob's trouble has arrived. Palestine is ripe for revolt and many begin looking for the Messiah. Herod's paranoia depends since many of his people do not consider him Jewish and he is not of Davidic blood. Herod decides to eliminate the princes of David to prevent any from claiming they are the Messiah since he must be of the House of David.

## 23 BCE

Jewish zealots rebel against Roman rule. It fails and its leaders are executed in Rome.

Herod falls in love with Mariamne, granddaughter of the Zadok Boethus and daughter of Simon IV Boethius, uncle to High Priest Yeshua (Jesus) III. To secure his divorce and new marriage, Herod executes High Priest Yeshua III to give the post to Simon IV. Yeshua is the father-in-law of Prince Alexander III Helios, 'Heli', the eldest and sole surviving son of Queen Alexandra from her first marriage to Davidic Prince Matthan ben Levi.

Davidic prince patriarch of Jerusalem Yaakov ben Matthan objects to Herod's plans to marry Mariamne. As a result, Herod executes him. Yaakov's eldest son Yosef 'the carpenter', as the eldest son of the eldest son and therefore heir to the family line goes into hiding from Herod as it becomes apparent that Herod's goal is to eliminate all the princes of David. Yaakov's other two sons (twins) are put in the care of his brother, Davidic Prince Hezekiah. Yaakov's daughter from his first wife marries Davidic Prince Theudas, who later sources will call a prophet and elder of the Nazarenes. Herod forces Yaakov's widow Cleopatra, to marry his new father-in-law and high priest, Simon IV Boethius. Herod will marry six more times before his death.

Alexandra Maccabee, former queen (sole ruler in 49BCE), is executed on orders by Herod.

## 20 BCE

Birth of Miryam, daughter of Prince Alexander II Helios. Through her father, she is a member of the Rhesaite line of Davidic princes (and a Maccabee) and from her maternal grandfather a Zadok.

Herod completes his rebuilding of the Second Temple.

Hillel the Great, a member of a previously illegitimate Davidic linage becomes Prince patriarch. He will rule until his death in 10 CE. Because of his great prestige among the people, Herod is unable to find an excuse to kill him.

## 19 BCE

Herod executes High Priest Simon IV Boethius, for sedition and marries his widow Cleopatra of Jerusalem. She is the mother of Davidic Prince Yosef 'the carpenter'. Herod and Cleopatra will give birth to two sons, both becoming half-brothers to Prince Yosef, 'the carpenter.'

## 17 BCE

Herod executes Prince Alexander III Helios, the last remaining son of former Queen Alexandra. With his family out of power, he is now a metal merchant along with his half-brother from his father's second wife, Joseph of Arimatheas. For a short period, Joseph becomes the daughter's guardian after his brother's death. He has another half-brother, Davidic Prince Gjor, by his father's third wife, Salome of Jerusalem, also called 'The Proselyte.' Prince Gjor fathers a son called Simon V Bar Gjor. Alexander's full sister, Alexandra, who is married to the exilarch in Babylonia, also survives him. She has three children. Her two sons will later lead a rebellion from Babylon against Rome and the daughter will become Queen of Persia. In addition, two nephews, both in line for secession to Herod's throne and two nieces, all from his half-sister Mariamne's ill-fated marriage to Herod, still live. All of his nephews and nieces are cousins to his daughter Miryam. Also still alive is his half-sister, Antigone, daughter of former King Antigonus and Queen Alexandra, who married Herod's son by his first wife, the Davidic Doris of Jerusalem, whom he divorced to marry Marianne.

## 7 BCE

As Herod progressively loses his mind, he executes for treason his two sons from his marriage to Mariamne Maccabee. He also kills his son by his first marriage to Doris of Jerusalem who is married to Antigone, the youngest daughter of former Queen Alexandra.

# 4 BCE

With Herod near death, zealots in Galilee stage a rebellion led by the uncle of Yosef 'the carpenter' Prince Hezekiah ben Matthan and his son, Judas ben Hezekiah. Hezekiah has been serving in Herod's army as a high officer. The rebellion is eventually subdued at the cost of many lives, including those of Hezekiah and his son at Sepphoris, a town only three miles from Nazareth. 2000 soldiers of the zealots are crucified and the inhabitants of Sepphoris sold into slavery. The brother of Hezekiah, (and hence another uncle of Yosef 'the carpenter'), Judas ben Matthan carries the banner of rebellion forward and is crucified by the Romans in 6CE for treason. Two sons of Judas ben Hezekiah will suffer the same fate in 47CE. Another son of Judas ben Matthan, one Barabbas, will escape death for rebellion through a pardon by a Roman governor by the name of Pontius Pilate.

Upon Herod's death, Simon V of Perea, one of the last remaining Davidic princes of the official linage, claims to be the Messiah and leads a revolt against Roman rule. He is captured and killed by the Romans in Jerusalem. With his death, the last heir of the halakhic approved lineage from genetically pure Jewish ancestors (of Jewish mothers) from King David has come to its end. As a result, the Rhesaite Line is made legitimate by the Sanhedrin to ensure that an heir of David still survives.

Miryam, the daughter of Davidic Prince (and Maccabee) Alexander III Helios, and granddaughter of Zadok High Priest Yeshua III (both murdered by Herod), weds Yosef 'the carpenter', son of the Davidic Prince Patriarch Yaakov ben Matthan (also murdered by Herod). They have a son who is one of the last remaining descendants of David, and will be a fusion of both the Zadok and Davidic bloodlines, making him eligible to be a Priest-King. Because of this, Herod's descendants will seek to take his life. In addition, because the son is a descendant of two formally illegitimate branches of the Davidic linage, some will not recognize his authenticity.

## 6 CE

The Zadok Sadducee Ananias, cousin of High Priest Yeshua III (the grandfather of Miryam), becomes high priest.

## 16-17 CE

Eleazar, son of Ananias, serves as high priest.

## 18 CE

Caiaphas, son-in-law of Ananias, becomes high priest. Both belong to the Pharisee Shammai's faction within the Sanhedrin.

## 66 CE

Rome ends the Herodian dynasty.

## 69 CE

Simon V Bar Gjora, nephew of Alexander III Helios and hence a cousin of Alexander's daughter Miryam, is crowned as king of the Jews in Jerusalem by High Priest Matthias III.

## 70 CE

Simon surrenders Jerusalem to the Roman general Titus. The city is sacked and burned.

## 73 CE

Simon V Bar Gjora is paraded naked and in chains through Rome by Titus. Afterwards, Titus crucifies him on a cross outside Rome.